A Little Bit of Love

Arva Bhavnagarwala

Published by Shush Books
Shush Books is a division of Shaherazad Shelves
shaherazadshelves.com
Copyright © 2023 by Arva Bhavnagarwala
All rights reserved.
Our books may be purchased in bulk for promotional, educational, or
business use. Please contact your local bookseller or Shaherazad
Shelves or by email at publishing@shaherazadshelves.com
Second edition, 2023
Cover design by Jay Aheer (Simply Defined Art)

ISBN 978-1-960323-09-5 (paperback)
ISBN 978-1-960323-21-7 (hardcover)
ISBN 978-1-960323-10-1 (ebook)

For Husain and Mohsin

Chapter 1
The Woman in the Water
Afrah

"Congratulations, the job is yours." Oh, how much I wanted to hear those words! I had marked today—the twenty-sixth of July 2005—in red on the calendar back home. It was the day of my interview. Instead, the receptionist said, "Ms. Farooqui, we will contact you once we decide. Thank you for coming."

After shaking hands with the lady, I stepped out of the office. The dark sky and torrential rain reflected my mood as I held tightly to the umbrella threatening to turn inside-out in the wind. I managed to reach the railway station, sheltering myself from the rainy mess and stuffed the umbrella into its cover to keep the sodden thing from leaking anywhere else.

The trains ran late, thanks to the rain. When one finally crawled into the station fifteen minutes later, I tied my dupatta across my body, held my bag close to my chest, and prepared to jump into the women's compartment. As the train screeched to a halt in front of me, I was jostled from all sides and pushed behind as a surge of women crowded to get on. *Uff...these women....* I had to reach home by three p.m. I'd promised Mom. If I didn't show up on time, she would roast me like the peanuts she put in all her favorite dishes for lying to her.

I elbowed my way to the front, ignoring the curses thrown at me, and managed to catch a pole in the middle of the compartment entrance just before the train's horn blared, signaling it was leaving the station. Hanging by the door looked neither enchanting nor safe with the lashing rain, very unromantic, not like the scenes in the Bollywood movies Mom enjoyed. I squeezed myself deeper into the compartment as the train took off.

Ah! This would be a daily thing if I were to get the job I'd interviewed for. Traveling from Kurla in the suburbs of Mumbai to Vashi, in New Mumbai, was going to be a nightmare. Shrugging at the thought, I smiled. *It would be a nightmare that paid.*

The train inched forward at a snail's pace as I gained my footing amongst the soaked bodies. Water or sweat-soaked? It didn't matter. After all, I was one of them too. Outside, the creek raged as we crossed the Vashi Bridge.

"Girl, your hair is getting into my mouth," a middle-aged woman standing behind me scowled.

"Can you hold me? Because if I leave the handlebar to tie my hair, I might fall on you." My lips curved in what I considered to be a sweet smile. But the woman snorted. I twisted my mouth and brought my frizzy hair over my right shoulder—with no intention of tying it up. And to make that irritating woman happy? Never.

People scrambled to get in and out of the train at the next station, and the annoyed woman moved to the opposite side of the compartment. Holding the handlebar above my head, I closed my eyes as my mind drifted back to the interview. I was so sure I'd get the job on the spot. It was my *seventh* interview, for Allah's sake! I knew the answers to most of the questions by heart and blabbered them optimistically. If only the interviewer hadn't asked me the last one.

'Where do you see yourself five years from now?'

A bubble of laughter had escaped me. I didn't know what to tell him. *Ask me more about Tally 7.2, the latest version of the accounting software, and I'll answer. Five years from now?* Clearing my throat, I'd said, 'I want to be a teacher. But my mother won't let my father pay the fees for college. She wants to see me married with a bunch of kids, but I want a career. So, this job will help me save money for the fees.' I had bitten my lip when the interviewer stared back at me wide-eyed.

I should have lied, manipulated the truth, and said something like I want to be a successful accountant... blah blah. *Argh, me and my big mouth.*

The train suddenly lurched to a halt, and someone bumped into me. Women toppled over, gasping and yelling. A pang of fear coursed through me. I checked the time. 3:30 p.m. Mom would be worried. Shaking my head, I raised my voice over the crowd, "What happened?"

"No electricity, the train will not move," replied a woman.

"There is water on the tracks. We are stuck in here," another said, grasping the pole and balancing to look outside.

"What should we do?" I asked. There were no intercoms or announcements made on these local trains. Only stations had them.

"Climb down and walk up to the next station?" someone suggested.

I looked from one woman to another, fear in my belly settling deeper, strengthening its roots. Many women had little kids with them. A baby cried. I made my way to the door and glanced outside. Yes, most men and women from other compartments were getting down and walking on the tracks.

"Mumbai is flooded," someone passing said. "It's like this everywhere."

Mumbai rains were always unpredictable. I'd been trapped in college once in a monsoon, but being stuck with friends and being cramped on a train with a bunch of strangers were totally different things.

"Crap," I murmured under my breath, voicing my concern aloud. "Should we get out or wait for the train to start?"

A woman preparing to exit said, "It is better if you leave with us. Soon the train will be empty. And it is not safe to stay alone. Come..." She held her hand out for me.

I stared at her, uncertain of what to do. The woman insisted I get down, but I couldn't move. She waited for a couple of minutes before giving up on me and began walking toward the station a few meters away. I strained my eyes to see the black letters on the yellow board. To my relief, it was Kurla station. Thank Allah, at least I could figure out a way home from here.

Passengers helped each other gain their footing on the waterlogged tracks. Holding the pole, I dangled my feet to reach the compartment steps, which were now visible as the train had halted away from the platform. But I missed them and slipped into the water.

Pain shot through my leg, and a woman nearby helped me up. I moved my foot and ankle, putting pressure on it as I stood. It didn't hurt much, so I was grateful that I could still walk home. Tying my hair into a bun, I followed the crowd to the station. I sat cross-legged on the damp platform, heaving a sigh of relief. A hundred meters seemed like a hundred kilometers. Drenched from head to toe, I shook my head to clear the water from my eyes. All I had to do was cross the overhead bridge toward the west side and walk home from there. It was ten to fifteen minutes away by bus or auto rickshaw, but it was unlikely that either of them was operating now.

"Oh Allah, help me," I muttered, walking toward the exit.

Outside, the sky was grey, and rain poured mercilessly. The roads were waterlogged, and shops were flooded with rainwater. Auto rickshaws and buses were stranded in the middle of the road. Ahead of me, people's calves were submerged. At my height, it would reach my knees. *How can I walk in this?*

I checked the time again. My watch, inevitably drenched, had stopped ticking a little after 4:30 p.m. I couldn't afford a waterproof one yet. I hoped I could make it home before it became too dark to see. Mom would have had mini heart attacks by now—no way to contact her either. Planning to buy a mobile phone with my first salary was still a distant dream.

Taking a deep breath, I stepped into the water. Immediately, goosebumps covered my body. The water was muddy, and I refused to think of its contents, or else I would never be able to bring myself to move. Setting my sight on people in front of me, I observed them to assess if there was a ditch or pothole that would trip me. It was like walking in a minefield; one wrong step, and bam! You'd sink deeper in the who-knows-what water or probably drown if a manhole was left uncovered.

The rain continued to pelt as I walked, muttering prayers under my breath and thoughts churning in my head. *Mom will kill me. Would I even make it home in one piece? And what about that interview?* I was sure I'd lost that job with the stupid answer I gave.

A human chain formed ahead of me, people holding hands to support each other as they waded deeper. I joined them, the water reaching my waist! Around us, buses, cars, and scooters were stranded. I wondered if the people in them had made it out safely and worried for those in my building—especially the ones on the ground floor. I lived in a low-lying area that flooded every monsoon, but not to *this* extent. If it was bad here, then the couple of hours of rain must have wrecked the entire city.

At last, I spotted familiar buildings and the outline of Sheetal Cinema. My building was right opposite the cinema. Three to four buses stood in the middle of the road. A handful of people helped those stranded to climb out and escorted them to the nearby mosque.

My clothes stuck to my body, my hair was dripping, and I was eager to go home and change, but the sight of a few young men from my building gathered outside one bus caught my attention. I slowed, curiosity getting the better of me. Torn between going home and being nosey, I hesitated at the bottom of the staircase of my building. I was already drenched and late; a few more minutes wouldn't do any harm.

More people gathered outside the bus as I approached. I couldn't determine who was inside at this distance, but it dawned on me that maybe a woman was trapped inside, scared of the men surrounding her.

Water hugged my knees as I reached the bus, and a teenage boy nearby said, "Be careful. It's a bit deep here." I shrugged at his warning, having waded through deeper waters already from the railway station. The boy continued, "Do you know the man inside? He refuses to come out. We all tried our best, but he won't listen."

"Man? I thought it was a woman," I replied. *Should I go back now? If it were a woman, I'd surely help her.*

But this man? Biting my lip, I made my decision. I had come this far...

Satisfying my curiosity finally, I stepped onto the bus and saw a figure seated toward the back, head resting on the window. He looked in my direction as I approached. I couldn't make out his face from where I stood, but I saw one thing clearly. He was clutching two huge blue plastic bags.

Chapter 2
The Man on the Bus
Sadiq

I steeled myself again, ready to drive off the next person who climbed into the bus to convince me to come down. Not that I didn't want to go to the mosque the boys had offered to take me to. I did—but I didn't trust anyone with the parcel I carried. Footsteps came nearer, and I did a double take. It was a woman this time, my age, maybe younger. Her hair was tied on the top of her head, and she exuded confidence in the way she walked as if on a mission. She took a seat across the aisle. I couldn't stop staring at her. Her eyes were a stunning grey. In the twenty-three years of my life, I had never seen someone with colored eyes in real life. Before I could even open my mouth to say anything, she smiled at me.

"Hi, my name is Afrah. Why don't you come and take refuge in the mosque? We don't know when the rain will stop, or when the bus will move. Even the bus drivers and conductors have left."

I cleared my throat and answered her the same as I had everyone before her. "Hi, Afrah. I can't come down. I'm fine here. Thank you." I did not want to change my reply just because she was a woman.

"Really?" She quirked her brow. "You are comfortable *here*?"

I nodded.

"Hmm..." She appeared to be thinking hard. "Ok, so if you need to pee, do you plan to go to the door and do your business in the water?"

Gob-smacked, I gaped at her. Of course, I hadn't thought about that. I assumed the bus would start and I'd reach home sooner rather than later.

"What?" She narrowed her eyes. "Don't tell me you are thinking of doing that, mister. Look at those people walking in the water. It is already full of sewage, and they probably know that, but how can you pee in front of everyone?"

I couldn't help myself and burst out laughing. It had been a while since I'd laughed this hard, and something in my chest fluttered. She chuckled, too. Three of the four teenage boys who were waiting outside came back onto the bus.

"Aapa, is he coming or not?" One of them asked Afrah.

Afrah looked at me and tilted her head.

Sighing, I pointed to the bags I clutched. "I want to, but I cannot leave these here."

A range of emotions flickered on her face, from surprise to confusion.

"What *is* that?"

"Books," I said.

"Books? Oh, that's not a problem. You can leave them here. It's not like the bus is going to start anytime soon."

Before I could reply, she stood and hovered near my seat, as if considering whether or not to pry my fingers away from the handle of the bag. She was close to me, shivering cold, and smelled of the reeking rainwater. I wanted to tell her to go home and change into dry clothes. Instead, I swallowed.

"Afrah, please. These are medical textbooks, and they aren't mine. I have borrowed them."

She narrowed her eyes. "That's alright. Nobody wants to read medical books here."

"But I need them!" I said in a louder than my normal voice and regretted it instantly. *I don't even know her, how can I talk to her like that?* In a softer voice this time, I continued, "You don't understand. I cannot leave without them. And look at the water out there. I cannot carry these and balance myself to safety."

Afrah thought for a while. "Okay. What if we help you to carry the books?"

I considered the viable option. Looking outside the window at all the water, my earlier assumption of reaching home wasn't going to happen soon. I *had* to trust these people.

Afrah didn't wait for my reply. Huffing, she said, "Look, mister. All of us want you to be safe. But we cannot drag you down against your will and we can't wait on you forever." She pointed at the boys waiting outside. "We will leave you here and then you will be alone, hungry, thirsty, *and* with a full bladder."

She turned away and walked off the bus.

I wanted to tell her I was ready to go wherever they took me. But she was gone. I leaned toward the window and spotted her talking to the boys waiting. Then she waded through the water toward an opposite building, where I assumed she lived.

A young man climbed up and approached me. "Listen, we have got some plastic bags. We will help you carry your books to the mosque where others have taken refuge. You can stay there until it is safe to go home."

I agreed and divided the books I carried into the plastic bags they gave me. In one bag I put Bailey's Principles of Surgery, which was a mammoth of a book, and folded it such that not even a drop of water could enter. In another bag, I put the three volumes of the Common Entrance Test books, and in the last one, I put Harrison's Principles of Medicine. This, I carried myself. These books were expensive, and because they weren't mine, they were my responsibility. I slowly stepped out into the rain, which had reduced to a drizzle, and walked through the cold water, following them toward the mosque. Glancing toward Afrah's building, I thought I saw her at the foot of the stairs, but the dim light was playing tricks on my eyes. I wanted to thank her for making me get off the bus.

Chapter 3
The Rebel
Afrah

The stranger on the bus followed his well-wishers toward the mosque, clutching a blue bag in his arms. I smiled at him, then shook my head, remembering he couldn't see me from that distance. *How foolish of me, I didn't even ask him his name.*

Turning, I climbed the stairs of my building. The water hugged my knees. My legs were tired and cold, but I somehow managed to reach the third floor. Mom was sitting outside the door with the neighbors. They gasped at me, and I grimaced. What a sight I must be to them! Drenched and stinky. Despite myself, I grinned when Mom hugged me and kissed my cheeks.

Her eyes were filled with tears as she kept saying, "Oh, thank you, Allah, for bringing my daughter safe."

Honestly, I, too, was relieved to see her. "Mom,

it's okay. I'm okay. I need to have a bath." After extracting myself from her hug, I stepped into the house.

"There is no electricity, and the water is very cold," she said to me, In the same breath, she called out to the neighbors, "Rukhsana, Farida...I need to take care of her."

"Nadira, give her something hot to drink," one of them replied as I headed straight to the attached bathroom in the bedroom.

I undressed in the bathroom, shivering, but it was a happy shiver.I soaked my dirty clothes in the bucket. It was one of my favorite salwar kameez, and now I'd have to discard it, considering the contents of the murky water I'd walked through. But when the cold, clean water caressed my body, my heart soared, and tears of joy flowed from my eyes. Ah, the relief of coming back *home*.

After changing clothes, I dusted a little talcum powder on my face and neck. The aroma of the brewing tea made my mouth water as soon as I opened the bathroom door.

Mom was ready with the chai. I devoured it with my favorite Parle-G biscuits.

"No more traveling in trains now," she said. "I'm going to tell your Abba to make you stop being so foolish. What is the need for a job?" She went on and on, pointing out all my inadequacies, but I shook my head and tuned her out.

Instead, I sank into the worn-out sofa we draped with bed sheets so that it looked sober. Our modest one-bedroom flat comforted me like never before. The kitchen was small; only one person at a time could work inside. But I loved churning out different delicacies here. We didn't have a bed in the bedroom—we slept on floor mattresses—but the thought of lying on it after the storm I endured seemed magical. Nothing could take away the gratitude I felt for all the little things that brought comfort to my life.

Yawning, I gazed sleepily out of the window at the soft rain. I got up to lie on the mattress in the bedroom that I used to share with my little sister and wondered what she was up to.

Two years younger than me, she was married and now six months pregnant. I missed her. Bushra and I used to be best friends, but now she had grown distant. I understood that priorities changed after getting married, but I wanted my sister to know that she could still share anything with me. Bushra was closer to Mom now than she was with me, but didn't share much with her, either. And Papa was a different matter altogether. He was far away from home, and I doubted he ever called her when she was at her in-laws.

I turned around on the mattress and squeezed my

eyes shut, only to see the image of that man on the bus. His obsession with his books, the way his hair flopped into his eyes, and how his Adam's apple bobbed up and down when I stood close to him wanting to peek in that bag....

I should have asked his name. He was so strange. I opened my eyes as a chuckle erupted from my throat. But I was a stranger. Who asks someone where they will pee? *Oh, my big mouth.*

I stood and looked out of the bedroom window. It was darker now. A few flashlights here and there. And...what was *that*? Something was moving on the water.

My heart jumped to my throat as I ran to the living room to confirm what I saw. I tried to spot it again, cupping my hands at the sides of my face to have a better look through the glass window.

Come on, where are you? I tried to concentrate on the scene outside through the chattering noise of aunties and mom gossiping at the door. I was so sure I saw a boat, but now I couldn't make out anything. After a while, I saw the flashlight again. Woohoo! A boat on the roads of Mumbai. This was the first time boats would've ever been used on the streets of the city. A few men illuminated by the flashlights in the boats seemed to be searching and yelling for anyone still trapped in the water.

A shriek broke out of my lips, and I clapped my hands. Those boats looked like inflatable ones, and I wanted to see them up close. Rummaging in the bedroom for my father's raincoat and not finding it, I yelled, "Mom, where is Papa's raincoat?"

Mom muttered, "Now, why do you need a raincoat? Stay put and pray. Or else sleep."

"Give na. Don't lecture me for everything." I stomped my feet.

"Oh, this girl and her tantrums." She removed the cushions on the sofa and opened a hidden storage place beneath it.

I whistled. "Wow, how many other hiding places in our house, Mom? How come I don't know about it?"

"As if you are interested in running the house," she scoffed.

"Mom, please. Raincoat?"

As soon as she handed me the raincoat, I dashed for the front door.

"Foolish girl! It's not even an hour since you walked in that water and returned home, and now again, where are you going?"

I giggled as Mom's voice floated toward me. Going down the stairs, I halted on the first floor. The ground flats were half-submerged in the water, their occupants safe on the upper floors. I didn't want my clothes to get wet again, so I hitched my salwar above my knees and prayed for them to stay there. Then donning the raincoat, I stepped in the water.

I didn't want to go in the middle of the road where the boats were. I planned on asking them to take me for a ride when they passed by me. I waited for a few minutes, but not a single boat came close to where I was. So, I ventured a little further into the water until my calves were submerged. Finally, a boat passed, carrying supplies —water bottles, biscuits, food packets. Oh, if I had brought some packets from home, I could have gone with them to the mosque and distributed them. Maybe even meet the man from the bus again to ask him his name.

Rukhsana Aapa, one of the ground floor residents, halted my wishful thinking when she yelled, "Afrah, your ammi is calling for you. You better go home."

Yes, of course. Who else would interrupt my wonderful dreams except for my sweet old mom? I didn't want to spoil my mood, so I went back to the building, sat on the topmost step of the first floor, and whistled. It was a satisfying day: I helped a man to safety *and* saw boats in Mumbai. Something that would not leave my memories for a while.

"Afrah! Come back inside and change your clothes!" Mom shouted from above.

I rubbed my eyes and yawned. Well, I wasn't wet one bit, except for the lower part of my legs. Even my salwar remained where I'd hitched it. What a miracle, indeed....

"Yes, you better go," Rukhsana Aapa said, sitting next to me, "or else Nadira will make sure you get married as soon as the water settles! She is that frustrated with you."

I snorted. I appreciated how Rukhsana was more of a friend to me, even though she was older than me by over a decade.

"Aapa, forget it. You tell me, where are you staying?"

"We are on the second floor, at Farida's house. Our home is...well..." She hiccuped and couldn't say anything further.

I'd seen how much the ground-floor residents suffered when I returned home earlier that evening. A sofa floated in the water and another table was on its last leg as Rukhsana Aapa's husband struggled to close the front door.

I hugged Rukhsana. Always well dressed in smart salwar-kurtis, with a matching dupatta covering her head, she ran a beauty parlor from her house. I couldn't imagine how many more things would be ruined once the rains stopped and the water drained.

"It will be all right, Aapa. Do not worry so much. We will help you clean up once the water settles. After all, you have such amazing neighbors." I wiggled my brows, and she smiled.

"Thank you. Now go."

I made my way to the flat, washed my hands and legs, and sat on a chair near the window, finger-combing my hair as I ignored Mom.

She muttered, "Change into other clothes, at least."

Here we go. I let out a tired sigh. "I'm good, Mom."

"At least Bushra listens to me. She married the man of my choice, and she is so happy. Why don't you listen?"

"Uff, stop nagging, mother. He wasn't the man of *your* choice," I challenged. When she didn't reply, I said, "Don't drag my little sister into our conversation every single time. I'm happy for her, too."

She chided. "What was so important that you had to rush out of here again? Going out in the water like that. Now, do not fall sick tomorrow. It's like you've made it your mission to never listen to me."

"Mom, there are boats outside. And I wanted to see..." I crossed my arms and pouted.

"You could have watched them from the window and not behaved like a spoiled child. It's not like you have never seen or sat in a boat before."

Mom was right, and I knew that. But in my defense, I had never seen an inflatable boat. Huffing, I went back to the bedroom, wishing for Papa to be with me. At least he let me do as I pleased.

I heard one of the neighboring aunties brainwashing my mother. "Why does she call you 'mom'? Why not Ammi?"

I couldn't help myself as I yelled back, "I'll call her whatever I want to! Stop interfering in our matters."

The main door shut, and Mom stopped toward the door of the bedroom, "What's wrong with you? You shouldn't talk like that to your elders. Wait till your abba calls."

I rolled my eyes. "What else can you do except grumble?"

"You have become shameless! I should have married you the day you turned eighteen, like Bushra. She is settled and now having her first child, too."

I narrowed my eyes at her. "She had a boyfriend when she was 17. I didn't. Yet, I am shameless?"

"No use talking to you!" She slammed the door of the bedroom on her way out.

I shrugged. I couldn't stand her comparison of Bushra and me. I was always happy for my sister but had enough of Mom's nagging. She wasn't like this before. We'd always had our differences, but her criticism of me started the day I told her I wanted to study. The thought reminded me of the interview again. I longed for the rain to stop so that I could continue job hunting. Staying here round the clock with Mother was going to make me insane.

After a dinner of roti and the sabzi I'd made that morning, I tried to sleep. I didn't call Mom to have dinner with me. She'd eat whenever she wanted to. Or not.

Sadiq

On reaching the mosque, I heaved a sigh of relief. *Thank Allah! I listened to Afrah. How could I have even thought of remaining on that bus all alone?* The lower floor was flooded. A few men and boys moved the chairs and other knick-knacks to higher ground. I followed them up to the first floor. It was sectioned off by curtains; one side was for men, and the other for women. I found a space near a window and deposited my books there. After thanking the boys again and greeting the others, I went to the washroom.

I returned after freshening up to the window where I'd deposited my books and pushed it open. There wasn't any other ventilation here and the mosque was filling up with people now. Raindrops covered my hands as I secured the window on the latch again, wondering when it would stop. Thoughts of my family crept into my mind. Still no way to contact Ammi. She would be hyperventilating with worry but being stuck here, I couldn't do anything about it.

The buildings across were flooded, and it was quiet outside. I assumed most of the stranded were either here or risked walking home in the dark. I would have too, if not for the books. And then what would've happened? Shaking my head, I sat, wondering if I could say my evening prayers, but my clothes...I had an idea of the contents of the muddy water I'd just walked through. *Thankfully, I didn't pee myself.* I gave a quiet chuckle thinking of Afrah.

The situation near my house would be so much worse. The cramped chawl that we lived in was on Pipe Road, a congested part of Kurla and an area prone to flooding with even a little rain. Resting my head on the wall behind me, I visualized the entire ground floor. I lived on the first floor with my parents, a small 150 square feet house with a tiny kitchen and a mezzanine of equal size. The houses shared a common toilet. My abbu's barber shop on the ground floor must be submerged.

"Assalamualaikum," an old man greeted me. His clothes were damp like mine, and his skull cap was drenched, too. "You are the man from the bus, right?"

"Wa alaikum assalam, yes. I'm Sadiq."

"I'm glad you chose to come here, Sadiq. See how dark it is outside."

I made small talk with him out of courtesy, but all I wanted was to curl up to sleep for a while Once he left, making his way around the room of men, I checked the condition of my books and tried reading a few questions. My entrance exams were next year. After my internship and graduation, cracking these exams would help me do my post-graduation in surgery. I had to clear these exams at any cost, had loans to repay, and so many dreams—the first being to find a better place to live with Ammi. Every moment lost made me restless. *Due to the floods, I can't report to work at the hospital tomorrow. What if I miss out? Ah!* I clutched my head with both hands as if to stop my anxious thoughts from churning in my head.

I closed my eyes and took a few deep breaths. The first thing that came to mind was a pair of grey eyes. *I need to thank her.* Maybe I could if I spotted her again tomorrow.

A few local teenagers carrying packets of biscuits and flasks of tea came to the floor. It wasn't much, but they were trying their best to make everyone comfortable. I smiled and thanked them for their generosity, also muttering my gratitude to Allah for keeping me safe. I shuddered to think how many people were lost or dead in this deluge.

One boy gave me a few candles and a matchbox. "Here, please light these. It will help to some extent."

I lit the candles in my section of the mosque, wondering if Afrah was on the women's side helping. But I didn't have a way to find out and going over there to invade women's privacy was out of the question. When our section was bright enough, I lay down and closed my eyes. Grey eyes flitted in and out of my mind, and so did the conversation I had with her. Why did I behave like a child? It was literally a tantrum—not getting out of the bus despite so many people requesting me to. Replays of that embarrassing moment kept all other dreams at bay, giving me a fitful sleep. I hoped I would get a chance to redeem myself in front of her.

Chapter 4
Mobile Phone in Dreams
Afrah

The next morning, water levels remained the same and vehicles were still stranded. No boats zipped by. Leaving the chai to brew for a while, I ate some biscuits in the living room. A lizard crawled on the opposite wall from me. Mom would do whatever she wanted to with it. I had no intention of disturbing the little creature who had gone as still as the world outside.

With the dead landline phones and no electricity, boredom enveloped me. *What should I do now?* Get on mother's nerves? She deserved it after comparing me with Bushra last night. Huffing around the house, I thought about my sister. I had no idea how she and her family were doing. They lived in another suburb, about fifteen minutes away. Was their area flooded like this, too? *Oh, water, water everywhere.*

What if the water supply in the taps dwindled, too? This could very well happen with the rain pouring outside and no information on when the electricity would be restored. I rushed to the bathroom and filled up all the buckets I could find. Why take the risk? Splashing water from the tap put me in a trance, and my mind drifted back to the man from the bus. I couldn't stop thinking about him. What was he doing? Did he attempt to walk home, or was he still at the mosque? If only I could ride in the boat, I could go to the mosque myself and find out.

Once my work in the bathroom was done, I peeked out of the window. One of the young men from my building was in a boat nearby. They were distributing supplies again. I called out to him, and with hardly anyone outside, he heard me easily. He told me how the nearby Mithi River was choked, and it would take another day or two for the water to recede completely.

It would be foolish to ask about the man from the bus. He wouldn't know anyway and my nosy neighbors were waiting to complain to mother about me. And Mom needn't know I had helped a man out of the bus last evening. She'd not want me going out of the house at all then. Not because she didn't want me to marry, but because she wouldn't be able to claim that she got me my match. Bushra had gotten her way. Now, I couldn't.

But I didn't want to jeopardize my happiness. I wanted to have my own income so I would not be dependent on anyone, be it a future husband or Mom. Besides, I loved teaching, and what could be better than doing the job you loved *and* getting paid for it? Papa had no problem with me working, and he had made it clear to me that I should do whatever I felt was right.

"Now, what are you up to?" Mom came out of the bedroom groggy. "Do you plan to cook food, or will it make itself?"

I couldn't hold back my sarcasm. "There are no vegetables or meat in the fridge. Do you want me to swim outside or take a ride in the boat to get you some?"

"You are impossible." She threw her hands up. "I'll make potatoes *sabzi*. Will you at least make rotis?"

"Yes, tell me once you are done in the kitchen, and I'll make." I didn't want her to complain while I cooked —the roti is not perfectly round, or the dough is too hard or too soft—I didn't have the patience to endure that so early in the morning.

Mom walked away and I stepped closer to the mirror on the old teakwood almirah in the living room, finding a hair growing on my upper lip.

"Arghh..." I'd threaded a few days back and didn't

want to endure that pain so soon. Why couldn't they stop growing for at least a month? My eyebrows had become bushy too, and a spot on my cheek hurt. That about-to-erupt pimple was a signal for my period to start. I checked the calendar again. Last month it was on the 30th. The local physician attributed my unpredictable periods to stress.

I didn't want it to break out, so I grabbed a little toothpaste from the bathroom and applied it to the area that was tender on my face. And then immediately washed it off, remembering Mom told me that applying toothpaste worsened the pimple. *What do I do now? Stupid pimples.* There were already enough scars on my face. I didn't want the pimple to hog the attention for my next interview. But what choice did I have?

The landline phone lay silent on the table outside the kitchen, mocking me as if to say, 'No calls, no job for you,' just like my mom.

"Shut up," I murmured in the phone's direction. "You are dead." And I would never stop waiting for 'the call.' It would come soon.

The list of things I wanted to buy with my first salary distracted me from falling into another spiral of disappointment over my interview. I had stuck the paper on the inside of the almirah's door. 'Mobile phone' was at the top, and I'd written a few models I liked next to it. Focusing on those words, I closed my eyes. *Oh, I'll buy the Nokia—it's the best model for the year. It has a fancy camera, too!* The image of the phone in my mind kept me sane. I needed money of my own. Earned money, not what I received as Eidi. And the dream of becoming a teacher...that would happen, too.

Chapter 5
Of Silence and Rage
Sadiq

It took two days for the water to subside. On the morning of the third day, I boarded a bus with my bags of books and gazed toward the building where the woman with grey eyes probably lived. Afrah. *What a beautiful name!* I prayed to meet her again one day.

The road leading to my home had dirt piled up on both sides and was sticky with muck. I pinched my nose to cut off the stale air. After reaching the chawl, I knocked on the door to my house. The silence around me was alarming. The neighbors' doors were all shut, too. The chawl, normally alive with a flurry of activity —neighbors sharing food and gossip alike—was still. I never carried the house keys as my ammi was always home. I knocked harder.

Footsteps shuffled from within the house, and

Ammi opened the door. Her eyes were puffy, and the shawl draped on her head was inside-out.

"Oh, Sadiq...oh, Allah *ka shukr*! Oh! My boy," she continued in Urdu. "We thought you...you...." She couldn't complete her sentence. Tears pooled in her eyes. "We couldn't find you," she whispered.

I hugged her. "Shhh. Ammi, shhh. I'm home. I'm safe. Stop crying."

"Shabana...what happened?" The frail Dilshad Aapa, our immediate neighbor, came out of her house, startled when she saw me. "Oh, thank Allah," she praised, and off she went to alert everyone.

I followed a hiccuping Ammi into the house and offered her water. "I need to take a bath," I said, going up to the mezzanine to get a towel and fresh clothes.

The water in the bucket was too cold. I used it in small amounts, shivering, but I didn't have any other choice. I scrubbed the dirt off from the last two days until my skin was raw. The water running off me became clear after using almost two buckets of it. My teeth wouldn't stop chattering, and after I got dressed, I draped a towel over my clothes, rubbing my hands together to warm them.

Ammi was ready with a cup of hot chai. As I sat cross-legged on the floor of our little room attached to the kitchen, she said, "Your *bade-abba* and abbu went searching for you the moment the water reduced. They left early in the morning today."

"How would they even know where to look for me? I never told you where I was going." And then it struck me. If my paternal uncle and father believed I was injured or, worse, dead, they would go to the hospitals nearby. "Any other way to contact them? Bade-abba has a phone, right?" Our landlines were still dead.

I went out and asked another neighbor to borrow a mobile phone. But its batteries were dead too. I would have to wait for them to come home.

Returning to the kitchen, I sipped on the tea and remembered the others stuck with me in the mosque. I hoped they all reached their destinations safely. And that image of Afrah telling me not to pee in the water had me chuckling again.

"What is it?" Ammi asked.

I pretended to cough, diverting the topic. "Nothing like homemade chai, Ammi. I missed you so much." Rain battered the roof, and the lone window banged shut. "I'm worried about Bade-abba and Abbu."

"Don't be," she said. "They will come home for lunch. I'm making fresh chapatis. You must be so hungry. Eat more now. Look at yourself." She clucked. "I can count your bones."

I laughed at my mother's antics. "Ammi, don't be

upset. This here, I reminded her, pointing at my head, "is very strong."

"So, tell your old ammi, where were you for two days?" She went to the kitchen and began kneading the dough for chapattis.

I explained to her how I was returning from a senior student's house with all the books when the bus was stranded. I told her about the kindness of strangers who escorted me to safety in a mosque and kept me fed for two days. As I spoke, I watched her cook, making magic with her deft hands. Everything she made was always tasty. She placed fresh chapattis layered with ghee on my plate, and I devoured them, satisfied. I didn't tell her about Afrah.

When I had my fill, I went up to the mezzanine with my books. Water dripped through the roof into the buckets I'd put throughout the house. But the damage notwithstanding, this small room was my home, my refuge. Even if it smelled musty all the time, even if there was only one window and no ventilation, even if I wasn't planning on staying here forever... I was accustomed to this place. Oh, Allah! How much I'd missed it over the last two days.

The sound of the dripping rain lulled me into a deep slumber.

By the time I woke up feeling energized, the rain had stopped, and it was time for the evening prayers.

Abbu's voice reached my ears. After rubbing my eyes and stretching, I climbed down.

"Good to see you are alright," Abbu said, greeting me.

"Did you sleep well?" Ammi asked while lighting some candles throughout our tiny abode.

"Yes, I did." I smiled at Ammi and nodded at Abbu.

Abbu's face danced in the shadows of candlelight. The beard on his face was turning grey, and the skull cap hid the baldness of his head. His tone edged with condescension, "Why didn't you walk back home yesterday? The water had reduced."

I gritted my teeth and bit back a spout of venom. He wouldn't understand even if I explained. He would blame me for going to my senior's house in the rain, and I wasn't in the mood to argue.

Ammi cut through the tension in the room. "Leave it, ji. He is home, safe. What more do we want?"

He dropped the subject and gestured with his hand outstretched. "Give me the two hundred rupees I gave you yesterday. I'll pay some poor fellow to get the shop cleaned up. And I'm going to the mosque for namaz."

Ammi did as Abbu asked while I stormed into the little kitchen. I poured some water into a vessel and put it on the stove, doing so with as much noise as possible.

"No use bashing up the vessels, dear son," Ammi said as Abbu left the house.

"Why did you give him the money? He doesn't need to spend it on some 'poor soul.' I could have cleaned the shop on my day off. Allah knows how we are getting by."

"Let it be, Sadiq. You concentrate on your studies. Do what you want to and make a better life for yourself."

I dashed toward my ammi and hugged her.

"Well, there, there," she said, looking up at me. She cradled my face in her hands, and my anger melted like butter in a hot pan. I remembered I had a two-day stubble on my face, and shaving it was the first thing I needed to do before going to the hospital. Ammi interrupted my thoughts, "What were you planning to make in that vessel?"

I gave her a sheepish smile and shrugged. "Are the phone lines up?"

"I haven't checked. But I don't think so." She confirmed it by lifting the receiver that hung on the wall right outside the kitchen.

"I'll study for a while then."

With a candle, I leafed through the books till I found the one I was looking for. But before I could open it, Bade-abba's voice thundered through our little house.

"Where is my *bachcha?* Come, hug this old man."

I dropped the book and rushed downstairs. Tall, well-built, with his long salt-and-pepper beard, Bade-abba Arshad looked quite intimidating to others. But I'd never seen him in that way. I hugged him.

"You scared us, young man," he said after releasing me.

"I know. But I couldn't help it." Once again, I explained in detail how I was stuck on the bus and how a bunch of strangers practically dragged me out to safety.

Bade-abba burst out laughing. "I can imagine you refusing to get down to protect a bundle of books. Did Haider meet you?"

"Yes, Abbu left a few minutes ago."

I loved my bade-abba more than Abbu. Even though Bade-abba was the most domineering member of the family, he treated me like a son. My uncle had worked hard to uplift his family; from selling dates on the roadside to developing a chain of stores selling his exclusive dates throughout the city, he had come a long way. He understood the value of hard work and dedication, unlike Abbu, who only liked to gather praise for himself.

"Am I keeping you from your studies?" Bade-abba asked me as Ammi brought tea and biscuits for him.

"Not really. I haven't started."

"It's too dark for you to study up there, anyway. Take your books and come with me. I have a battery-operated lamp. It is fully charged, and I haven't let Farheen use it, no matter how much she begged." His raucous laughter reverberated in the room.

I thought about his offer for a moment. Bade-abba lived a few minutes away in a housing complex. But I wouldn't get a minute's study in, not with Farheen, my cousin, there. Although she was younger than me by a few years, she spoke to me as if I was a small baby—always cooing and flipping her hair. It got on my nerves. I looked at Ammi, who waited with bated breath for my answer.

"No, Bade-abba. I'll stay back here. I may not even read anything today. Will just rest."

"Ha, okay. But if you change your mind, do come. The water has gone from our area. Only this part is flooded."

"Bade-abba, do you have any idea when the trains will start?" He was always well-informed, and I wanted to go to the hospital as soon as I could.

"Oh, they have started, bachcha. Electricity and phone lines might start tomorrow." He finished his tea and took leave, hollering to the neighbors.

Ammi sighed. "Your sisters will be so worried about us. Allah knows how they are doing."

Knowing how much Ammi worried about every

single thing, I was glad I didn't take up Bade-abba's offer of leaving the house. She needed me here. I held her hand and said, "They must be alright. We will talk to them as soon as we can. Okay?"

My sisters had found stability in their married lives. I couldn't thank Bade-abba any more than I already had. If it were up to my abbu, he wouldn't have even bothered to check what family he was marrying them. Some or other acquaintance would promise it was a good family, a good match, and he would go ahead with it. I shuddered to think where my sisters would have landed. Thank Allah, Bade-abba was actively involved in arranging matches for my sisters.

As for myself, I felt lucky I had a chance to follow my dreams. And all of it, once again, because of Bade-abba. Whenever anyone from my family would ask what I wanted to be as a grown-up, I always said a doctor. It would amuse my relatives, and they would laugh, saying nobody had studied so much in their family. But I'd wanted to change that. I had the brains. The art of treating others through knowledge fascinated me. And I wanted that knowledge. When I fell short of money to pay the fees, Bade-abba helped me out by paying them.

I went to the mezzanine again and finally opened a book to read. Toxicology was my weakness, along with microbiology. I had somehow managed to clear these subjects in the second year, but having to study them again for the post-graduate entrance exam gave me jitters. What other choice did I have? If I wanted to be a surgeon, I had to score high to secure admission to a good hospital in the city, or I would have to go out of the city or even the state. I didn't mind going some-where else, but the thought of leaving my Ammi alone didn't sit well with me. *No, I'd score well enough and take Ammi to live somewhere nice with me in the city.*

I opened the page to toxins and their antidotes, but a banging sound from below disturbed me. *Can't even read a single line.* That's why I preferred to stay at my college library to study.

"Sadiq, come eat something," Ammi shouted from the kitchen as if she had a sense of whenever I opened my books. I always obeyed her.

"Spend some time with your old ammi today," she said as I climbed down the steps. "Tomorrow you'll disappear early and come home late again."

The rains thudded on the tin roof, causing the ceiling to leak more this year than ever, and I would have to put a plastic sheet over it. The roof needed proper repairs with tar, but nobody in the chawl wanted to take the initiative or contribute to fixing it up. They were happy living with the buckets or putting up temporary plastic sheets to save money.

After I finished eating the rice and dal, I went

down to survey the roads. The water was ankle-deep, and I thought it might recede completely by morning. I looked forward to going to the hospital; it was the last few days of my pediatric posting in my internship. Next week, I would start my favorite—surgery.

Chapter 6
Prime Age
Afrah

I went to the terrace of my five-floor building. It was relieving to be out in the open and not cramped up inside now that the rain had stopped. Grayish clouds hovered above me, the sun yet to be seen. A few birds chirped and cawed as if glad they could fly again. Breathing the fresh air brought a smile to my face. Then I looked down. And cringed.

The water from the roads had drained, but there was garbage strewn all over. It would take many days to clear the roads, and only if it didn't flood again. In the distance, some of the stranded vehicles were starting up , but with the phone lines dead there was still no other connection to the outside world. I had no idea what was going on in the city. People from the locality had said that the electricity would be restored by tonight or tomorrow morning. Until then, it was candlelight.

I stayed on the terrace for a while, alternating my gaze between the sky and the traffic below. A few neighbors from my building joined me. Tuba, my friend, was among them. Her long hair was braided , and her shoulders slumped.

"What nasty last few days," she said.

"Yes, indeed. Are you alright?"

"We haven't been able to contact my abbu. He was at his work office when the flooding started. He called once, saying he would try to make it home, but as we told him to stay put, the line disconnected. I'm really worried." Her eyes glazed into tears.

I hugged her. "Don't worry, he'll come home soon." I really hoped he would.

After squeezing her hand, I made my way home.

"There was a call for you," Mom said as I entered. "From APK Consulting."

The dratted phone came alive the moment I stepped out of the house. My heart jumped to my throat. It was the same company where I'd last interviewed at! I promptly dialed them back.

"Miss Farooqui, yes. I had called. I'm glad to inform you that you have got the job. Please report to work at 9:00 a.m. on the first of August, Monday.

You'll receive training for a month, and then we'll take it from there."

I swear I could've screamed, but controlled myself. "Thank you so much, ma'am. Yes. I'll be there at nine. Bye." I put down the receiver and then released a squeal. "Woohoo! Yay!" I let it all out.

Mom came out of the bedroom. I hugged her and turned her around in the living room. "What are you doing? I'm dizzy." She extricated herself from my grip and sat down on the sofa.

I plonked right next to her and heaved a sigh of relief. "Oh, sorry. I got carried away." I screeched, "But I finally got a job!"

Mom looked pale. "You did?"

"Oh, come on, Mom, don't be a spoilsport. I have given so many interviews but doing that Tally course finally helped me. Your precious money did not go to waste." I wiggled my brows, but she wasn't amused.

"And what about the rishtas I have arranged for you? What will I say when you won't be available at home?"

Oh, of course, marriage was the reason she wasn't happy I got the job. I held her hand. "Mom, we can always adjust the timings. Have I ever not been present for the suitors?"

Mom smiled. "Of course, you are very cooperative.

Except when you say you want to work after marriage, and they look at you horrified."

"Yeah, yeah. Why can't I work after marriage? Or study, for that matter? My husband can pay my fees for the teacher's college or let me work so I can save and then study. Simple."

"It's not that simple. You are twenty-one. Your prime age is fading. You need to act like a to-be-bride and get yourself a good man. You can't do that if your head is somewhere else."

"I'm *only* twenty-one, Mom. Not fifty. And even if I do get married, I will not have a baby so soon. I'm a baby myself, as you always say, so how will I take care of another one?"

"Nonsense. I don't know from where you get all these ideas. Look at your sister. She married at eighteen, and now within a year, she is going to be a mother. Sometimes, she shows more maturity than you."

"Don't compare me with anyone, okay? I hate it!" With my heart pounding in my chest, I went to the window. Mom grabbed my shoulders and turned me around.

"How dare you talk to me like that? Let me talk to your abba when he comes back. Till then, you enjoy your few months of freedom. Then you'll see."

I mocked her. "*Then you'll see.* Papa is on my side,

whether he is in Saudi Arabia or here, it will not make a difference." I wagged my tongue at her and walked to the front door.

"Now, where are you going?"

"Jahannum."

Mom gasped and muttered, "This girl will be the death of me."

Giggling, I escaped upstairs to the terrace again. A fresh breeze soothed me. I did not like exasperating Mom, but she left no stone unturned to irritate me. Why couldn't she understand this little thing? Bushra chose her path in life, and I wanted the freedom to choose for myself, too. It wasn't too much to ask. Papa understood what I wanted. He always encouraged us to pursue our dreams. If Bushra's dream was to get married and have a baby, then that was her choice. I wanted to get married too, but I wanted a career as well. Any man who didn't want me *and* my career need not marry me. I wouldn't ever settle for anything less.

When my heart calmed, I went back into the house, determination coursing through me. Mom was talking to someone over the phone. I assumed it to be Bushra, and I wanted to give her the good news about my new job, but it would have to wait.

"Tuba's abbu is back," she told me as she put the receiver down.

Oh, so it wasn't Bushra. I closed my eyes, thanking Allah for reuniting Tuba's family.

In the bedroom, I glanced at myself in the mirror. *I'll have to get my eyebrows tweezed.* Mom didn't like it when I threaded my brows either. She'd often say, 'Be proud of how Allah made you, and don't get lost in this make-believe world.' I understood this, I really did, but I liked looking this way.

I counted the spots on my face. Ten. Or more than that? I couldn't make out now. Some were large, others tiny. There were too many. I sighed. I'd have to let the pimples take their course. If I fiddled with them, they would leave more scars.

I analyzed the hair growth on my forearms and legs. I would have to wax before Monday. A visit to Rukhsana Aapa was due. But considering the state of her house, I doubted she would be available for the next few days. *Maybe I'll wear all my full-sleeved kurtis until then.*

I opened the steel cupboard of clothes and made a mental checklist of things I needed to do while rummaging inside for something smart that I could wear on my first day. *Buy a train pass, some comfortable shoes or sandals for daily travel, more kurtis, and jeans.*

A mint green kurta caught my eye on the shelf. I took it out and searched for the black salwar and dupatta to wear with it. *Cleaning the mess of my cupboard...* Another thing added to my checklist. Placing the kurta and leggings on the bed, I clapped my hands.

"Perfect!"

Monday morning came soon, but my nerves kept me from breakfast. I hadn't felt this anxious even on the first day of junior college when the "well-meaning" people in my building told me to be careful and blend in the crowd, or I might be ragged as the junior-most. However, nothing of that sort happened, and those were the best years of my life. I'd graduated in March earlier this year, and these last few months had been a nightmare as I was stuck at home.

I bid goodbye to my mother, who surprisingly smiled and wished me safe travels. She told me to call her from the office once I arrived. Sometimes, her behavior boggled me, but I was glad she boosted my morale. I needed some confidence to handle the day.

At the station, seeing the snaking ticket counter queues made me more nervous. It was important to reach the office on time on my first day, so jumping the queue was the only option if I didn't want to be late. A few people hollered at me as I tried to cheat my way to the front. Embarrassed, I asked an old man for help. He refused at first, but after some pleading, he agreed to buy me a return ticket to Vashi. Then, on Platform 7, I struggled to get on the train. The women jostled together, behaving as if they missed it, their lives would be over. I was one of them. Elbows were used as weapons to disarm or, in this case, dissuade each other from boarding first. But I didn't give up and caught hold of the pole in the center of the entrance, then moved inside the compartment.

After arriving at Vashi station, I smoothed my crumpled kurti and combed my hair, which was both a mess, all thanks to the crowd inside the train. At the office, I was pleased to see many new recruits like me waiting for our training to begin.

I struck up a conversation with Roshni, who, like me, was a fresh graduate. She was wearing a kurti and jeans, and her hair was tied in a top bun. I couldn't ever do the top bun!

"I come from Bandra," she said. "Changed a train at Vadala station. What about you?"

"I live in Kurla. My goodness, how do you manage two trains? I had a body massage today for twenty minutes by protruding elbows!"

Roshni laughed. "I know. Get a first-class pass. It is slightly better," she said, indicating so by raising her thumb to her index finger with marginal space between them. "Also, we can catch the same train. You can get in the—wait," she mentally calculated something before continuing, "8:03 train at Kurla. We'll reach Vashi by 8:30, and then we can either take a bus or an auto till here."

I looked at her in awe. "You are so good at this!"

"Oh, that's because I have been using this route for the last five years." Roshni grinned. "My college was in Chembur."

I nodded. A smartly dressed man entered the conference room. I liked this place. The small cubicles were arranged in circles, so each could see what their counterpart was doing. "Today's training is a crash course in Tally 7.2, amongst a few other things," the man started.

Thank Allah, I already know Tally. This would be a good revision.

I yawned multiple times throughout the lecture until one of the senior coworkers threw a pointed look at me, and I kept my mouth closed for the rest of the session. I didn't want to get fired on my first day. *At least pretend to listen, even if you already know it all.* Then we were each given a file of an accounting sheet and asked to demonstrate what we had learned. I had fun doing that and even helped Roshni finish hers. Another newcomer asked me for help too, so I toned down my confidence a little; no use being bombarded with others' work too, right?

After a short lunch break, everyone dispersed to the different departments we were assigned. Luckily, Roshni was with me. The remaining day passed in a blur.

Back home exhausted, I splashed cold water on my face. Mom wasn't home. *She must be at one of the neighbors.*

I hugged a pillow on the sofa and closed my eyes, remembering the days after I'd gotten the acceptance phone call for my new job. On the third day, post floods, I sat talking to Mom and the lights blinked on. Overjoyed, we rushed to switch on the television. She couldn't stay away from her daily soaps, but the cable connection was still out. We looked at each other and burst out laughing.

"Oh, you are home," Mom said, pulling me out of my reverie. "How was it?"

I opened my eyes. "It was good. They are making us learn Tally again, and then they'll tell us what our jobs will be."

"Good. Made some friends?"

"Yes, one. We'll be working together."

Mom hugged me. "I love you so much. Remember that."

I hugged her back, wondering what had put her in such a good mood. "I know." I kissed her cheek. "I love you, too." Then I pouted. "But you make me *so* angry sometimes!"

Mom sighed. "I'm your mother, and you will understand one day when you become one."

I scoffed and crossed my legs on the sofa, my pajamas shifting up.

Mom gasped at a white patch over my ankle. "What is this?"

"I don't know. It's been there for a year, I think."

"A year? Why didn't I know about this?"

"Is it important? Somebody told me it happens in calcium deficiency. I use Nivea cream every night on it." I peeked at it more closely. I could see the clear margins. "Has it increased in size?"

"How would I know, *beta*? I have not seen it before. See, if it doesn't get better, go to our doctor, okay?"

I saluted and giggled. "Yes, Mom."

"I'm worried about you," she said. "How will you travel so far daily?"

"It's just five stops by train. No big deal, and it takes only about twenty-five minutes."

"But you have never traveled by train before."

"Mom, I have. Don't forget those five years of junior college and graduation."

"But that was in Sion. Half the time, you went by bus."

"Yes, I know. But I'll figure it out. Don't worry so much." I stood, feeling something flutter in my chest. All I craved was this little bit of love from my mother, and when I did get that...it...I swallowed and blinked back tears. I turned my face away so that she wouldn't see my glazed eyes.

"Now, where are you going?" Mom asked.

"Oh, Mom. Nowhere. Just looking out of the window." I tied my hair into a bun and parted the curtains for the view outside, a teary smile plastered on my face.

Chapter 7
Coincidence or Fate?
Sadiq

My first day of surgery postings at the hospital after leaving the confines of my tiny house consisted of ward rounds. To my disappointment, we had yet to step into the operation theater, but the month ahead looked exciting, and I couldn't wait to hold a scalpel.

Today could be the day. It was our unit's emergency duty.

Over breakfast, I'd tried to explain to Ammi the different unit systems at the hospital. "I'm in Unit 2 this time, which means I will not come home Tuesday and Friday."

"As if I understand what you say. Unit 1, 2, or 3. Doesn't matter if you give me a call at least once during the day."

"I'll try, Ammi. I'll see if there's a direct line from the ward."

At the station, I had to run to catch the train, else I'd have missed it by a fraction of a second. Being a Tuesday, it was a little less crowded. I could enter the compartment without too much shoving. Mondays were always crazy, and yesterday was no exception. After placing my heavy bag of books on the overhead racks, I rolled my neck to reduce the knotted muscles. That's when my gaze fell on a woman in the adjacent compartment. It wasn't a compartment as such, but a small block barricaded with a grill that served as a first-class area for women. The familiar woman looked in my direction. Her face lit up like an electric bulb, and she waved at me.

Afrah. Instead of returning her wave, I looked at my feet, my hands involuntarily rubbing my nape. I didn't know why, but I was suddenly shy at the thought of being the one she was directing her gaze at. *I should have at least smiled at her.* My heart pounded as I glanced up again. She was still staring at me. Before I could raise my hand to return her wave, Ashish, my colleague and friend, called out for me as the train halted at the next station. I turned away from Afrah to look in his direction.

"Buddy, please take this," Ashish said, hauling his

bag over the heads of commuters and hearing a few choice words in the process.

I grabbed it before it fell on an unsuspecting man's head and placed it on the rack. Ashish stood near the door, and I waited for him to find a way toward me as the train emptied at the next stop. I glanced in Afrah's direction, but she seemed busy talking to the woman beside her. Her red salwar kameez stood out in the crowd.

Ashish yelled, "Bro, whatsup?"

I didn't want to shout over the crowd, so I waited for him to move closer. Ashish was the one who convinced me to buy a first-class pass for traveling way back in our first year. I wanted to travel in second class, but after being squeezed from all sides for several days and coming out of it looking harrowed, I gave in. Saving as much money as possible was important for me, but traveling like that wasn't going to get me closer to my goals. It would be a waste of my energy.

Ashish joined me as the next stop went by.

"Where were you yesterday?" I asked.

"Oh, I woke up late," he shrugged. "And then I missed the allotment of units at the hospital. I can't believe they've put me in Unit 3. I can't do a fifty-six-hour shift...simply cannot. I'm asking for a repeat allotment today."

"Let it be, Ashish. You have to put in the work," I tried to explain.

"Yeah, yeah. Your posting last month was in Medicine, right? How was it?"

"It was good. I was in Unit 1. But we managed it well since the work was light when we had our shift. I guess I was lucky." Internal Medicine was hectic but fun. It gave me a lot of practical experience, and I always volunteered to assist in most procedures, be it intubation or central line insertion at intensive care units. I didn't mind helping Ashish in case he landed in Unit 1 or Unit 3 and voiced my thoughts aloud.

"Really? You are awesome." Ashish backslapped me. "I'm so relieved to hear that. I wouldn't mind Unit 3 now, but I'll still try to change it to two."

I shrugged. "No harm in trying, but don't fight. A few more months together, and then we are all going our separate ways."

"We'll see about that when the time comes." Ashish looked back and forth from the adjacent ladies' compartment. "Dude, there's a chick staring at you," he whispered suddenly.

"What?" I played dumb.

Scoffing, Ashish turned my head toward the women's compartment and raised his index finger. "See, in the red dress with her hair loose."

Afrah narrowed her eyes at us, then returned her gaze to the woman next to her.

"Stop it. She's not looking at me."

"Oh, she was. I can ask her if you want."

Ashish was about to open his mouth to call out to her, and I did not want to embarrass myself further, so I blurted, "That's Afrah."

"What? How do you know her? I have never seen you talk to any chick in our batch."

"Stop saying chick, chick. It's degrading."

"Yeah, whatever. Don't change the topic. How do you know that ch—girl?"

That's when I told him how I was stuck in a bus during the floods last week but was lucky to get through it almost unscathed, all because of that woman.

"What a horrible flood that was!" Ashish concurred. "Even our area was flooded. We gave refuge to those stranded in our community hall."

But my mind was somewhere else. I felt a certain pair of grey eyes on me, so I glanced in Afrah's direction again. She looked at me, and this time, I smiled at her. But she twisted her mouth in a frown and looked away. It startled me, as I wasn't expecting a frown from her, but then a chuckle escaped my lips.

"What?" Ashish asked.

"Nothing. I'm saying that at the end of it, we survived. I think that's what matters."

"Yeah, bro, you are right. We survived. Ah, let's not talk about it. It's too depressing."

We stood in silence for some time.

"Do you ever plan to actually talk to her?" Ashish nagged me. He'd never let it go.

I shook my head, not knowing the answer myself. "I don't know, maybe if I get a chance."

Our conversation drifted to the post-graduate entrance exams coming up. I was relieved by the change in topic, though it was overwhelming to think about.

"I won't take the exams this year," I said.

"Why not?" Ashish looked at me. "It's practice."

"I know, but we have enough of these to practice." I showed the Triple-A textbook I carried.

"But a live exam is different."

"I want to clear my exam on the first attempt," I tried again.

Ashish didn't need to know why I was not taking the exams. Not because I feared failing but because I couldn't afford to. I would have to pay for each entrance application form, which could be anywhere between 2000 to 2500 rupees. My plan was to appear for the state entrance exams only next year. Some of my batch mates planned to skip the internship to study and crack those exams this year itself, but the practical experience of an internship was more important for me as reality was different from theory. I needed to be confident enough to diagnose and treat the illnesses of the people in my chawl and other relatives.

Ashish interrupted my thoughts. "Clear in the first attempt? It's the dream, isn't it?"

"I know," I replied. "We should aim high." That was my motto in life, anyway. Aim for the highest and dream your dreams. Then they will, one day, come true.

When we reached the station, we climbed down and went to the hospital together. I sensed a busy day ahead.

Chapter 8
Sisterly Shenanigans
Afrah

The next morning, I craned my neck to look for the man in the adjacent compartment. I kind of felt guilty for not smiling back at him yesterday, but the way he first stared and then pretended as if he didn't recognize me made my blood boil. Now I couldn't find him amidst the crowds.

I had discussed it with Roshni, and she believed he really didn't recognize me. It wasn't particularly bright on the bus the evening we met. I had accepted that notion, and my cheeks burned at my foolishness. Then my skin prickled and when I looked at him, he smiled at me. *He did remember me.*

Today, he was nowhere to be found. What were the chances I would see him again?

"Afrah...Afrah...!" Roshni called.

"Yes, I'm listening." I tried to. That girl never

stopped talking. She began describing her journey in a shared auto-rickshaw in vivid detail. I tuned her out. I didn't even know the man's name, so why couldn't I stop thinking of him?

Blabbering non-stop, Roshni and I reached our destination in no time.

I enjoyed work. It was the traveling that drained me. The first-class compartment wasn't any better than the second. Women jumped onto the train even before it halted. I couldn't, for the life of me, do that. Once, I lost a sandal in the crowd while trying to get on board. Thankfully, I found it again, but I'd missed the train.

Because Roshni had my back, I found it a bit easier in the last two days. She waited at Vashi station for me in case I missed the train again and kept a place for me to squeeze in by the door. In a short span, we had come to know each other well.

No matter how my day went, I always came back home smiling. I didn't want Mom to know about my difficulties. I wasn't about to give her any opportunity to berate me for having a job.

The week flew by, and my heart brimmed with excitement as Saturday arrived. I would meet my little sister after almost a month.

I woke up earlier than usual that morning, took the meat out to thaw, and prepared the mixture to marinate it. Biryani was Bushra's favorite dish—and not just any biryani. It had to be the one made by me. She always said no one could beat mine, and that was something I held in high regard.

I didn't know if Asif, Bushra's husband, would be visiting too. She hadn't mentioned it, and even if he did, he wouldn't enter our house. It was a custom in their family to never enter or even drink water at their in-laws' place. Her in-laws had weird practices. I always thought it was quite strange. Who did such things nowadays? But I kept quiet about it because Bushra wouldn't listen to even a single word against her in-laws, and it wasn't my business anyway.

I liked Asif initially. He was Bushra's boyfriend for six months before he asked for her hand in marriage. Both sets of parents were wary of the arrangement at first, as Asif had just turned twenty-one and was yet to have a stable income. And Bushra hadn't finished junior college. But then they gave in. The wedding was a grand affair. It had always upset me, though, that my sister didn't complete her studies. Maybe I would find the time to talk to her about it today.

"Oh my, where has the sun risen from?" Mom greeted me.

"From the east, Mom." I rolled my eyes at the

mention of doomsday because I'd woken up earlier than her. "Don't behave like a foolish old lady."

She gasped. "I'm not that old." Then she looked around the kitchen, eyebrows raised at the meal in progress. "Do you need any help?"

"No, I'll make tea and breakfast for us. You can change the bed sheets. I'll dust the rooms later."

"Yes, this is good." She left to follow my orders.

I was surprised. Mom never listened to me on the first attempt. Maybe it was the excitement of her becoming a *nani* that mellowed her. I shrugged. The reason didn't matter if she let me be and do what I wanted to do.

By noon, Bushra arrived. Asif accompanied her. He stood stone-faced at the door, refusing to come in.

"Ammi...Appi!" Bushra hugged Mom and me in turn. She bid her goodbyes to her husband, and as soon as she made herself comfortable, I offered to make her a cup of hot masala milk.

"I won't have it. Milk makes me too gassy," Bushra said.

"So, black tea?" I questioned.

"Eww...no...normal tea will do."

I narrowed my eyes. "Normal tea has milk."

Bushra laughed. "There's no winning with you. Come here."

We hugged again, and I put my hand lovingly on

Bushra's stomach. "Can you feel the kicks yet?" I asked.

"Yes. I'll tell you when. Now I guess she is sleeping."

"She?"

"Well. The old aunties tell me I'm carrying a girl because my stomach looks like a watermelon."

"Oh, it's too early to comment on the shape of your stomach. You are barely showing," Mom interjected and then went to the kitchen to check the biryani.

We talked about how Bushra would stay with us for her delivery and up until the baby turned two months old. It was a ritual most new mothers practiced. Seeing Bushra so excited brought a smile to my face.

"So, how is Asif treating you?" I asked.

"Good." Bushra shrugged. "He treats me like a princess. I'm bringing a child into their family after years of his sister trying and being unable to get pregnant. I know she is upset with me because she treats me strangely when she comes to visit. But otherwise, it is all fine."

"That's good to know. Be careful of his sister, though."

"Yes, I am. She comes to visit every other day. There's so much negativity in the house when she is around. It's like we are walking on eggshells."

"What are you both talking about?" Mom's voice startled both of us from the kitchen doorway.

"Nothing, Mom, let us have lunch," Bushra said. "Afrah is hungry."

Mom went back to get us plates. I swatted Bushra's hand at the lie she told, but she winked at me.

"Ammi doesn't need to know all this. You know how she'll react."

"Of course." I mimicked locking my lips and throwing the key away. *Is that why Asif's parents agreed to the marriage so fast—not letting Bushra finish her graduation—because they wanted a child in their family?*

Bushra sighed in relief. "He cares for me but loves his sister, too. And it is understandable, although sometimes it does get overwhelming for me."

"As long as you are happy, nothing else matters," I put stray strands of hair behind her ear. "Come, let's hog my special biryani."

Laughing, we sat to eat. After a sumptuous lunch of mutton biryani and curd salad, we relaxed for an afternoon siesta.

"That was a killer meal, Appi. Teach me your secrets. I can never make it so good."

"Yeah, yeah, little sister. Didn't you get gas after eating so much basmati rice?" I teased.

"Oh, let it drop."

"Not in a hundred years." I poked my tongue out and went to the kitchen to clean up.

"Let it be, do it later," Mom said. "Come, talk to your sister."

I spoke from the kitchen, "You both talk. I will chat with my sister later."

"Do you need any help?" Bushra asked.

"As if Mom will let you," I replied with a chuckle.

"Ammi is not so bad."

"Enough, you two. I'm right here." Mom laughed.

I tuned them out and did the dishes. We had domestic help before, but when news arrived that Papa was returning for good, we decided to cut the unnecessary costs. His return before retirement meant only one thing. He was going to lose his job, and no one knew whether he would get one here because he wasn't highly qualified. He'd told me that he wanted to start his business. But until then, we needed to tread carefully and not finish off all our savings.

Not that I minded doing the household chores. It hardly took any time. We were the only two people living here, after all. As I arranged the crockery on the shelves where they belonged, Bushra hugged me from behind.

"Appi! How is your new job going?"

I smiled, "Good, so far. We have a training period for a month."

"Wow. Now you are going to be a high-flying career woman. You are getting to live your dream!"

"Come, let's go to the terrace. I have so much to share with you."

I told my sister about the interview and how I struggled to reach home in the floods, about the boats I saw, and how people helped one another in a heart-warming gesture of unity.

"Yes, it was a horrible thing to have happened," Bushra said. "So much loss. But I'm proud to live in this city, no matter what."

Then I told Bushra about the strange man on the bus whose name I'd not bothered to ask. And how I saw him again on the train.

"Oh, that's so nice of you, Appi. It is okay if you don't know his name. I bet he'll remember you. You are not easy to forget." Bushra wiggled her brows.

I laughed. "So, when are *you* getting back to finish your graduation?"

Bushra gave a sheepish smile. "How's it possible now? With this one coming into our lives," she pointed to her tummy, "what will I do with a degree? I don't want to work."

"It's not about having to work. You have completed one year of your graduate studies, and only two more remain. You can also do a correspondence course. I'm sure Asif will back you."

"Drop it, Appi, I don't want to. You know how much I hated academics."

Sighing, I looked at my sister. I did try to talk some sense into her. That's all I could do. Any more pressure, and she would drift away from me, thinking I don't respect her choices. I liked the camaraderie we shared. It reminded me of the times before she had a boyfriend.

We sat gazing at the cloudy skies until a fat drop of rain fell onto our heads, and we headed back.

The next day, I cooked aloo parathas and made coriander and coconut chutney. Mom and Bushra finished all of it and even licked the chutney off their fingers. What better way to satisfy my culinary skills? We chatted as we waited for Asif to come pick her up.

When we'd finished, I opened the almirah in the living room and removed the old family photo albums. I sat down on the sofa and looked through the photos. Me, a chubby little baby trying to stand, and Bushra, a newborn in Mom's lap. Papa hovering in the background. Our content family of four. These photos always made me forget my worries, working like a balm to my stressed self. I wanted so much from my life, and it always felt like time was running away from me, like the local trains I missed by a fraction of a second.

My mood lifted as I turned each page of the album. Smiling and sometimes giggling at that motley of pictures: one with me wearing sunglasses and red lipstick when I must be...two years old? Bushra crying and Papa gifting us dolls and frocks. I felt Mom's gaze on me and shut the albums, putting them back in the almirah. She'd start explaining the story behind each photo, and I had heard them enough times already. I just wanted to look at the photos by myself.

"It was a fun two days, wasn't it?" I asked.

"Yes. It was. You look sad, though. All good? You can tell me."

"I do miss Bushra." Then I grinned. "You know what would truly rejuvenate me?" Her worry about my health transformed into a worry about what I was going to say next. "Shopping, Mom, shopping!"

Before she could stop me from executing this amazing idea, I grabbed some cash I'd saved and knocked on my friend's door downstairs.

Chapter 9
Opposites Attract
Sadiq

Although it was exhausting and I could barely keep my eyes open after a night shift, I enjoyed my surgery postings. I'd made it a point to read about all the cases I helped in the treatment of throughout the day so that I could answer most of the questions the professors threw at me while in the outpatient department and ward rounds. And it was my turn for a case presentation next week.

I had a day off on Sunday, and I absolutely hated that. Usually, I'd go to the college library to study on my off days, but the college was shut on Sundays, so I was stuck at home. Making use of this opportunity, I paid a visit to the barbershop. Abbu hadn't opened it for business yet, and for good reason. Inside the shop, the floor still had a layer of muck, and a musty smell permeated each and everything. I wondered what exactly the 'poor fellow' to whom Abbu had paid a huge sum of money had done to clean the place.

Scoffing, I picked a broom and kept a bucket to fill in the tiny washroom. The place needed some air and opening it daily for customers would do the job.

"Sadiq, how come you are here?" Abbu asked, entering the shop. He was dressed in a loose shirt, lungi, and a skull cap.

"I'll leave now that you are here." I was in no mood to get into an argument with him.

"Karim hasn't cleaned it that well," Abbu started, but I walked past him. "You know he needs the money—"

"Yeah, distribute all the meager income to the whole world and starve your own family." I grimaced, hoping he hadn't heard me muttering. I never understood my father's logic of charity. We were barely getting by ourselves, so why did he think it was okay to give away our money?

Ammi stepped out of the kitchen as soon as I stepped into the house.

"What's gotten you upset?" she asked.

The small mirror behind the door reflected my frowning face. "Nothing, Ammi."

She shrugged and went back to her cooking. The aroma of the nihari lifted my spirits. Ammi was a marvelous cook. I peeked into the kitchen.

"So much? Whom are you cooking for?" I asked, looking at the size of the vessel.

Ammi cleared her throat. "It's for an order."

Before I could ask anything more, a neighbor called out, "Shabbo Aapa, this woman is looking for you," with another woman in tow.

"Farzana, the dish is almost ready." Ammi greeted the woman. "I have chopped the coriander and ginger to garnish it when you serve. How will you carry it?"

"Oh, I've got this." Farzana brought out a huge tiffin carrier.

"Wonderful!" Ammi started to fill the individual dabbas of the carrier, and after she was done, Farzana paid her five hundred rupees.

"Shabana Aapa, thank you so much. No one was ready to take the order at such short notice. I'm really grateful to you." Farzana said as she left.

I gaped at the whole exchange. Ammi looked at me with a sheepish smile.

"Oh, Ammi, I'm so proud of you. But you don't have to do this."

She sat on the floor, heaving a sigh of relief. "I thought you would be angry."

"I am angry, but not at you. You shouldn't be slogging to put food in our stomachs when *he* is hobnobbing with the world, talking about his charity."

"Don't say that. He is your abbu."

"Ammi, you know what he's doing. Why is the flattery of him by others more important to him than us? I hate coming here. It's only because of you that I do."

"Here, taste this." She offered a plate of food.

I dipped the roti in the nihari and tasted it. "Hmm." The spices and the meat cooked in ghee were so full of flavor, it shut me up. "This is a nice way to change the topic, Ammi."

"Look at yourself. You have become so thin. And how will that brain of yours work if you won't eat?"

I smiled. *As long as Ammi is with me, I can fight the world.*

Outside, the chawl was alive once again, as if the flood never happened. A few neighbors came knocking to share the special dishes they had made. Ammi, in turn, filled bowls with nihari and offered it to them. I forgot Sundays were feast days in our chawl and was now glad that I got to spend it with people who cared for us.

Another woman came asking for Ammi to place an order of biryani. Ammi looked at me, and I grinned, gesturing for her to carry on. Shabana—the caterer— was slowly gaining a name for herself.

I climbed up to the mezzanine. Switching on the tube light, I poured over my books, simultaneously going over the plan in my head: to read how much I could on the subject I was posted in and to keep solving questions on the subjects I had already covered so I would not forget them.

Afrah

A new week and a new wardrobe! I couldn't suppress the bubbles of joy in my tummy as I stepped out of the house. Shopping always cheered me up, and I'd bought three sets of clothes, along with new hair clips and a pair of shoes to prevent my toes from being crushed in the crowd. I'd gone to Linking Road in Bandra, a popular spot for roadside shopping, with my building friend Tuba after Bushra left with her husband. I enjoyed bargaining with the sellers and used all tricks to get the lowest possible price for a thing I liked.

Now, waiting at the station, I stood tall, with new confidence in me, like I could take on the whole world. That's what new clothes and shoes did. I fiddled with the chain I wore, an exact replica of a branded one I'd seen in a fashion magazine. Looking at the indicator clock once again, I sighed. The train was running late.

That's when I spotted a familiar mop of hair in the crowd. *The man from the bus.* Before I could change my mind, I squared my shoulders and walked in his direction.

"Hi," I said the moment I was within hearing distance of him.

But the man didn't even look in my direction. I repeated myself louder this time. Exasperated, I tapped on his shoulder. He was about a head taller than me.

He looked down at me and blinked, his mouth agape.

"I said 'hi' to you twice." I grimaced, thinking *that* shouldn't have been the first thing I said to him. But my heart fluttered like the wings of the sparrows that nibble on the grains Mom puts for them on the windowsill, and my mouth moved on its own. "I need to know your name. It's so foolish of me, I always ask the name of the person I'm talking to, and since I did you such a big favor by getting you off the bus..." I put a palm over my mouth as he looked at me with wide eyes. *Arghh...me and my big mouth.*

"I'm Sadiq. And thank you so much for helping me off the bus."

He opened his mouth to say more, but the train sped into the station. I took a deep breath to calm my speeding heart and rushed to my spot, trying the 'jumping in the train before it stopped' stunt one more time. My shoes fit well; no chance they would slip from my feet. Before the train stopped, and even before the women who wanted to get down could alight, I jumped.

"Whoa!" Roshni caught my hand.

A woman who threw me dirty looks called me 'stupid.' I showed my tongue to her and smiled at Roshni.

"Someone went shopping and is showing off," she teased.

I giggled. "Yes, and I tried to call your landline. We came to Bandra, but nobody answered at your place."

"Oh well, I went out with my cousins. These earrings are cute," she touched the little silver rings that hung from my ears.

"Thank you."

My gaze fell on Sadiq once again. He stood facing me but averted his eyes when I looked at him. I couldn't help myself and burst out laughing.

Roshni asked, "Are you alright?"

"Yes, remember I told you about the man on the bus?" When Roshni nodded, I continued, "Look, his name is Sadiq."

Roshni followed my finger. "Oh. Why doesn't he cut his hair?" she asked. Sadiq's hair fell into his eyes.

"Yes, I'll ask him that when I talk to him next."

Roshni laughed, and we blabbered our way until our stop arrived. Occasionally, I glanced at Sadiq. He smiled at me once or twice, but neither was a proper smile, only a flicker of one.

The following morning, I once again dressed in my new clothes, but I didn't feel well and couldn't figure out why. Mom didn't bother me too much on weekdays; she was too engrossed in watching the TV serials. My training was fun, and I had supportive colleagues. Still, I couldn't shake off that sad feeling.

I reached the station just as the train arrived and was one of the last to get in. The place beside Roshni was occupied, so I stood in front of her.

"You don't look well, Afrah. Why did you even come?"

"I don't know. I didn't feel like staying at home. I've been feeling low since yesterday evening."

Roshni remained silent for a while. "Is it your date?" she whispered.

It took some time for me to realize what she meant. "I haven't had it for two months now."

"Oh, so all this must be what is called premenstrual symptoms. It affects some women worse than others. I read it in a magazine once," she whispered again, although no one was paying any attention to us. The other women were either listening to music on their MP3 players or taking a nap. "Don't worry. The feeling will pass when you get your period."

"But I'm scared. My periods are bad. Very bad. I need to lie down for one whole day, along with hot water bags and painkillers. What'll happen if I get them today?"

"Afrah, relax. What's the point of thinking about something that hasn't even happened? By the way, you have an admirer in the adjacent compartment." She tried to divert my attention.

But I didn't take the bait. I didn't turn to acknowledge Sadiq. I'd seen him get into the compartment earlier.

"Okay, forget about this period talk. What do you think of Ishaan?" Roshni asked.

I flashed a smile. Ishaan was a new recruit. "I don't like him. He appears to be overly- smart."

Roshni scoffed. "As if I'm asking for yourself."

"I know. Well, you should talk to him and figure it out." I narrowed my eyes. "Oh, you'll make a perfect couple. Both 'know-it-all'." Then I giggled, angling my head to peek at Sadiq.

"How mean." Roshni crossed her arms. "I know you want to wave at Sadiq. So why don't you go ahead?"

I shrugged and turned my head again to where he stood. But his eyes weren't in my direction anymore. "He doesn't want to say hi to me now."

"How do you know? I'll tell you when he looks here."

I stood in silence for a while. Thoughts running in

various directions. The training, then a permanent job. Saving for teacher's college, mobile phone, and those white patches on my legs...and Mom. Oh, Mom. Sometimes I couldn't understand her at all. She hadn't been talking properly with me for the last few days, and it kind of bothered me now. I thought it was because she was busy watching television, but this morning too, Mom didn't acknowledge my presence. As if I was invisible. I would try to talk to her tonight.

The train rumbled over Vashi Creek, and the otherwise serene water rippled violently, like my racing thoughts.

Chapter 10
Grey Eyes on Platform no.7
Sadiq

My heart beat a little faster when I saw Afrah on the platform. I wanted to talk to her, so I rushed in her direction, but then the train arrived. After I got on, I watched her climb in just as the train began to move. I wanted to wave at her, but she stood with her back to me. Yesterday when she spoke to me, I wanted to tell her more than a mere thank you. But as if my tongue had been depressed by a spatula, I couldn't get more words out.

Ashish didn't get in at the next station. Surrounded by people chatting nonstop, I wondered where he was. He was the only friend I had in the last five years of medical college. I preferred to stay alone and would've stayed a loner among my batch mates if not for Ashish. *I'll give him a call from the hospital.* I had a small phonebook where I wrote the contact numbers: Ashish, a few other batch mates, resident doctors at the hospital, the number of the hospital itself, and the extension numbers of the wards. I even had the numbers of a few professors. Touching the back pocket of my pants, I confirmed its presence.

The train lurched to a halt at another station, and I looked at Afrah again. I couldn't get her grey eyes out of my head. She got off at Vashi station. Maybe she was a student, too. I would ask her the next time I got a chance. Being a Tuesday, I had a night shift and wouldn't meet her until Thursday.

The surgery posting kept me busy. I was allowed in the operation theater but was relegated to background work. The anesthetist would ask for help in checking the patient's blood pressure or to help with an extra intravenous line insertion. The scrubs called to me, and I had to suppress my desire to assist in the surgeries for the time being. I had to prove myself to my seniors that I was good enough and hoped to achieve that by the end of my forty-five-day posting.

Thursday morning, I walked to the station with a spring in my step. I so looked forward to meeting Afrah. But she wasn't there. Thinking she might just be late, I skipped my usual train to wait for her. But there was no sign of her. Dejected, I went to the hospital and immersed myself in the rounds and dressings.

The next morning when I had convinced myself that I wouldn't see her again, I finally spotted her at the station. I increased my pace but stopped before reaching out to her. What would I say? She was tapping her feet and looking around. I prepared to duck, but her gaze met mine at that moment. Her mouth curved into a slow smile. I couldn't help but smile back.

She glanced at the time on the indicator, and I followed her gaze—a minute for the train to come. A minute was enough for me. I stepped ahead to meet her. She did the same.

"I wondered if it was a fluke to see you these last few times," she started.

"You wouldn't believe I thought the same as I walked here."

"Ah, at least I know your name now."

I raised my brows. Afrah raised one of hers. It arched perfectly over her eye. I could never do *that*.

"You don't talk much, do you?"

A sound escaped my throat, and I shrugged.

She clucked her tongue. "It's quite rare to see a man my age so protective of his books. That's why I remembered you. Not because you are handsome or anything—" She put her palm over her mouth.

"I know." I grinned. "And I remembered you because...." I wondered whether I could tell her because of her eyes, but she continued the sentence for me.

"Because I made a valid point that evening. Or you would have had to pee in the water outside, which already had lots of pee...."

I laughed and sensed a few onlookers glancing in our direction. Afrah looked at me with her mouth open. She cleared her throat, ready to say something, but the horn of the incoming train sounded.

"Where do you get down?" she quickly asked. "And will I see you tomorrow?"

"Two stops after Vashi. And no. I'll see you on Monday." I walked a few steps ahead to where the door of the general compartment would be. But then I retraced them toward Afrah and before I could stop myself, added, "I remembered you because of your eyes."

Afrah

Feeling giddy with something I couldn't pinpoint, I jumped into the compartment before the train stopped and stood beside Roshni.

"Hey, you feeling good?" she asked.

"Yes, much better. I had my period yesterday."

"I figured. Is Sadiq there?" Roshni asked when she saw I couldn't stop smiling and staring into the other section.

"He was, but now I can't see him."

"He must have gotten into the next compartment."

"What color are my eyes? Can you make out?"

Roshni looked into my eyes and shrugged. "Greenish grey? I don't know. Looks like Aishwarya Rai's. Why, what is the matter?"

"Nothing," I said dreamily. *He remembered me because of them.* "I think they are bluish-grey, but different people tell me different things."

"If it doesn't matter, leave it. Anyway, you don't have to ever describe the color of your eyes in your biodata," Roshni said.

She did have a point.

"You are cute," Roshni suddenly said.

"Huh?"

"I said you look cute."

I tilted my head. "Don't pull my leg. I know how I look. Is there too much hair on my upper lip?"

She inspected it. "Not too much. If anyone sees us like this staring at each other's eyes and lips, what will they think?"

We giggled.

"We are young women debating standards of beauty."

"We aren't debating. Only you think less of yourself."

I sighed. "Forget that. Tell me, what did I miss at work yesterday?"

Later, returning home, I couldn't stop smiling. Not because Sadiq told me he remembered me because of my eyes. No, not at all. I will be receiving my first-ever salary the next week. That's why. I practically skipped my way home, and the moment Mom opened the door, I hugged her.

"Oho, what's the matter?"

"Nothing, I'm happy. Can't I hug you now?"

"Hmm...Sunday, be ready. You have another rishta. They'll be coming to see you."

I didn't want to sour my mood by thinking about another suitor, so I muttered an okay and went to change. When I came out to make a cup of chai for myself, Mom was in the kitchen doing the same thing.

"Did you listen to what I said earlier?"

"Yes, Mom."

"No protests? I'm surprised."

"Don't provoke me, Mom. I'm happy today, so I'll wear my uniform and be ready to greet our guests."

"Uniform?"

"The pink and yellow kurti-churidaar I always wear?"

"Oh yes," she said, "Wear some other jewelry with that, though. I'll loan you mine."

I quirked my brows, "Loaning me your jewelry! Who are they?"

"A distant relative of Rukhsana downstairs."

Traitor. I shared my experiences with her during the flood, and now she brought her own relative. Hmm. I'll have to change my beautician now. Mom watched me like a hawk, but I wouldn't be intimidated. No, not now. *Oh, what a brilliant idea! Why didn't it strike me before?*

Mom interjected. "What is going on in that wicked brain of yours?"

"Wicked, ha?" I opened the cabinets, thinking about Mom and her sixth sense. Or was it really sixth sense? She watched so many soap operas, and something or the other was bound to rub on her. "Aha!" I exclaimed as I found our sugar storage jar. Then scooping a few spoons into a bowl, I told her, "This is for our morning tea. Don't worry, I'll bring more tomorrow."

"And what are you going to do with the rest?" Mom asked, horrified.

"I'm making my own wax, Mother!"

"Ya Allah," she muttered, walking to the living room. "Bushra might talk some sense into you." She dialed a number.

Meanwhile, I was engaged in my experiment.

When Mom peeked into the kitchen sometime later, the sugar in the pan had turned brown. "Where did you learn to make this?" she asked, her eyes narrowed with suspicion.

"I watched a video at the office," I smiled.

"Do you go there to work or learn all this nonsense?"

"Mom, this is not nonsense. This is saving money. I go to Rukhsana Aapa every fifteen days and pay her seventy rupees. I'll save that na."

Mom nodded her head and went back to the living room. "Call up Bushra later. She wants to talk."

"Not until I get my own phone," I murmured. I had started to mark the days in the calendar. "Nokia 3310, I'm coming for you, baby."

The weekend flew by. I had my sights set on the end of August when my first check would be in my hand. I'd discussed the same thing with Roshni on the train last week. The company had given us ATM cards while opening our salary accounts. We'd also talked about changing the pin number of the card.

Now, on the train, Roshni started, "I heard there was a fire last night in..."

"Hmm." I was distracted. Mom's complaints about me going to work had been extra harsh this morning.

"Did you speak to your lover boy today?"

I snapped back to attention. "Lover boy? No. We met only once. I didn't like him. He complained that the tea was too sweet. I mean, everyone in my building knows I make amazing chai, and how dare he say that? I made it clear when we had a few minutes to talk with each other—I planned to continue working after marriage and even after having kids. He looked at me as if the hair on my upper lip had grown into a mustache. And then he tells me, 'You crack good jokes.' I wanted to slap him there. Huh."

"Wait, wait...Sadiq came to visit you at your place?"

"Sadiq?" When I realized he was the one whom

Roshni was talking about, I gasped. "*He* is not my 'lover boy.'"

Roshni laughed. "Not your lover boy? Then why does he keep looking at you? He has eyes only for you, sweetheart."

I glanced at the other compartment. When our gazes met, he waved and smiled at me. I returned the gesture. Reaching late to the station today due to the horrible traffic, I couldn't talk to him earlier on the platform.

"By the way, whom were you describing?" Roshni asked.

"I had a suitor to 'see' me yesterday," I informed her.

Roshni laughed. "It sounded like it was one hell of an experience!"

"Huh! How is our overly smart Ishaan?" I asked.

"Not *our*," she replied, fiddling with her bangs.

"Hmm...he doesn't like women whose hair falls into their eyes," I told her in all seriousness.

"As if you would know," Roshni scoffed. Then she narrowed her eyes. "Have you ever spoken to him?"

I gave her a huge smile. "For that matter, yes. We spoke about a certain girl who shuttles two trains to get to work. And then he told me how much it irritates him when women fiddle too much with their hair."

"*Kuch bhi*...you are making it up." Roshni's blush worked its way across her fair-skinned face.

"It's up to you if you want to believe me or not." I shrugged.

Roshni tied her bangs with a clip and sighed. "What else?"

"What...what else?"

"I mean, what else did you talk about?"

"Oh, you mean Ishaan and me? I totally made that up. We never spoke." I chuckled in delight. My poor friend was so gullible.

Roshni shook her head and screamed in irritation, but it only made me laugh harder. The spectacle we made got attention from near us as well as from the men's compartment.

When I looked at Sadiq, he was trying to hide a smile. There was also a question in his eyes. I gestured to whether I'd see him tomorrow. He shook his head. I pursed my lips. Maybe the next time I spoke to him, I would get his schedule so that I'd know when to expect him.

To my pleasant surprise, I found Sadiq sitting on a bench the next morning. He appeared to be reading something from a huge book. The bench was occupied, so I stood next to him and bent a little to see the cover of the book on his lap. I tried to turn the cover when Sadiq slapped my hand.

"Ouch..." I cried.

He looked up and grimaced. "Sorry, I didn't know it was you. I don't like anyone else touching my books."

I snorted, thinking this was the most he'd spoken since I met him, and waved him off. "It's alright. You should give me your schedule so that I can know when I'll see you. Not that I like talking to you, you don't talk anyway. But still..."

"My schedule is complicated." Sadiq packed the book in his bag and stood. The train would be here in another two minutes. "I'm completing my medical internship."

I waited for him to say more.

"Umm...so I have night shifts twice a week and sometimes one or two Sundays."

"Woohoo. You do know how to talk. This is super interesting. So which days will I see you? I can come a few minutes early to know more about these night shifts and you," I rambled, my heart thudding faster than normal. Yes, I did want to know more about him, but I chided myself internally for being so bossy. What if he wasn't looking forward to talking to me as much as I was to him?

Sadiq rubbed his neck and stared at the tracks.

"Umm...I'm here all days—except Wednesday and Saturday. I leave the hospital in the evening on these days. And from fifteenth September, I'll be starting different postings, so then I'll be here daily."

"Fantastic. I'll see you Thursday then. Bye!" I waved and rushed to take my spot on the train before I rambled any more nonsense to him.

Chapter 11
Birthday Party
Sadiq

"Sadiq, we have an invitation to join Bade-abba at his house for dinner today. I forgot to tell you when you called," Ammi said as soon as I entered the house that evening.

My night shift was hectic, and I wouldn't have the strength to sit through dinner, but I couldn't say no to Bade-abba. After dropping my bag near the steps to the mezzanine, I sagged to the floor.

This last week, I couldn't study much. The OPD and ward rounds kept me so busy. And the fire tragedy yesterday...my colleague and I were up the whole night tending to the patients with varying degrees of burns. Stabilizing them, dressing their wounds, and inserting intravenous lines. So far, dressings and intravenous lines were all that I'd done in my surgery postings. It irritated me that I still didn't get the chance to enter the operation theater.

"Oh, my bachcha. You must have had a bad night," Ammi patted my head. "Let me apply some oil into your hair, come. And you need to cut them, they are falling into your eyes."

I smiled at that as an image of Afrah popped into my mind. I met her quite often these days. And she'd asked me the same thing. "How do you see with your hair falling into your eyes?"

"Yes, Ammi, I'll get them cut. I don't understand why they grow so fast."

"Your abba is a barber, that's why." Ammi meant it as a joke, but I didn't laugh.

"Yes, Abbu is a barber." It pained me to talk about him. "I'll be getting my check soon. I'll give you some for the house."

"No, no. I don't need it. You spend it on yourself. Buy a new bag," she said, looking at the patched-up one I carried for the last four years. "And shoes, too. By Allah's grace, my catering business is going well. I can manage to put food in your stomach."

I sighed, running my fingers through my hair. "Is *he* not giving anything for the house?" Then I stood. "Forget I said that. I'll freshen up, then we can go to Bade-abba's."

I thought about splurging a bit for myself. Although we were paid a measly sum of two thousand rupees for all the slogging we did, I had saved ten thousand over the last few months. I used to give half of it to Ammi to help in the house, but she refused to take any more from me. If I did buy a new bag and shoes, even a few shirts, I would still have enough to pay for the exam fees..

After a quick shower, I changed into my best shirt and trousers. "I need a new lab coat," I muttered, uncovering the stained one from my bag to put it into washing. I would have to do my shopping on my next day off.

We hitched a ride to Bade-abba's house in an auto-rickshaw. I would have preferred to walk, and so would Ammi, but Abbu insisted, and I didn't want to create a spectacle in the middle of the road. Allah knows what he wanted to achieve—getting down from a rickshaw to make an entrance was different than walking.

The atmosphere at Bade-abba's apartment was quite festive. I failed to remember why we were invited, but when Ammi brought out a gift-wrapped parcel and handed it to Farheen, it struck me. It was her birthday.

"Happy birthday," I greeted her at my turn. She looked regal in her white, floor-length sequined dress.

"No gift for me?" she asked at my empty hands.

I was taken aback. I'd never gifted her before, then why this demand now?

"Oh, relax, I'm kidding." She pouted.

I did relax but found it weird when Farheen sat beside me as people greeted her. Most faces were familiar, distant relatives and a few of their friends. Bade-abba always splurged on his daughter's birthday. He also threw a party for everyone during the two Eids.

Anam, my older sister, dragged me away and gushed about Farheen's dress. I thanked her for pulling me away from Farheen, but not before telling her to stop talking about the Anarkali dress.

"You are so boring," she finally said and left me on my own. My heart soared to see her happy.

Seeing all the flurry of activity around me, I suddenly wished for Afrah to be at my side. I didn't know what to talk about with these people, and Afrah.... She was so fearless. Spoke whatever was on her mind. Not caring about the repercussions. She lit up my world in the same way the dark classrooms would light up when I was first to reach class and flicked the switch on.

I didn't realize I was smiling, not until Madiha Aapa, my oldest sister, sidled up to me and cleared her throat.

"Hmm, whom are we thinking about?" she asked,

quirking a brow. I ignored her question, but she followed the direction of my gaze. Farheen gushed around with her friends.

"Oho, so that's your dream girl?"

I jerked my head, startled. "What?"

"Who amongst those has caught your eye?" Madiha Aapa pointed to Farheen and her girlfriends.

I rubbed the back of my neck. "No one from them, Aapa."

"No one from them? Ha? So, someone has...hmm... tell me. You can share this tidbit with your aapa," she teased. When I didn't reply, she insisted. "Come on, little brother. You are always surrounded by books. Live a little. Tell me."

I didn't want to admit that the image of Afrah crept up on me when she said the words 'dream girl.' I shrugged. "I'm not thinking about anyone, Aapa."

"So why that wistful smile on your face?"

I sighed. "Okay. I *was* thinking about someone."

"Tell me fast," she nudged me into a corner, away from anyone's earshot, "before my little monster of a son comes looking for me."

"Hmm. I was thinking about Harrison. He is an enigma."

"Harrison?"

I shrugged, "Yes, Aapa. Harrison's Principles of Internal Medicine."

She huffed in mock anger, leaving as she muttered, "And *you* are a useless enigma."

"Come on now, do not call my nephew useless," Bade-abba laughed as he back-slapped me. "Come into the party. Why are you standing here alone?" He pulled me into the living room. "Dr. Sadiq Shaikh. We are proud of you."

Everyone looked at me, and I didn't like being the center of attention, so I tried to pull away. But Bade-abba didn't let go of my hand.

"I'm not a doctor yet," I mumbled.

"You'll be soon." He smiled and made me sit at the dining table next to Farheen again.

Everyone around me was cheerful and happy, so I let it go and pretended to enjoy the plate of dinner offered to me when all I wanted to do was sleep.

"What are your plans for tomorrow?" Farheen asked me.

I looked at her with wide eyes, not expecting this question from her. After swallowing the morsel of chicken in my mouth, I replied, "I have to study."

"Only studying, right? Take a break and come with me and my friends. We are planning to watch a movie and then dip our feet at Bandra Bandstand or Juhu Chowpatty. Either of the two."

I remembered the last time I'd been to the beach. *Before my tenth grade?* And that too because Bade-abba always took my sisters and me whenever he went for his Sunday outings.

"Don't think so much," Farheen said. "I know how much you loved playing in the sea."

I did, indeed. Loved frolicking in the ocean. We used to play at Chowpatty, half-naked in the water. Oh, how much I missed those days!

"No, Farheen. I'm sorry, I can't. I have to study for my exams in December."

"December? That's so far...surely if you spend one day with us, it's not going to make you fail."

I found no way out of this. How could I make her understand that studying for medical entrance was different from studying in school, where even cramming up notes a day before could ensure you passed the exam?

"Oh, leave him alone, Farheen. If he doesn't want to come, fine. Ask one of your friend's brothers to accompany you," Bade-abba stated. He wouldn't allow the girls to travel alone. "Sadiq," he gestured to follow him.

I excused myself from Farheen. "Thanks, Bade-abba. I have to study. I hope you understand."

"Don't worry about them." He waved me off and closed the bedroom door.

Taking note of the privacy, I had an idea of what

this conversation was going to be about. I braced myself.

Bade-abba started. "I feel the tension between Haider and you. He is your abbu. When do you plan to repair your relationship with him?"

I groaned internally. I didn't want this conversation. Not now, not ever.

Back home, I was overwhelmed with relief. I'd told Bade-abba—more like complained—to him about Abbu's antics. Abbu had always been this way from the beginning, only I had realized recently. Ammi had learned to live with the man, but I often found myself arguing with him, unable to bear it. I preferred staying out of his sight, that way I wouldn't have to talk to him at all.

It was better that way. Daily skirmishes made me restless; I didn't like a hostile environment. Staying away from home as much as possible was an easy solution. But for how long could I do that?

It was past 10:00 p.m., and I was about to retire for the night when a scream from one of the neighbors caught my attention.

Abbu came running inside. "Shabana! Shabana... give me my bag, I'm going to the mosque to get the maulvi. Imran is possessed...Ya Allah!" I was sitting on the floor, right across from my abbu. He looked at me and asked, "Do you want to come with me?"

I grunted. He understood what it meant.

As soon as Abbu got what he came for, he rushed out, and so did Ammi. Then she returned and said, "You should have gone with him."

"Fine," I clucked. "Let me see Imran once. I don't think he's possessed, anyway."

In my early days of medical college, I used to refuse to treat anyone in my chawl for two reasons; first, I didn't know how, and second, I didn't still have a degree. But I never shared the first reason with anyone for obvious reasons. Now, I had a fair idea of what to do in such emergencies. I still couldn't treat them, but at least I could guide them.

As I entered Imran's house, the nineteen-year-old lay on the floor, covered in blankets, muttering nonstop. I touched his forehead. It was blazing hot. Throwing away all the blankets from his body, I asked for a bowl of water and a clean cloth and demonstrated to Imran's mother how to sponge him and bring down the temperature. Some of the other neighbors were whispering about possession like Abbu had.

I grimaced. These people relied on superstition too much. But I didn't want to argue with them right now. This boy needed *proper* medical treatment.

"He has a high fever. That's why he is muttering like this," I said, placing the wet cloth on the boy's fore-arms. *It's called delirium.* I doubted the boy could swallow a paracetamol tablet considering how drowsy he was. "Take him to the hospital, they'll give him an injection for immediate fever relief. He is not possessed," I couldn't help but state. His mother only nodded. "Imran... Imran?" I shook him. "Come on, help me," I urged the boy's father.

Together we took Imran down the stairs.

"Your abba has gone to get a maulvi," the man said.

"He needs a doctor, not a maulvi right now. Come...Rickshaw!" I yelled into the night.

At the hospital, I gave a brief history of what happened to the doctor on duty. The doctor planned to run some tests and find out the cause of the fever. Once sure that Imran was in safe hands, I made my way home and jotted the differential diagnosis in my head out of habit. I'd then compare my reasoning with that of the treating doctor's to know whether I was on the right track.

'The most important thing you need to know when you start your general practice,' one of the professors I admired had told us during our ward rounds, 'is to identify a patient needing emergency care.' That statement stuck with me. And Imran did need emergency care.

I had to leave early the next morning for rounds, but I found time to ask, "How is Imran, do you know Ammi?" as I drank my morning chai.

"Yes, the doctors will keep him there. They did many tests. Reports will come today."

"I'll visit Imran on my way home."

"You won't study at the library?"

"It's Sunday, Ammi."

She sighed. "Sunday, Monday. All days are the same for me."

Something seemed off with Ammi. Her brows were furrowed, and she kept fidgeting with her hands. "What is it?"

She shook from her reverie but looked at me blankly.

"I asked what it is," I repeated.

"Oh, nothing." She smiled, but it was strained. "I'm just tired."

"Tell me, Ammi. What is troubling you?"

She folded the mattress on which she slept, sat on the lone chair in the house, and whispered, "Your abbu took the little cash I had for household expenses. And I don't have any more cooking orders yet"

I clenched my fists. Thank Allah Abbu wasn't at home, or I didn't know what I would do. Every day a new problem! How could I engage in studying with these petty issues at the same time? But I was sure there was something more bothering my ammi.

"What else?"

"That's it."

I'd be late for the hospital rounds if I stayed any longer, but this was more important. "Look at me," I said and sat in front of her, kneeling. "Tell me."

"He told me to ask my dear son to help out with the household expenses as henceforth he'll not let me do my business." Ammi couldn't help herself as tears dropped from her eyes. "It's the only thing I love to do. And now..." She sniffled.

"I'll talk to him, and don't worry about the household expenses. I can handle that."

"No, no," she stood, "You'll not talk to him. He is angry about yesterday. You went behind his back and became the hero, saving Imran. That is *his* job, son. Let him cool down a bit. Please."

I nodded. Ammi knew how to live with my abbu, and I wouldn't argue with her about that. I hugged her fiercely.

"A few months more, Ammi. A few months more."

I'd shared my plans with her. After I received my degree in March, I'd apply to private hospitals to work as a resident doctor. The big corporate hospitals always needed fresh graduates. They paid well, too. I would then rent out a house, a better one than this, and go to live there. Although Ammi always said she couldn't leave Abbu behind, I would figure out a way when the time was right.

I picked up my torn bag and made my way out of the house.

"Buy a new bag and new shoes," Ammi said.

I smiled. Yes, I will need a new bag as of now. But shoes could wait.

Chapter 12
Salary Day
Afrah

Pay day had finally come. I bounced in my seat and remained fidgety throughout the long day that seemed to never end. I so wanted to feel that salary slip in my hands! Then, I had to rush to the ATM, get the cash, and make one of my dreams come true... Nokia, you're mine.

"Afrah...Afrah," Roshni whispered from next to me. "Our bosses are watching you. If you waste your day just bouncing in your seat, you'll not get your salary."

"Shut up." I laughed. Nothing could spoil my mood today.

The hours inched slowly until the time for us to leave arrived. But I didn't see the bosses giving salary slips to the employees.

"What's wrong?" I murmured. Roshni had gone to

the washroom to freshen up, so I asked a senior employee who was about to leave. "Ma'am, what about our salary slips?"

The woman looked at me, her face tired from work. "Yeah, what about it?"

"Umm. Today is the thirty-first. Shouldn't we be getting our salaries?"

"Dear, didn't Riya in HR tell you that we do not give salaries on the thirty-first? The management releases them in the first week of the month. So, you'll be getting yours anytime between first to seventh September. Sometimes up to tenth."

My heart deflated like a burst balloon. I rushed to the washroom to give the news to Roshni.

"Oh, sweety, I already knew." I looked at my friend in accusation. Roshni raised her hands. "I'm sorry, I tried to tell you, but you were so excited and energetic these last few days. I didn't want to break your heart."

I could feel the tears threatening to spill. But no. I wouldn't cry for a silly thing like this. It was a matter of a few days more. My dream could wait until then. And besides, getting a mobile phone wasn't an emergency, was it? I splashed some water on my face and then we made our way back home.

"Our training period is over babes," Roshni gushed while I stared at the train wall. Not even the Vashi

Creek looked pretty to me. "Now we'll do some real work."

I reached home in a sour mood. All I wanted was to curl up on the mattress and forget about the day. But while climbing the steps to my flat, Rukhsana told me Bushra was visiting for a few days. So, I plastered a smile on my face; I didn't want to greet my little sister in a grumpy mood.

"Appi...!" Bushra cried as soon as I stepped inside. "Surprise!"

I hugged her, being cautious not to crush her belly. "Oh well, I had an inkling you were here."

"Huh, really?"

"Yes, I could smell the gas from your farts as soon as I stepped inside the building!"

"Eww...not fair, Appi."

Both of us laughed and sat on the sofa.

"If you had called about your arrival, I would have brought our favorite seekh kebab from the shop outside the railway station. And please don't give me any excuse you cannot eat it."

"No, no excuse for seekh kebab! Let the smell of the farts reach Asif too." Bushra snickered.

"Where's Mom?" I asked.

"Ammi's gone to get some clothes from the tailor. She has made a few for me."

"Hmm." I turned to face my sister. "Now tell me, how *are* you?"

"I'm good. They look after me well," Bushra said, smiling.

"Great, so did you come alone, or did that grumpy husband of yours drop you off?

Bushra grimaced. "Don't say that. Yes, he did come by to drop me. He asked about you."

"Oh my, the great Asif *miah* asked about poor me?"

"Stop the drama, Appi. He wanted to know what kind of work you did, whether your work would influence me and our baby."

"Huh, tell him your baby will learn tally 7.2 from birth," I laughed. "Seriously Bushra, who have you married?" The smile on my face vanished. I could see in her eyes that my sister didn't have one problem but loads of them. I, however, didn't want to pester her. Bushra would share when she was ready. If she was here, I would make sure my sweet, little sister laughed.

Mom came home just then, huffing, and muttering curses for the tailor.

"Chill, Mom," I said from the kitchen while making masala tea for everyone.

"What is 'chill Mom?' Bushra, teach her something. Look how she talks."

"Appi, if you talk like this, no one will marry you," Bushra started. We both burst out laughing.

"You both!" Mom huffed again.

"Ammi, let Appi be. Why do you pester her so much?"

"Yeah, Bushra *ki* Ammi, why do you pester me so much?" I echoed. "It's not like I'll tell my husband 'Chill, bro.'" I couldn't stop giggling.

Mom narrowed her eyes at both of us. She clucked her tongue and sat on the sofa. "Forget all of that." She brought out a loose kaftan from her bag and handed it to Bushra. "See, I got this stitched for you, but she charged 250 rupees for this. Only the top, no salwar. Now check whether it fits you, or else tomorrow I will go and show her my true colors."

I stood behind my complaining mother and massaged her shoulders.

"Mom. Chill. For real. Close your eyes and relax. Enjoy the massage."

"This is not massaging. You are going to break my bones!" She laughed.

And just like that, all three of us were laughing together again.

That night after dinner, I asked Bushra, "Does Papa know you are here?" We were lying on the mattress, talking in the dark.

"No. I haven't spoken to him for a long time."

"Hmm..." I glanced at the clock. "He'll call in some time. Maybe after he finishes his dinner."

We always spoke around ten at night, twice or thrice a week, after he was done with the day's work. The time difference suited us well. It was five minutes after ten, and the phone rang. I gestured for Bushra to answer the call.

She spoke in monosyllables, and I smiled, thinking about Papa's response to Bushra's questions. He was a man of few words. He listened to us well, and I loved him so much. The calls at night were to hear each other's voices, and Papa was an expert in gauging my mood from the tone of my voice.

At that moment, my mind conjured up an image of Sadiq. I was startled and shook my head. *Why him?* I barely knew him; I didn't even know where he studied or worked. We hadn't shared that piece of information yet.

"You know, Appi, you may have to get a proper bed, at least a single one, once I come to stay here for my delivery," Bushra said after returning to lie down beside me on the floor mattress.

"Yes, ma'am." I giggled. "Anything else?" Bushra only sighed. I wanted to ask what troubled her, but I didn't want to rush her. Still, I couldn't control myself and followed up on the momentary silence with, "What is it?"

"What?" Bushra looked at me.

"While I may appear to be in my own world, I do

notice things. And you don't seem happy to me. Like your fake smile or fake cheerfulness," I said, finger-combing her hair. I loved Bushra's smooth straight hair. She had dyed it light brown, and it suited her. I thought of streaking my hair burgundy—I learned that word from Roshni, who raved about it as one of her cousins had gotten it—but one thing at a time. Phone first. Then everything else. Besides, the most important thing was to save up the fees for the teachers' college.

I glanced at Bushra, waiting for a reply. But she was fast asleep. I smiled, unsurprised that fiddling with Bushra's hair had put her to sleep. I longed for someone to do that for me. Mom used to give my hair an oil massage, but she stopped a long time ago. Was she *so* annoyed by me that she refused to do anything that made me happy? When had we grown so distant?

I dozed off into a restless sleep. The last thing on my mind was that if I married the man of Mom's choice, maybe things would be normal. But by then, I would've grown up so much that an oil massage wouldn't matter.

Sadiq

I reached home in a daze. My batch mates were way ahead of me in preparing for the entrance exams. They had joined extra classes that gave them mock tests. I couldn't afford those. And when I did ask them to share the mock tests with me, it shocked me to know I could barely answer a fifth of the questions. How could I stand a chance at the state or national level when I couldn't even get past my colleagues? I didn't want to compare myself with them, but it was clear that what I was doing wouldn't be enough. Yes, my circumstances were different. Way more different than any of them. I should be grateful that I could finish the MBBS course despite everything. And in a few months, I'd be receiving my degree. Officially, the most educated member of my entire family—even in my neighborhood. It made my heart flutter, and I chuckled. When Bade-abba called me 'Doctor Sadiq,' it would be *real*.

"Did you visit Imran?" Ammi asked me.

I didn't reply to her, a little embarrassed. Yes, I was supposed to do that, but my mind was preoccupied with academics. I was grateful Ammi didn't pester me for my moodiness, but sooner or later, she would. And I couldn't lie to her—only omit the details—otherwise, she would insist on asking for help from Bade-abba once again. He would willingly help me if I asked, but

I was already in his debt and didn't know how long it would take to return the loans.

On the mezzanine, I opened my books. But no matter how much I tried, I couldn't concentrate. The words lost their meaning, and my mind was cloudy. The internship was difficult, and the hours were tiring. I'd be able to get more time once these surgery postings were over. My memory was good, and I could cover up the syllabus. Also, I wanted to learn practical things as much as I could because once I received my degree, I imagined a queue of neighbors and relatives would come to me for treatment once they heard the news. And I couldn't fumble in front of them—it was also a matter of my pride. Doing the internship diligently ensured that my reputation wouldn't be scarred even before I built it.

I closed the books and got ready to visit my neighbor, Imran, at the hospital. After checking on him, I'd pick up a new bag from the market. And a stethoscope. Using the ones at the hospital or borrowing from co-interns wasn't always feasible. Having made the decision, I kissed Ammi on the cheek and told her my plans.

"Khuda hafiz," she said, "Also, buy new shoes."

I waved and left, pretending not to hear the last part. I got my shoes stitched from all sides by a cobbler.

That would last me three-four months, if not more—it was cheaper than getting a new pair.

Once I reached the hospital where Imran was admitted, I spoke to the doctor on duty.

"Looks like enteric fever," the doctor said, "the spikes are less frequent but still there. Let's see what his blood culture says."

I nodded and entered the room Imran was in. The boy and his mother wouldn't stop thanking me. I accepted their gratitude but also waved them off.

"It was my duty. And I'm so happy he is doing well now."

With Imran in good hands, I went shopping. After haggling with the shopkeeper for the lowest possible price, I bought a bag that would suit my needs and went home.

I was surprised to see Bade-abba and Farheen there. As far as I remembered, my cousin hated this place. When we were kids, and whenever the family gathered here for Eid, Farheen would cry her lungs out if she had to visit the toilet. We had a common one in the chawl, and it was at the far end. A bit secluded and dark. I would leave no stone unturned to scare her— making weird noises, hooting, switching off the light once she went inside—until Ammi would pull my ear and drag me out of there, scolding me, "Do not trouble my beautiful Farheen". I attempted these jokes only when Hamid, Farheen's older brother, who was the oldest of us all cousins, wasn't around. He was huge, had a roaring voice, and hit or punched anyone who got in his way.

"Sadiq beta, here eat this." Bade-abba stuffed a gulab jamun into my mouth. The syrupy mithai melted in my mouth and I smiled in pleasure. I had to wait till I swallowed it to speak.

"What is the occasion, Bade-abba?"

"Hamid has married again," he said, bursting with joy. "We arranged the match for him in Dubai. He'll come here with his wife, and then we'll have a grand celebration."

I was delighted for my cousin. Hamid's first wife had died of dengue, and only now did I understand the hemorrhagic fever must have caused her death. Unable to bear the shock, Hamid went to Dubai and started a date business out there along with a partner. The business flourished, and now he had settled again.

"Where is Haider?" Bade-abba asked Ammi.

"I don't know. He said he was going to the mosque to oversee some repairs."

"Oh, is it? Hmm..." Bade-abba scratched his cheek. Then he looked at me. "Why don't you go and call him? Let's celebrate. I'll order biryani, meanwhile." He smiled and strode off toward the phone, leaving no room for argument.

I walked out, resigned. Bade-abba was trying his best to mend our relationship. But I wasn't in the mood to reconcile with Abbu. As soon as I reached the barbershop below, I found Karim—who worked to keep the shop clean—loitering outside.

I tapped his shoulder, "Run to the masjid and tell my abbu to come home. Fast. Tell him his brother has come and calls for him." Karim nodded and started in the direction of the mosque. "Wait," I called out, "Don't tell him I sent you. Say Bade-abba sent, okay?" Karim nodded his assent again and rushed off. I waited outside the shop, leaning on its wooden door.

My mind churned with thoughts of how to cover up the syllabus for the exam. I had skin postings for fifteen days and then psychiatry for another fifteen. One month of no night shifts would definitely help. I could go to the library after my postings and study there. It sounded perfect. And I hoped it would be so.

Chapter 13
Heavy Dresses and Gold
Afrah

Bushra and I spent the next couple of days teasing each other and Mom. One evening, we were discussing baby names.

"Shifa, if it's a girl," I said.

"No, Iqra for a girl," Mom insisted.

"You both, it doesn't matter. Asif and his family will decide on the name. So why should we quarrel?"

"Hmm, you're right," I said. "Now, stand up, I want to see you." I assisted her. "What happened in the last month since we saw you after those floods? You are *huge*...." Then I walked around her, inspecting her from top to bottom. "Hmm..."

Bushra laughed. "What are you doing?"

"You will surely deliver a boy. Let's discuss boy names," I said in finality.

"Stop badgering your sister, Afrah." Mom voiced

her opinion from the kitchen, where she was making soup for Bushra. "Let her rest."

"How can you be so sure it's a boy?" Bushra asked, curious.

"Your tummy is like a basketball!" I squealed and then laughed when Bushra tried to grab me.

"Nonsense," Mom said.

"Mom, you concentrate on making soup. Bushra will vomit it out if it becomes even a bit salty," I muttered.

"You wait, Appi. You wait. Once you are in my shoes, I'll take my revenge."

"Long time for that." I flopped on the sofa and yawned.

Bushra sat beside me. "I'm exhausted. My back aches, and even I'm wondering how did I get so huge? Still, two months to go..." Then she shook her head. "Ammi, come here, please. I forgot to tell you the main reason why I'm here."

"You mean you aren't here because you miss us? How mean!" I pouted.

"And here I thought only Ammi is obsessed with melodrama," Bushra replied. When Mom sat across us on the cane chair she recently bought, Bushra continued, "My in-laws are hosting a baby shower as soon as I start my ninth month. Then after the function, you have to bring me here."

Mom nodded, already knowing about this custom. She raised her brows and asked her to continue.

"So...umm," Bushra fumbled.

"Just get it out," I said, crossing my legs on the sofa.

Bushra widened her eyes. "What is that?" she pointed to the white patch near my ankle.

"Oh, something. I don't know." I shrugged.

"See, it's on this leg too..." Bushra pointed to my left leg.

I hadn't noticed the patch on my left leg. "Oh yes..." The one on my right leg appeared to have increased in size. "How come I didn't notice it?"

"If you live in your dream world, how will you see reality?" Mom interjected. She dragged her chair forward to look at the patch again.

I sighed, "Looks like Nivea cream is not working."

"You better get it checked from Dr. Wasim," Bushra said.

"No, she cannot go to him now," Mom muttered. "She rejected his son's rishta quite cruelly. He was so smitten with her. And I don't want to give any reason for him to gloat that it was good she rejected...that she has so many health problems. Huh."

"Many health problems?" Bushra asked. "Ammi, this is the only one."

"No, Bushra, what Mom means is I have so many other issues too. Not getting periods regularly, so many pimples, and this perpetual state of living in a funk."

Bushra sighed. "Fine. There are many other doctors. Go to anyone else and get yourself checked."

"Yes, ma'am." I straightened my legs. *Enough discussion about my problems.* "Bushra, what were you saying earlier?"

"Oh…umm…they want you to give me three heavy dresses and one gold set for the *god-bharai* ceremony." Bushra averted her eyes. "I said okay."

I stayed silent. It took me a lot of effort to do that when all I wanted was to yell my lungs out at her. How could she even agree to such a thing?

But before I could say a word, Mom declared, "Consider it done."

"Mom!" I yelled. "What do they think we are? We don't have a gold mine. On the one hand, you refuse to pay fees for my B. Ed course, and on the other, you are willing to spend so much for a bunch of gold-diggers?" Bushra flinched, but I didn't care. Right from the time Bushra married, her in-laws kept asking for something or the other on various occasions. They had already borrowed 25,000 rupees as a loan. I never said anything because I wanted to keep my little sister happy. But this was too much. "First, tell them to return our loan."

"You cannot talk like that, Afrah. You don't understand these things. Don't you want your sister to live comfortably?" Mom yelled back.

"As if she is living happily now." I pointed at my sister, "Look at her mom, can you say she is happy? She hides her feelings well, don't you, Bushra?"

"Appi..."

"Afrah! Enough. Bushra, we will give all that. You relax, don't listen to your sister. She has no sense, only thinks about herself."

I stomped my feet. "Fine, do whatever you want. Sell the house, sell your soul..." I headed to the bedroom. "Don't ask me for anything, though!"

As I brewed tea in the kitchen the next morning before work, Bushra hugged me from behind. "Morning, Appi. I love you so much!"

"Hmm...morning, Bushra. So would you like boiled eggs or omelets?"

"Anything is fine. I'm sorry."

I blew on the tea as the milk in the pot threatened to spill over. I liked to make milk tea; just add milk to the water, tea leaves, and sugar. It tasted creamy, and I loved it.

I turned to face my sister. "What are you sorry for?"

"For putting you all in a tough spot. I thought of being stronger and refusing them to ask you all for what they demanded, but I couldn't do it. I so want to be stubborn as you, but..."

"Shhh. Don't let Mom hear you want to be like me. She'll roast you like chicken tikka on a barbecue!" I grinned, though I really wanted to slap her. I also wanted to tell her that it wasn't too late for her to become strong-willed.

Bushra should have finished her studies so she could learn to have her own voice and not give in to the pressure of her future in-laws. Asif loved her, and Bushra loved him back; their love wouldn't diminish if the wedding got delayed by a year or two. Bushra was supposed to say all this and remain firm in her decision. But no, she gave in like the docile little girl she was then as she did now, and we had to bear the brunt of it all.

I sighed. I couldn't share this with her. I shuddered to think about the consequences of causing so much stress to the little sister that she might have an early delivery. I didn't need more black marks on my name.

"Come now. Let's have breakfast, then, I have a job to do."

"Yes, Appi." We sat to eat the omelets and toasted bread. After taking a bite, Bushra asked, "How is your job going?"

"It's good. I'm enjoying it. And I'm now also used to traveling by train." I smiled.

"Oh, I cannot imagine traveling alone on a local train. And Kurla station? It's so crowded, and it has so many platforms. How would one even know where to go?"

I clucked my tongue. "You speak as if you are illiterate. Agreed, it's a bit complicated, but if you start going daily, it'll be a cakewalk. Which you aren't going to, by the way, so why stress about it? Enjoy your life."

"You are right."

I washed our plates in the sink. "There is tea for Ammi. But she'll have to make something to eat," I instructed Bushra. Mom had gone to the morning bazaar for fresh fruits and vegetables with the neighbors. "I'm leaving now. See you later."

Bushra stopped me. "I won't be home when you return. Asif is coming to pick me up. So, I'll now see you in October."

"Hmm. At your baby shower. Yes. We'll talk on the phone." *By that time, I'll have my mobile.* But I shook my head at the thought. I wouldn't get excited about anything. What was the use? The salary slip caused me so much heartbreak.

Later, I renewed my train pass at the station and rushed to the platform. An announcement said the train was running late again, but I did spot a familiar face. I went up to him.

"Hi, Sadiq." I grinned when he looked at me, his brows furrowed.

He rubbed the back of his neck and smiled. "Hi, Afrah."

"So why the sad face?" I asked.

He shrugged. "Conflicts at home."

I rolled my eyes. "Tell me about them." Then I straightened and said, "Actually, let's make a pact. Whenever we talk, we'll not bring up any of our problems at home in our conversation. We don't need that gloom to follow us everywhere. Yeah?" I quirked one brow, then the other.

Sadiq looked at me with wide eyes. Then he nodded. "Good idea."

"Great then. So, cheer up. Smile. You are handsome when you do."

He turned away and his Adam's apple bobbed up and down as if he was gathering up the courage to talk with me. He had the same flicker of a smile whenever I complimented him.

"So, are you still doing night shifts at the hospital?" I went on.

"Yes," he said, and I could see his eyes shining in enthusiasm. Looked like he loved to talk about his work.

"Which hospital do you work in?"

"The municipal hospital in Nerul."

"Wow. I have never been beyond Vashi. How is it?"

"Busy?"

I laughed. "No, I meant Nerul?"

"Oh, it's good," he shrugged.

I concluded from this that he hadn't seen the sights of Nerul. He appeared to be the kind who went from hospital to home and vice versa.

The speaker made another grating announcement saying the train was canceled. Collective sighs and groans filled the platform. The next train would be impossible to get into.

"Why can't she announce something positive?" I complained.

"That's how it always is," Sadiq said, his voice a whisper.

I glanced in his direction, at the sadness his words conveyed. What was he fighting against? Why did he have a look that said he was resigned to his life? I cleared my throat. "Where did you say you lived?"

"The Mastan chawl at Pipe Road. Do you know about it?"

I nodded. I'd been to that area once; I remembered it vividly. It was congested, so full of people, with hardly any place to walk. Mom had to hold me tight so that I wouldn't get lost in the crowd like I once had at Dadar station. Chawl-like buildings flanked either side of the small road. And street vendors occupied the remaining space on the road. Their shouts, coupled with the honking of the rickshaws, scooters, and bikes, gave a cacophony of sounds that could even put the noise level at the airport to shame.

"Oh look, our train is arriving," Sadiq said.

The women around me geared up to get on the train. I had no intention of getting mangled today. I didn't have the strength to jump on the train.

"I'm going to skip this," I said in finality and took a few steps back. "Bye. I'll see you?"

Sadiq waved. "Tomorrow."

I watched him in awe as he made his way into the train—not like me, jumping inside—but weaving his way through the crowd until he finally grabbed the pole and hauled himself into the compartment. He raised his hand as the train started, and I wondered whether he waved at me again, but then I brushed it off. Why would he think about me more than he should? Or maybe he does? Ignoring the fluttering in my chest, I adjusted my dupatta. As the train crawled its way out, I braced myself to get into the next one.

and when he came, they spoke about me as if I wasn't present in the room.

"A few flats are vacant in my building. Come to live in one of them. We'll work out something for the rent. It will be better for Sadiq; at least he can study in peace," Bade-abba had said, and Abbu concurred.

Of course, my abbu would agree, but working out something for the rent meant Bade-abba was paying it. And I didn't want any more debt in my life. Also, I didn't want to live so close to Farheen. Though she was my cousin, I preferred her company once or twice a year, at the most.

"I don't think that is wise, Bade-abba." I had jumped into the conversation without permission. "My academics are my responsibility. And I'm hardly home. I prefer to study at the library."

"Don't interfere when elders are talking," Abbu reprimanded.

"I wouldn't if I wasn't the subject of the conversation. And besides, Ammi and my decision should matter. We earn, after all," I'd added, my tone scathing. I didn't want to engage with Abbu, but my future was at stake here, and I wanted to hurt him with my words.

"Sadiq," Ammi pleaded, "it would be better if you go out now."

"No, Ammi. A decision for me has to be made in my presence."

"You earn peanuts and act like you are earning lakhs. I have raised you, son. Don't forget that," Abbu growled.

I clenched my fists. I had hit him once before, and I would do it again. In a heartbeat. Instead, I picked up my bag and stomped out of the room. Whether my anger was justified or not, that man brought out the worst in me, and I preferred to stay as far away from him as possible.

I didn't know what happened after I left. I didn't get a chance to ask Ammi. She was asleep by the time I came home. I ate a cold dinner from the plate she had left in the kitchen. Then I tried to read a few pages of Toxicology. How much my brain retained would be revealed to me later.

Ammi had whispered to me this morning—things were left as they were after I'd stormed off. But I would have to sit with Abbu and Bade-abba at some point in time and discuss matters like a grown adult.

To which I had replied, "*He* has to behave like a grown adult. Bade-abba and me, we already are."

Now, as I got off the train, I stuffed all those problems into a corner of my mind. I needed to be alert for the day ahead. I might get to scrub and hold an instrument at the operating table.

The next morning, I reached the station way ahead of time and sat on a bench just vacated by another commuter. Not long after, Afrah rushed toward me. She looked radiant today, her eyes twinkling. "Hi," she said, a little breathless.

"Hi, Afrah," I smiled and stood, offering her the seat.

She waved me off, saying, "Train is due in a minute. Listen, we forgot to shake hands on our pact."

I stared at her.

Then, she further said, "Arrey, remember we decided to not talk about our problems at home whenever we are together? The pact we made?" She snapped her fingers.

Oh yes. I remembered. It seemed a good idea. "Yes."

"Good then, so deal?" She offered her hand for a shake.

I looked at her long fingers, hesitating not so much for religious reasons, but the idea of touching her made my heart race. Her hand was soft, and I had a strange feeling of how they would feel if I were to kiss them. I shook my head to disrupt the visual.

"What?" Afrah asked.

"Nothing. Deal."

She held my hand and released it only after the train sounded its horn. She cleared her throat. "Bye."

"I won't be here tomorrow. Tuesday night shift."

"I know."

My heart skipped a beat. *She remembers my schedule.* I didn't expect her to. Like I didn't expect so many things—the probability of ever seeing her again. Of talking to her. I wondered why she still hadn't made a joke out of how we first met. Rescuing a gentleman in distress. Chuckling, I boarded the train.

Afrah

I reached home, skipping and bouncing all the way. Yay! I had my dream phone in my bag. All I needed now was a SIM card. I made a note to go back to the shop to check out the plans available that best suited my needs—sending text messages to Bushra, Roshni, and talking freely to a couple of my college friends with whom I was still in touch. I knocked at the door of my house and hugged Mom as soon as she opened the door.

"Careful, beta," she said, laughing. She had applied some kind of face mask and kept her face away. "What makes you so happy today?"

I rushed to the kitchen, drank a glass of water, and

then sat on the sofa. "Wait for it, Mom. Dun dun dun!" I took out the packet from my bag. "I bought a phone!"

Mom laughed at my delightful squealing and inspected the package.

"Go on and open it. It will not bite you," I teased.

She hesitated, so I grabbed the box myself and opened the seal.

"Huh, wasn't I supposed to open it?"

"Oh, you are too slow, Mom." I brought out the phone, switched it on, and handed it to her. "Here."

Mom turned the device in her hands.

"See? Press this." I showed her all the features of the phone. "It has a camera, Mom! I can click lovely photos of you."

"Hmm...I don't understand all this, but how much did it cost you?"

I grimaced. My entire first month's salary was gone, plus most of my savings. I didn't want to settle for a cheaper one. It had to be the best. I wasn't going to buy a phone every few months. This was a once-in-a-life-time investment. Wasn't it? After justifying my actions and promising myself to save my future salaries, I took the plunge. The travel allowance from my job would help me get a SIM card. But Mom didn't need to know all of that. And anyway, she had refused to take even a penny from my salary.

So, I gave her a reply she'd have liked to hear, "It's

not that costly. But now, life will be fun!" Kissing my mother's cheek, I said, "Eww...what's this? It tastes bitter."

Mom laughed. "I told you to be careful."

The month of September flew by. The last rains, coupled with thunder and lightning, gave me an opportunity to click many pictures. I took them from my office window, from the moving train, and sometimes from my bedroom window. Then, I went through the pictures and deleted the blurry ones.

Mom's September went by differently. Since I had refused to help her with the demands put forth by Bushra's in-laws, she kept herself busy arranging for the gold set and dresses they'd asked for. I did try to remain oblivious to her struggles, but I was aware of how difficult it was for her. I'd overheard her grumbling conversation with her friend that she had been shopping all across the town to find good dresses for Bushra's baby shower, but her budget was too thin to afford them.

One Saturday morning, as I was going through the collection of pictures on my phone, Mom sat next to me. The TV was on, but she wasn't focused on her soaps. It was as if she'd aged so much in the past month. More wrinkles round her eyes. Bags underneath them.

I gave in and held her hand. "Mom, I'll bring the 'heavy dresses.' You can relax."

"When will you have time to do that? The function is next Sunday. You have only eight days."

"That's enough time. I know of a place where I'll get those, so it won't be a problem."

I took a picture of her deep in thought.

She swatted me. "Oh hush, how many pictures will you click?"

Giggling, I said, "Now, you sleep well, get a facial, and then I'll click another one. I'll show them to you then. 'Before and after your not-so-favorite daughter helped you.' Ok?"

"You think that Bushra is my favorite?" Mom snorted. "But it's nothing of that sort. I only want what is best for you. Perhaps you'll understand when you have kids yourself."

I didn't know what to reply to that. How many times had I told her to leave my future to me? But she was relentless, and I didn't want to begin another argument. I browsed through the phone's gallery—pictures of the crowded station, the rains, and lightning, a few pics of Roshni and myself, hair flying as the train moved full speed. And I had even clicked a few of Sadiq in the next compartment.

I had his landline number now, although I never called him. I didn't get an opportunity to do it yet. Besides, I only wanted to call him at home for the fun of it, but he laughed and said he would hardly be home as he studied in the library until late at night.

I met him daily at the station for the last fifteen days or so, and most of the time, I did the talking, but I did learn a few things about him. Like how he wanted to be a surgeon, how he waited for his internship to be over so he could get a better-paying job. I smiled, looking at the various pictures of him. Those few minutes with him made me feel as if I was in a different world where there weren't any problems at all.

Putting my phone down to charge, I looked out of the window. The traffic moved at a snail's pace. My next goal was to get the stuff for Bushra. And Tuba was an expert in this matter. It was time to knock on her door again.

Chapter 15
White and Other Colors
Afrah

Monday morning, I slogged my way to the station. It was that feeling again—the one that made me feel as if all the world's problems were on my shoulders and nothing could make me happy. Was it my period? I had stopped tracking my cycle. Did I get it last month?

"Hey, chirpy bird, what's wrong?" Roshni asked as soon as I entered the compartment. We now had a fixed place by the door.

"Nothing. Or maybe premenstrual something, I forgot what you had said last time."

Roshni gave me a sideways hug. "Oh, my baby," she cooed, "premenstrual symptoms. Don't worry, you'll be fine."

"I'll have to skip a day again," I groaned. Typing the entries in the Tally software and then cross-checking with the accounts books made me feel as if I was doing an important job. The most important job. Plus, the few minutes of internet surfing were a bonus. The connection was painfully slow, but still. I could get so much new information on various things.

"That's alright. But hey, cheer up. October has started, and it's salary week." Roshni wiggled her brows.

I narrowed my eyes. "Yeah, but I'm not falling for it this time. They'll give us whenever they want to."

"That's also fine. But don't be grumpy. Come, let's click some pics of the creek."

"You click, and then if they turn out nice, I'll take them via Bluetooth."

I looked over in the men's compartment. Sadiq stood there, talking to his friend. I prepared to wave at him when he glanced in my direction. But he never did. He was late today too it seemed since I didn't see him on the platform earlier.

My day at work passed in a blur, and soon we were heading to the station. "Roshni, I want to eat something."

"Something? Do you have anything specific in mind?"

"Something spicy?" I suggested.

"Hmm...oh!" Roshni snapped her fingers, "I know of something that'll instantly uplift your spirits and satisfy your hunger. Come. Come here," she repeated, taking a detour. Instead of heading toward the platform, we went to the food stalls at the station.

"Wow, I didn't know about this," I said, looking around at the stalls. The smells of the delicacies cooking made my mouth water. "Okay, so what are we gonna eat?"

"Bhaiyya, cheese wada pav...make it two and put lots of cheese," Roshni said in Marathi to the stall owner.

"Cheese wada pav?" I asked.

"Yup, it's heavenly."

I took a bite and moaned. Heavenly they were. The gooey cheese melted in my mouth, and the deep-fried potato wada was just perfect. It was a bit spicy, but the cheese and the bread bun in which it was placed balanced the taste.

"Amazing!" I said in delight.

"Aren't they?" Roshni laughed. "Look, is that your friend?" she pointed to a man not far from us.

I followed her index finger and spotted the familiar figure. My heart skipped a beat. Sadiq. "Yeah. I wonder what he's doing here."

"Come, let's ask. You can also introduce me. Your friends are my friends." Roshni grinned.

"I don't even know if we are friends," I said but my

heart pounded faster with each step I took in his direction.

When we were close enough, I noticed he wasn't alone. The same man who accompanied him on the train was with him.

"Hey, hello," Roshni said before I could say anything.

Sadiq looked at us, surprised. His friend grinned.

"Hi," I said, smiling. I had finished the wada pav and now wanted to drink water. "Do you have some water?" I blurted, not knowing whether he did have it, just as Roshni said, "Fancy seeing you here."

Sadiq nodded and opened his backpack. I was elated when he offered me the water bottle.

"I'm Ashish," Sadiq's friend introduced himself.

"I'm Roshni. She's Afrah. You might have seen us on the train."

"So, what brings you here?" I asked Sadiq.

"Why? Aren't you glad to see us?" Ashish replied.

I cleared my throat. "Of course I am," I said and muttered my thanks while handing the bottle back to Sadiq.

"Well, I had to buy some things from the mall, so I dragged my buddy here to accompany me," Ashish said.

"Are you headed home?" Roshni asked, "There's a

Vashi local starting in—" she glanced at her watch and then the train indicator, "—exactly five minutes."

We walked down the steps toward the platform together. Vashi station was underground, like many stations in New Mumbai. I lagged while Roshni and Ashish were busy talking. Sadiq noticed, and he reduced his pace to walk in step with me.

"I plan to go to the library to study after this," he said.

I smiled. "I know. I remember you don't have peace at home, and you need to get those huge books in that tiny brain of yours."

Sadiq shrugged and sighed. "I have obstetrics and gynecology postings from next month. It is again busy, and I won't get much time to study."

"Yes, I understand."

"Dude, I really don't want Unit 1 or Unit 3 this time," Ashish said over his shoulder.

"What's that?" I asked Sadiq.

"Ashish has surgery posting next and is a bit anxious about it. I need to go this way." He pointed with his thumb. "Bye, Ashish. See you tomorrow."

Ashish stopped. Then he looked at me. "How can he leave a beautiful girl like you to travel alone on the train? Ask him to drop you home."

I felt my cheeks heat, but then I cleared my throat. "What do you even mean by that? I don't need a bodyguard. Besides, he has more important things to do, and you are there na," I said in a sweet voice. "Won't you escort Roshni and me?" Oh, I was enjoying this.

"I... uh..." Ashish appeared to be at a loss for words, "Yes. Yes, of course, I will."

"Come on, guys, we'll miss the train," Roshni called out.

I bid goodbye to Sadiq, who flashed me a smile.

"I'll see you tomorrow!" I said, and he waved a hand in return.

We waited by the platform where the train's men's compartment would stop. As the train arrived, Roshni insisted it would be rude to leave Ashish alone.

"It's not only men's compartment," Ashish said when I tried to drag Roshni toward the women's section. "It's called a general compartment. Both men and women use it."

"Yeah." I forced a smile. It was always crowded, and I had no intention of being pinched at places where I did not want to be pinched. "Except we need a separate one coz men cannot keep their hands to themselves."

"Hey, don't generalize," Ashish said.

"Yes, yeah, whatever."

"There are good men around. Take me, for example."

I rolled my eyes while Roshni giggled. I understood

he wanted to flirt with her. And I wasn't going to inter-fere if Roshni didn't mind—or was rather enjoying—the attention.

I sat by the window seat, with Roshni next to me and Ashish next to her. They talked and laughed all the way while I relegated myself to the background. I thought about the dresses I bought for Bushra two days back and how Mom made a face looking at them.

'What? You didn't like them?' I'd asked.

'They are pretty, but aren't the colors gaudy?'

'Well, heavy dresses are gaudy. Pastel shades are meant for subtlety, which apparently Bushra's in-laws do not understand.' I was spewing venom when I had no business to be doing so, but I couldn't help myself. That discussion always got me in a sour mood. I wondered whether Papa was aware of all of this. *He would be, or else from where would Mom get the money needed to buy the gold set?* I wished he would come home sooner to sort everything out.

Now on the train returning home, I wondered whether I would be in a similar position when I got married. No more suitors had come my way since the last month. I felt I had more energy because of that; the entire ritual tired me. I didn't like to fake smile at my prospective husband or serve him and his family tea and biscuits. It felt as if I was deceiving everyone—all prepped up for display. They would never know the real me. If it were up to Mom, I would not have been allowed to even see the man I was marrying until the day of the wedding. But I had put my foot down and refused to follow that custom.

Thank goodness for small mercies. I was glad Papa stood firmly by my side when I voiced my opinion on the matter. Mom couldn't do much and had to oblige.

Ashish stood up and bowed to us when his station arrived. "It was nice to meet you, ladies." He winked at Roshni.

"Likewise, Ashish," I replied.

After he got off, Roshni shuddered.

"What?" I raised my eyebrow. "I thought you enjoyed talking to him."

"I did, but I don't know. He shared his number with me and grabbed my phone from my hand and saved his number in my phone. All of it without even asking me!"

"Good, one task less for you. Don't worry, I'm sure he means no harm. Or else I cannot imagine Sadiq being friends with him."

"Hmm...you do have a point. So, what do you plan with this month's salary?"

I shrugged.

"How about streaking your hair burgundy?"

"No. I don't think so. I need to save my salary

now," I said. "Two years of teacher's training is forty thousand rupees. I'll need it."

"True. Have you decided which colleges to apply to?"

"Yes, sort of. I have two places in mind." I stood as my stop arrived. "I'll tell you later. Bye." I quickly got down. As I crossed the foot overbridge, my phone vibrated. Fishing it out of my bag, I read the message from Roshni: *It's fun traveling in the general compartment. Maybe we can do it more, at least for the return journeys.*

I didn't bother replying. I didn't want to waste money on messaging when I could tell her in person what I thought. If the train started from Vashi, it would be fine. But if it came from ahead, then the general would be crowded, so there was no chance of getting in.

"Do you have anything to wear for the function this Sunday?" Mom asked once I got home.

Oh, right. Bushra's baby shower. The one thing I was glad of was that it meant Bushra would be living with us for the next three months—her entire ninth month and then two months with the baby. I was excited that it would be like the earlier days when we had loads of fun. Or maybe not. Bushra might be too busy with her new baby. I wondered how difficult or easy it might be. The baby only needed milk and clean diapers. What else?

"Where did you go? Afrah?"

"Oh, I'm here only, Mom. Yeah, I'll wear *my uniform*," I said, using air quotes.

She gasped. "Not that. Don't you have anything else?"

"Shhh...relax, mother. It's not my function anyway, nobody is gonna look at me. Let Bushra shine, it's her day."

"What gonna...gonna? From where did you learn it? I'm telling you, this job-wob is not doing any good. I keep telling your abba, but I don't understand what you've told him. He doesn't listen to me."

I kissed Mom on the cheek. "I'm gonna freshen up." Laughing, I went to the washroom. All the uneasiness I'd felt that morning, the dour mood, had evaporated. Roshni called it Monday Blues. 'It happens,' she said, 'when you've had a relaxing Sunday, you feel lazy to wake up early in the morning and come to work.'

I hadn't asked her why it was called 'blues' and not any other color. Maybe I would ask tomorrow.

I took a bath and while patting myself dry, I noticed another white patch on my body. This time, it was on the inside of my left wrist. It was a small one, but it made my heart beat a little faster. I rushed out and called for Mom.

"What?" she shouted from the kitchen.

"Mom, see this." I jutted my hand forward. "Now what to do? You don't even want me to go to the doctor."

"Oho, apply some cream or something, it'll go away. And I didn't tell you to not go to the doctor, I told you to find a different doctor."

I went back to the bedroom and examined the patch. Applying more Nivea, I prayed for it to go away. I had stopped taking calcium tablets, could that be the reason? I didn't know what to think anymore. Maybe I should find another doctor soon.

Chapter 16
The Fight
Sadiq

At the college library, I opened the Microbiology textbook. Those few hours with Ashish, which I earlier thought would be a waste of time, were refreshing. It had been a while since I had such an outing. That's why Ashish kept telling me that some time out is good for the brain. And now, I agreed with him. I might not go to the mall every time, but a visit to the beach or even a nearby park would clear my mind.

Staphylococcus failed to grab my attention. I turned to the next chapter. But my mind drifted to Afrah. I wondered if she felt bad when I refused to travel with her and left her with Ashish. She did say she understood. Or had she only said it for appearance's sake? I shook my head. Those few minutes at the railway station with her had become the most exciting time in my day, and I looked forward to meeting her every time. She brought so many stories with her. *Maybe I should contribute more to the conversation. What if she considers me a bore and then refuses to talk to me?* The chapter on gram-negative bacilli floated in front of me. I needed to stop being negative.

The bacilli were soon replaced by other images in my head. What would Afrah think of me when she'd know I had raised a hand on my abbu? I always had anger problems right from when I was a little boy, but people around me handled my anger and tantrums. Being the only boy and the youngest in the family, I'd been a pampered child. Especially by Ammi. I didn't remember Abbu looking after me that much. He never took us for any outings either. It was always Bade-abba. As I grew older, I tried to channel that anger into academics. And I succeeded, except a few times when I burst out—or rather, popped like popcorn cooking in a pressure cooker.

I remembered that day vividly. It was two and a half years back. I'd just returned from a tiring day of lectures and more lectures. Second year of medical college was busy. Abbu was at home and was discussing something when I stepped into the house.

'Oh, good, you're back,' Abbu had said. He didn't even give me a chance to wash my hands and face. 'You can take a bath later. This will not take much time.'

With reluctance and convincing myself that this must be important, I sat with my parents.

Abbu started. 'I have decided we will sell this house and move in to stay with your bade-abba.'

It took some time for those words to sink in. Bade-abba was newly widowed; his wife passed away due to a sudden cardiac arrest.

'What good will it do?' I answered.

'What do you mean? He is alone, he'll feel good if we are around him.'

'You don't have to sell the house for that. We can go and stay with him for a few days.'

'But he insisted we stay with him for longer. In fact, he only suggested we sell this dump of a house. There's an extra room at his place. We can all fit in that.'

'This is foolishness. You cannot make us homeless. Even if this place needs repairs, it is our home. My home. How long before things get back to normal and Bade-abba tells us we are no longer welcome? And he has his children to look after him. They are adults.'

Abbu all but shouted. 'So now you'll disobey your bade-abba's orders?'

'It's not disobeying, it's self-preservation. We are already in his debt—he is paying my fees, and I have accepted that. But now, nothing more. There is no need to sell this house!' I shouted back. The veins in my head throbbed. Ammi squeezed my hand, attempting to calm me down.

'But we have to. I promised to loan money to a few people. And we cannot get that until I do this.'

That did it. 'You cannot make your family homeless to please a bunch of strangers, you piece of shit!' I stood.

Abbu stood, too, and jabbed a finger at my chest, 'Don't you forget, I'm your father.'

'What have you done for me as a father?' I was shaking.

Ammi tried to pull me away. 'Sadiq, please, stop it. Go upstairs, I'll give you something to eat.'

'No, Ammi, now that it is out, I want to know. What has this man done for me? For you or my sisters?'

Ammi had tears in her eyes. She went and closed the door of the house. I knew what she was trying to do. But it wasn't of much use as the doors and walls were paper thin, and sooner or later, everyone in the chawl would know about it.

'I have fed you and clothed you. How can you forget that?'

'So? Did you do it as a favor, or was it your duty? Bade-abba has done more for this family than you ever have. When I wanted money to study, you didn't even try to arrange for it. And you keep saying so many people owe you, now where is it? I even suggested we shut the barbershop since there is no money from it. We could have given it on rent, which would have helped run the house, but no. It looks good to your 'friends' to have the shop. Why would you listen to me?'

'As if you know business skills.'

'Oh, and you know a lot. Selling the house, making us homeless, and then squandering all the money...for what, Abbu? For what? Why are outsiders more important to you than us?'

But my words didn't affect him one bit. 'I need to sell this house. Discussion over.'

'And I will not let you sell this house. Not even over our dead bodies,' I sneered, my voice was cold, and in my daze, I pushed him.

Abbu fell backward, and his head hit the wall.

'Sadiq! What are you doing?' Ammi yelled. 'For Allah's sake, leave him. Please...'

Ammi's fearful voice jolted me from any more violence I was about to commit. Shaking my head and clenching my fist, I'd stormed out of the house.

Now, in the library, with E. Coli in front of me and Afrah inside my head, I wondered about that outburst of mine. The topic of selling the house had been shelved completely since then.

Bade-abba tried to talk some sense into me about reconciling, but I did not budge. We managed the house by cutting costs. Ammi used her savings, and I sold off my ring given to me by my grandmother. What use was the ring if we had nothing to fill our stomachs with?

I hadn't gotten that angry since then. Many incidents would trigger me, but I diverted my attention. Anger made me a monster. And I needed that monster contained in its cage. I had bigger goals in life now.

Shaking my head to focus, I reminded myself that I needed to concentrate on the chapter before me. I wanted to solve the test papers Ashish had given, but when I'd tried one a few days back, I could barely answer ten to twelve questions out of the hundred. I needed to work harder. Much harder to even stand a chance of clearing the exams next year.

Chapter 17
Baby Shower
Afrah

It was a few days before the holy month of Ramadan. Mom was stoked with happiness. However, I woke up not feeling well. A visit to the washroom revealed the reason. Clots of blood dropped down, and I sighed. Partly in pain and partly in relief. I wouldn't have to go to that damn baby shower. Bushra's mother-in-law had sent a list of prospective grooms for me to Mom. And Mom had badgered me so much over the last few days about it that the excitement I had for the event evaporated.

Mom needed my help to wrap the jewelry and the dresses in an eye-catching way. I tried—even watched some videos online at my office—but I couldn't replicate it quite the same.

'You can't do even a single thing well,' she taunted me.

'Please, Mom.' I rolled my eyes. 'I can cook. What more would a man want from his wife?'

She scoffed. 'Babies, too.'

'Urghh...leave me in peace, please. I know how to act with my potential suitors.'

After dragging myself to the kitchen, I filled a hot water bag and popped a painkiller. Back in the bedroom, I lay on the mattress, and my thoughts drifted to Bushra. I'd spoken to her last night. Her in-laws had hired a few henna artists to apply designs on the hands of all the females of the house. *Why do they pressure us for jewelry if they can splurge so much?* Bushra was equal parts excited and nervous, but she had promised me it would be one of the grandest baby showers in their generation.

"Come on, Afrah, wake up! We have to get there early," Mom called from the living room.

"I'm awake only, Mom. But I don't think I can make it." I groaned.

"Don't talk rubbish. Why can't you make it?"

"Isn't it obvious?" I replied, pointing to the hot water bag on my tummy. When Mom still appeared clueless, I scoffed. "I'm chumming."

"What?"

I chuckled. Of course, Mom wouldn't know the slang for periods. I had learned the word in junior college and found it cool. I'd even checked its meaning in the dictionary—it actually meant 'friends.' When I discussed it with my friends, they laughed it off. 'Yes, but if you become friends with your periods, life becomes simpler,' they'd justified the term.

"Periods, Mom. Periods. I just got it. And you know how bad my first day is."

"I know, it's bad for all women who get periods, but we don't stop working, do we? Come on, take some pills in your bag. You can eat them at the ceremony hall."

I arranged some pillows behind my back and sat up against them. "Mom, I can't come. You know I bleed so heavy and need to change pads too often."

"I know, beta. But this is important. We are Bushra's only family. And we will leave as early as we can, okay? You also take one or two sanitary pads. You need to divert your attention from that pain. It'll be all good. Come now, start getting ready."

When she put it that way, it did make sense. We were Bushra's only close family here. And if I kept my mind busy, the pain would seem less. Wouldn't it? Begrudgingly, I decided to listen to her for once.

After getting ready, we took the gifts in a suitcase. It would be easier to carry and safe, too. Outside, rains lashed at us, and I hitched up my white salwar with a frown; I didn't wear my uniform after all.

"See, Mom, Allah doesn't want me to go. Those

clouds thundering with the special effects of lightning all indicate this. Don't you think it seems like that ominous background music in your TV serials?" I couldn't resist trying Mom's melodrama on her.

"Stop blabbering nonsense, Afrah. Ask that auto-rickshaw if he'll come." She gestured toward one of them down the street.

We went to the ceremony hall by an auto-rickshaw, hoping the rain would end soon. I didn't want the city to flood again. I had no intention of staying even a minute longer than required at Bushra's place.

Finally, we reached our destination. The local school hall. Real flowers decorated the entrance. A few bouquets and potted plants were kept at strategic locations. More flowers decorated the stage. The backdrop had a baby's face, with chubby cheeks and brown eyes, and fairy lights twinkled around its head. A comfy-looking chair sat alone on the stage. I had a sudden longing to occupy that chair and take a nap.

A sweet aroma drifted toward me, and I glanced toward the buffet. No harm in checking out the food. The waiters were busy, so I lifted the lid of the first dish. Carrot halwa! I breathed in its scintillating aroma. I wouldn't mind taking a few bites. It looked so good....

"Afrah!" From afar, Mom waved at me in a frenzy.

Taking one last longing look at the carrot halwa, I

walked in her direction. *I should have told her to leave me alone as a condition for attending this ceremony.*

"This is Afrah, my older daughter. She has a job, you know. So, she's busy. Hardly home." Mom laughed. "Oh, but she makes a mean biryani, right?" She looked at me, and I gaped at her. It was unbelievable. Mom was actually showing me off as a working woman. Oh, I wanted to giggle, but I controlled my impulse and greeted the women. Then I excused myself and found an empty chair to sit back and relax.

Bushra was yet to arrive, although I did spot her in-laws. I ground my teeth, thinking about the demands they made. What would they ask for next after the baby was born? Wasn't it enough that we'd look after Bushra post-delivery? And her in-laws wouldn't have to spend anything for the hospital admission and everything that a delivery entailed. *Now if they ask for anything, I will show them their place. Consequences be damned. Huh!*

I glanced at the time on my watch. Mom had loaned me this rose-gold one; it was delicate but suited my wrist. Though I wanted to wear my usual black one, I made an exception at Mom's insistence. I had to stay alert and keep looking at my wrist, as I didn't want this fancy watch to fall anywhere or get scuffed.

My gaze fell on the white patch on the inside of my wrist. I'd considered it to be a trick of the light earlier and then forgotten about it. But now, it could be seen clearly, and it didn't look like I had a calcium deficiency.

"Mind if I sit?" a hoarse voice asked.

Startled at the intrusion, I quickly tugged at the sleeves of my kurti. *Thank goodness I wore a long-sleeved one.* I didn't have it in me to explain the patch in case anyone noticed and asked about it. And people here were extra inquisitive, this was more like a gossip party than a baby shower.

I took a deep breath and clutched my stomach, feeling my insides cramp. The last thing I wanted was a conversation with a stranger. I looked up, and instead of finding an old lady—as I assumed it would be judging by the voice—my eyes widened seeing a man. Older than me, in his late twenties or early thirties. He cleared his throat, preparing to make small talk. I turned my head and ignored him.

"Nice decorations," he said finally.

I quirked my brows. "Nice?" *More like over the top,* I wanted to say. The man looked blank. I shrugged, "Yeah, nice indeed."

"Are you related to the pregnant woman?"

No, I got bored at home, so I gatecrashed a baby shower in the middle of a rainstorm. I gave him a huge smile and fake laughed. "Of course, can't you see the resemblance? Bushra is my younger sister."

"Oh...now I get it."

The spasms in my stomach increased in intensity. I couldn't bear them anymore. I found the pill in my bag, and after excusing myself from the stranger, I walked toward the buffet to get some water.

"Afrah, where did you disappear? Come with me, I want you to meet a few more women."

"*Mom*," I whined. "Please, I'm hurting, don't make me do that. I'm here for Bushra. Why isn't she still here?" As if on cue, Bushra entered amidst fanfare. "Good, she's here. Now you give her the gifts, and then let's go."

"Uh," Mom muttered. "I guess I forgot to tell you we have to take Bushra back with us today. It might be evening until she's seen everyone."

"Very nice, Mom, very nice. Now do me a favor and find me someplace where I can lie down for a while. Somewhere closer to the bathroom." When she hesitated, I asked, "Or do you want me to roam around here, vomiting and with blood-stained clothes?"

Mom took a deep breath. "Fine, come with me," she said through clenched teeth. I giggled mentally and followed her. I wondered how she ever spoke like that. I, for the life of me, couldn't speak without even moving my lips.

Being as popular as she was, Mom was stopped by a number of women on the way, and I was introduced like a rag doll. Plastering a smile on my face throughout the short walk, I sighed in relief once she found me an empty classroom. I lay down on one of the benches.

"Thanks, Mom. I'll find you once the effect of the pill kicks in. Can you find me a hot water bag?"

"Yes, My Queen, what else do you need?" she stomped her feet and banged the classroom door shut behind her.

"Easy, Mom. This is not your house," I whispered and chuckled. Then I grimaced in pain. All I wanted was to go back home and sleep. *I still have to meet Bushra,* I thought, yawning. *Later. She's going to come home anyway.* Just as I was about to doze, I heard footsteps outside the door. Sitting up, I straightened my dupatta over my dress. The door opened, and in walked the same man with the hoarse voice.

"Oh, so you are here," he said, "I wondered where you disappeared."

I found it creepy that this man was out looking for me. I cleared my throat and stood. *Damn the bleeding!* I couldn't stay here with him. The thought alone gave me goosebumps.

"I was just leaving," I said, walking toward the door. But I couldn't resist also asking him his name. I had to know who was stalking me.

"Mirza. And you are Afrah."

My palms turned clammy; this man knew my

name. So, he was definitely stalking me? It would be better if I were in the crowd. Not saying anything to him, I rushed out of the classroom.

Bushra had settled on the stage, and I went to meet her. My little sister looked tired, despite the layers of make-up, and she wore a heavily embroidered kurti and salwar. The sequined dupatta wrapped around her head and pinned at her shoulder made her look so much older than she was. I wondered what was heavier, Bushra or her outfit. Then my gaze fell on Bushra's hands. The color of her henna was dark maroon, and it looked beautiful. I grasped her hands and brought them closer to me. I loved the smell of henna.

I hugged Bushra and muttered in her ear, "When can we go home?"

Bushra smiled and whispered back, "Why, Appi? You enjoy these functions so much."

"I do, but I'm not feeling good."

"Okay, Bushra and Afrah, you can talk later. There are others who want to meet you." Bushra's mother-in-law interrupted.

"Of course, Auntie." I gave a wide smile. "Did you like our gifts?"

Mom came out of nowhere and slyly pinched me on my arm. "Come, Afrah, let's eat something," she said, smiling coolly. When out of earshot, I could feel the heat emanating from her. "How shameless can you get?"

"What was shameless? Did I ask anything wrong?"

"Oh, for Allah's sake, stop being so selfish. Go now. Do whatever you want, but don't come near Bushra till this is over."

"You know what, Mom? I'm going home. You get Bushra and come back when all this nonsense is over. Maybe her in-laws should have had a competition— whoever brought the most gifts would get a prize." Saying the last part in a sing-song voice, I left the venue.

It had stopped raining, but the roads were mucky. My sandals and white salwar would be stained black by the time I reached home. *I don't care.* My stomach growled and I turned, thinking of going back to eat something, but then decided against it. I bought a wada pav, and ate it, not wanting to worry whether eating bread would increase the stomach pain, and asked for directions to the nearest station.

I climbed onto the first train that arrived, ticketless. I wanted December to come fast. Papa would be home. I longed to hug him and talk to him. He was the only one who listened to me. Really listened, without passing any judgments. I rested my head beside the window and closed my eyes.

Chapter 18
Of Internship and Manipulation
Sadiq

It was the beginning of my obstetrics and gynecology postings. The month of Ramadan would start in a few days, and Ammi was too worried for me.

"How will you manage to fast with this hectic schedule?" she asked me. "Where will you break your fast? And those night shifts...where will you eat your sehri? You cannot eat junk food, Sadiq."

"Shhh...relax, Ammi. I'll manage everything. Don't worry so much. Because I'll be busy in the ward, the day will pass so quickly that I won't even realize I'm fasting. As it is, we go a long time without eating or drinking much."

Ammi hadn't looked convinced, but she let it go.

Now, in the labor room, I cringed as the woman shouted. While I prided myself in doing surgeries, I couldn't stand seeing a woman bleeding and yelling in pain. I'd almost fainted on the first day. But a few deep breaths brought me back on track while one of my colleagues fainted. We had attended normal deliveries in our final year at medical college, but conducting them made me nervous. *No, no. Buckle up.*

The resident doctor informed us, "So, guys, monitor the blood pressure and heart rate every two hours for all these patients. For bed numbers twenty-three and twenty-five, monitor every hour. They are pre-eclamptic and have separate BP monitors. Keep the cuff attached to their arms only—that would make checking their blood pressures easier and faster."

I nodded in reply and got to work. I didn't want to spend the whole month only doing this. But in a way, I was also glad. It would give me some time to adjust with fasting for Ramadan. While checking their blood pressures, I tried to recollect more about pre-eclampsia. All I could remember was that if a pregnant woman had high blood pressure, it affected the growth of the baby. *I have to read more about this.*

My days in the posting passed quickly. It was tiring as I was also fasting. Ammi had insisted I shouldn't fast, but I had never missed even a single day. No matter what, I always completed the fasts.

I'd met Afrah only once at the train station; she

looked tired as well. Even though it was the first time I'd seen her in a while, we couldn't talk much that day.

In the ward, I graduated from checking blood pressure to assisting in deliveries that entailed pushing on the woman's stomach to let the baby out. Many women refused the presence of a male while they delivered. The resident doctors argued with them that we had many good obstetricians who were male, but some of the women refused to budge. In such cases, I was relegated to the wards to again monitor blood pressure.

At home, the atmosphere remained the same. If Abbu was there and he asked me something, I would answer in monosyllables. Ammi had started her catering again—after cajoling Abbu a lot—for *iftaar* parties this month, so I did get to eat treats from time to time. She always saved a little from the order for me.

"Hamid is coming in a few days. Your bade-abba will host a party for him and his new wife."

"Hmm...if I'm free, I'll attend, Ammi."

"There is no pressure from me. But your abbu and bade-abba will not let you remain absent. I'll tell you the date as soon as I know, so you can make arrangements to come for some time."

I smiled at her. She always put my interest first. "Okay, Ammi. I'll do anything for you."

The day of the party arrived sooner than I had anticipated. Hamid arrived in the city on the twenty-third of October, and the party was set for the following day. *Why couldn't they rest and keep it next week? On a weekend. After Ramadan. On Eid day?* Not that it mattered to me, as I was too busy prepping for my Preventive and Social Medicine postings for three months, out of which one month would be a rural one where I would have to live in the village and work at the primary health center. I looked forward to that month. It would be a welcome break from the tensions at home. Plus, I would learn new things and get more time to study. I hadn't told Ammi yet. I had no idea how she would react, but I would convince her. It wasn't a choice—I had to do it for my sake. To preserve my sanity.

The morning of the party, I woke up with much trepidation. It was an iftaar party, but I did not want to go. One, because I wasn't quite fond of Hamid; he had always been a bully to me and all the other kids in the family. Second, these parties always had a bunch of giggling girls who went silent the moment I passed by. It irked me, to say the least. I really wished for a miracle to get me out of this quandary.

I went to the hospital as soon as I could.

"Remember to come early," Ammi told me for the hundredth time.

"I know, Ammi. I'm not a child," I answered, my voice pitching louder than usual. I caught Ammi's grimace and rubbed my neck. I didn't want to hurt her, not even in my dreams. "I'll try my best. But Ammi, you know how things are at the hospital, and I'm in the gyneac ward. Do you understand? It's so unpredictable. I promised you I'll return home early instead of going to the library, right?" When Ammi nodded, I continued, "Do not worry so much. I'm going to come here as soon as I'm done with the rounds. Okay?"

I smiled in relief. Her badgering me to come early gave me this wonderful idea. It wouldn't be the first time I would be manipulating the truth—a little self-preservation was my need of the hour.

I reached the hospital with a smile on my face.

"Intern!" the head nurse shouted the moment I stepped into the ward. "Blood collection, bed numbers twenty-one, twenty-two, twenty-five, twenty-eight, and thirty-one." She grabbed my hand and put a piece of paper in it with a list of the tests. "You know where to find the needles and bottles."

I wanted to laugh. The world at the hospital was so different; no one called me a doctor there. And they were right in doing so. I still had a few months to graduate. Yet at home and in my neighborhood, everyone called me 'Doctor Saab.' I had stopped correcting them because they simply didn't understand.

While doing my work, Afrah kept invading my thoughts. I hadn't seen her in over a week now. I'd caught a glimpse of her friend, Roshni or Rohini? I wasn't sure of her name. When we met a month back at Vashi, I wasn't paying attention to anyone else but Afrah. It almost broke my heart when I had to part ways—I would have given anything to sit next to her—but she said she understood. My chest ached by the time I reached the library. But academics were important. Being together on the train could wait.

After depositing all the bottles at the nurse's station and filling up all the relevant forms, I sat on an empty bench and browsed through the phonebook. Of late, I had used it to jot down interesting points and mnemonics taught by the seniors on rounds. Now, I was using it for something entirely different.

I finally found it. Afrah's cell number. *Should I call her? What if she's at work and is busy?* I paused and put the diary back in my coat pocket. I stood, then sat again. *No, I'll call her. What if she hasn't been on the trains because she's in some trouble?*

For the first time in my life, I dialed a number other than my home.

Chapter 19
A Phone Call and Dabeli
Afrah

I couldn't stop yawning. The last few days were a nightmare. I tried to imagine how life would be once the baby came out. *Better or worse? Better. Certainly, the baby would feed and sleep.*

Bushra couldn't sleep the whole night. She often felt breathless and had to visit the washroom a hundred times. I tried to cajole her to sleep, but as if a switch had turned in her system, she stayed up the night and slept through the day. While it was okay for her to do that, I found it difficult. Not to mention the two missed workdays because my sister thought her labor pains had started. We rushed her to the hospital only to be told to come back after a few days; it was a false alarm.

The lack of sleep made me tardy, and often I missed my usual train. Add to it the Ramadan fasting. I normally couldn't stay hungry for a long time, and this month was a test of self-control for me every single year. I did manage to fast daily unless I got my period. The latter, despite the pains, was a relief.

Roshni supported me the most on these difficult days. She waited for me at the station, and we always went to the office together. She didn't mind reaching a few minutes late almost every other day. It had been a while since I'd met Sadiq, too. What was he up to? Maybe I should give him a call.

Rubbing my eyes, I yawned again. I so wanted to rest my head on the worktable and nap for a while, but Tally seemed to call out to me to complete the entries. *No, enough.* The dratted entries could wait. A teeny-weeny power nap couldn't.

As I was about to enter dreamland, my phone rang. I cursed the caller. "Hello," I started, "if you tell me anything about any offer, I swear to Allah, I'll come through the phone and snap your neck in two and then make *kheema* pulao out of it!"

"Um, Afrah?" a tentative voice asked from the other end.

Out of all the things I so desperately wanted, the topmost being a good night's sleep, I wasn't expecting a call from him. Yes. I did glance in the general compartment on the train in case he was late. And wasn't I just wondering what he was up to? And here he was. Such telepathy. A throat clearing from the other end snapped me out of my thoughts.

I opened my mouth. "Oh my! Sadiq?"

"Y—yes, hi. How are you?" he asked.

"Oh, I'm so not good, Sadiq." No, I didn't want to burden him with my problems. "Leave that. You say, how are you?"

"I'm okay. But what happened to you? You don't sound well either."

I really wanted to tell him everything. Groaning, I said, "I know, but I can't talk so much on the phone. You see, I'm at work."

"Um...so will I see you tomorrow?" he asked.

I didn't know that either. What new thing awaited me at home? "I have no idea. But I can see you today. Can you come to Vashi station at 4:30? Meet me near that stall of cheese wada-pav?" Oh, how much I wanted to eat that gooey lump of cheese.

"I can try. If I get late, I'll give you a call."

"Okay, that's great." I spotted my supervisor coming toward me, and I whispered, "Listen. I gotta go. I'll meet you later," and disconnected the call.

I shook my head, still not believing Sadiq had called me. *Me*, whom bheveryone called a spoilt and selfish brat. It almost brought tears to my eyes. I again shook myself to start working before the one thing I loved—my job—would be taken away from me.

I rushed to the station after work, hoping Sadiq would come; he hadn't called yet to change the time. I really wanted to share my burden with him. I'd told Roshni about my struggles on the train rides to work, but she had brushed it off as a phase.

"Be patient, you'll be fine. Think about your poor sister. How must she be feeling? She needs all the support."

I sighed. Yes, my sister needed all the support. But what about supporting the people who supported her?

Now, I reached the station sans Roshni. It was difficult to get rid of her—I had to tell her I was going to meet a distant relative, and surprisingly Roshni had bought that. I didn't like lying to her, but Allah knew how much I wanted this alone time.

I looked at the wada-pav longingly, and then my gaze fell on the *dabeli* stall. The shopkeeper filled the pav with potatoes and chutney. He then roasted it in butter and served it to customers after garnishing it with some pomegranate, sev, and onions. My mouth began to salivate. I had tried it only once and still remembered its sweet yet tangy and spicy taste. Unable to resist the aroma, I bought two dabelis on a whim and asked the man to wrap them separately. I would eat it at iftaar—a little treat for me.

I returned to the wada-pav shop with my goodies and grinned. Sadiq was standing there.

"Hi," he greeted me.

I smiled at him. "Thank you for coming, let's go to the platform and sit?" I handed him the packed dabeli and put mine in my bag. "Careful, it's hot."

"I...uh...don't want to eat this," Sadiq said, his fingers gently wrapping around it.

"But it's really yummy. You don't have to eat it now. Eat it later."

Sadiq put the parcel in his bag. We went to the platform and found a place to sit. We didn't talk for a while, the honking of the trains coming and going filling our ears.

"My sister has come to live with us for a while," I started, and when Sadiq tilted his head and raised his brows, I raised my index finger and continued, "I know we had made a pact to not talk about our families, but if I don't talk about it, I'll go mad."

Sadiq gave a flicker of a smile. "No, go on. I'm listening."

"Thanks," I grinned. "So yes, my sister Bushra— she is nine months pregnant and could pop out any time." I paused to wait for the train horn to stop blaring and then I told him all about my experience over the last few days. When I stopped to look at Sadiq, he had this half-grin on his face.

"Hmmm," he said. "I understand how difficult it

must be since I'm posted in that same department at the hospital, but...."

I was sure to hit him if he asked me to be patient with this issue.

"...What you can do is give her soft pillows to support herself when she sleeps."

I looked at him wide-eyed. "What?"

"We do that at the hospital, and it works. The pillows support the belly, they take the pressure from the diaphragm—the breathing muscle—and then the women don't get that breathless feeling that keeps them awake at night. I know you will then ask why is that they can sleep during the day, so let me tell you, the sleep-wake cycle gets reversed. If you stay up the whole night, you will have to sleep in the mornings to make up for it, right?"

I nodded, but I was in a daze, not because Sadiq had provided a solution to me, but because I heard him talk *so* much for the first time. I beamed at him. "You are amazing."

Sadiq smiled and rubbed the back of his neck. "Uh, thanks."

"I'm going to try this tonight," I said as my phone rang. "Oh, a call from home, excuse me?" Sadiq nodded. "What?" It was my mom, but most of her words were eaten by the noisy station. "Can you be clear and slow? I'm not understanding anything." I put a finger in the other ear to block out the sounds.

"I said, Bushra's water broke. Where are you? I'm taking her to the nursing home."

"Okay."

"What okay? Where are you? Come fast!" Mom yelled.

"I'll meet you at the nursing home directly. Bye." Sighing, I turned to Sadiq. "The pillow trick might not be needed anymore. My sister is finally going to pop out. Thank you for helping me, though."

"It's nothing. I was worried as I didn't see you for so many days."

I didn't know what came over me at that moment, but before I could change my mind or give thought to maintaining Ramadan self-control, I kissed him on his cheek. A little bit of kindness always melted my heart.

Chapter 20
The Kiss and Some Screams
Sadiq

I could still feel Afrah's lips on my cheeks. I couldn't believe it. My heart was beating at twice its usual rate, and I feared I would get an arrhythmia. Sitting on that same bench long after Afrah left, I tried to recover from that unexpected gesture of hers. Maybe she didn't realize it was Ramadan and got carried away with her happy emotions. She seemed so relieved when I told her about the pillow trick. The furrows on her brows had disappeared. Shaking my head, I again touched the spot where she'd kissed. Only my mother and sisters had ever pecked me.

Several trains came and went. I couldn't bring myself to get on any of them. I sat as if I was in a fugue-like state—not knowing how or why I landed up here. Then as if on autopilot, I got on the next train that arrived on the platform. The jingle of the train bell brought me out of my trance, and I realized I was going in the wrong direction and jumped down just as the train started.

I didn't want to go home, didn't want to attend the party. I hadn't felt this light-hearted in such a long time, and going to Bade-abba's and interacting with Abbu and Hamid would spoil my mood. Retracing my steps back to the hospital, I dialed home. Having laid the groundwork earlier this morning, I had to take my idea forward. The ward was so chaotic. It would be perfect. The call connected.

"Hello?" Ammi said.

I won't be lying, only manipulating the truth. Repeating this mantra in the back of my head, I said, "Ammi, I am stuck in the ward here. It is very busy."

As if on cue, the nurse yelled, "Intern! Keep down the phone and go...that patient is full...the head is out. Go, go fast!"

"Ammi, I need to go. I'll call you again, later."

"Sadiq," Ammi almost yelled, "Don't call now, we are going to your bade-abba's house. Try to come, if not, I'll explain it to them. Don't worry, do your work."

I sighed in relief and rushed to the labor room. The ward was indeed crazy. With three women delivering simultaneously, the labor room was full. I prided myself in conducting normal deliveries, though I couldn't yet use forceps or vacuum. And I had no intention to, either. I'd managed to overcome my initial hesitation, and if the patients were comfortable in my presence, I did my best. How did Afrah's sister fare? I wanted to call her again; my mind wouldn't stop thinking about her. *Later, once this madness settles.*

I was happy with one thing—I didn't have to endure the giggles of Farheen and her friends, or the backslapping by Hamid.

"Thanks, bro," Saumil, a fellow intern said. "It's so busy today. I don't know how we'll manage till tomorrow."

My colleagues had been on call since yesterday. Oh, poor Unit 1 people.

"Don't worry, if you want, you can rest for a while. I'll wait here till ten," I offered to help. I wouldn't be able to study anyway because if I remained by myself, my mind would drift to Afrah. The shouts by the patients and the nurses would keep me occupied until it was safe to return home.

"You are amazing, Sadiq. Thanks again. We'll catch a quick nap and recharge ourselves for the night," Saumil said and called for his co-intern.

I gave a nod and got back to completing the paperwork.

Afrah

"What was I thinking?" I spoke aloud, heart hammering in my chest. I still couldn't believe I'd actually kissed that unsuspecting man. Even if it was just a peck on his cheek. It happened so fast that for a moment, I did not realize what I'd done.

Now, on the train, I stood near the door, fidgeting with the split ends of my hair. It would be a nightmare untangling them, but it didn't bother me. I had too much energy in me for a Muslim who was supposed to abstain from an action like that.

Leaning out of the door, I held the pole for dear life and whooped. The creek passed by, and the wind blew my hair all over my face. It was such a thrilling moment. I'd always wanted to yell over the water from the time I started this job, but the crowded train didn't give me an opportunity. Roshni would have squealed in fear at this stunt of mine.

Even I was not sure if Bushra kissed Asif before they married. I slapped a hand over my mouth at the comparison.

My racing heart settled, and I sat in the window seat. But I couldn't sit still. Going to the door and coming back again, I wondered what the handful of women in the compartment thought of my restlessness. One of them had earphones plugged in.

The stations passed by, and I closed my eyes. All I could see was the stunned face of Sadiq. What must he think of me? Should I call him and ask? Biting my lips, I felt my cheeks heating up. He was the only one of the opposite gender, after my papa, whom I had kissed. Grinning like a fool, I shook my head.

Soon it was my turn to alight from the train. Back to the mundane.

Outside the station, I was about to sit in the auto-rickshaw to go home. But then I remembered that Bushra was about to deliver. *Finally*. Or she must have already delivered. I didn't want to predict what was happening, so I rushed to the nursing home, grateful that it was within walking distance of the station.

"Excuse me, where is the gynecology ward?" I asked at the reception and turned around in the lobby in case I spotted my mother or one of Bushra's in-laws.

"First floor, take a right from the stairs," the surly lady at the reception replied.

I didn't feel like thanking her because of her tone. Mom or Bushra would have. But it didn't bother me. I went in the direction she told me to.

A woman screamed. *Is that Bushra?* I ran the remaining distance and opened the door. I could make out my sister's voice, "I'm done...I'm done! I can't do this...ahh!" She shouted. There was another door with Labor Room written in bold. The screams came from the other side. Yes, it was Bushra. I pushed open the door, and there she was, behind the curtain. "Aahh…" she yelled again.

"Oh, thank Allah, you are here." Mom grabbed my arm. "Your sister refuses to listen—tell her something. Tell her to cooperate with the doctor and push," she pleaded with teary eyes.

I was at a loss for words. Mom prodded me again. I cleared my throat and nodded. "Bushra. I'm here," I spoke through the curtain when Bushra's shouting ceased. "You are my brave sister, do as the doctor says, please?" Should I part the curtain and see what was going on? No! I didn't think I could handle watching all that blood.

"Appi, you're here," Bushra moaned. "Tell them to do an operation, I cannot do this. Please, Appi."

"Bushra, it will only take a few minutes more. Push hard. Come on."

"Few minutes? Bloody, I'm doing this…ahh…for more than an hour… ahh!" The screams started again.

"Bloody?" I wanted to laugh. But I looked at Mom and asked, "One hour?"

"Don't listen to her, she's exaggerating." Mom replied as the doctor inside started, "Push… push…."

"Push Bushra, come on, you can do it!" I went on repeating it like a mantra, much to the doctor's amusement.

She later parted the curtains and said, "The baby is out. You can stop shouting."

"Oh.," I grimaced. "Can't hear the cry."

"You will," the doctor replied, and at that moment, an ear-piercing scream came from behind the curtain.

Mom rushed inside. I still couldn't do it and remained planted outside.

"Bushra...Bushra?" I asked tentatively.

"Appi, it's a boy."

"Okay, are you alright? You were brave, indeed."

"No, no. I'm not alright...ouch!"

Mom came out holding a tray with a tiny creature wrapped in a green towel.

The nurse and another doctor cleaned up the baby as he went on crying. I stood transfixed, marveling at the little thing. *He looks like a monkey.* I wanted to ask Mom about the way he looked but stopped myself.

After the doctor was done with whatever she was doing, she wrapped the baby and handed him to Mom. "The baby is alright. Start breastfeeding as soon as the mother is shifted to the ward." She gave a nod to Mom and me.

Mom muttered prayers in the child's ears. I went out of the room and sat in the visitor's section, wondering how painful the whole thing was. I didn't want to know how I would go through all of it if and when that day ever came. An image of Sadiq popped into my head. He was so calm and collected and always had a solution to any problem. *I should tell him this. Good qualities in others should be praised.* I didn't like flattery, though I often engaged in it at the office with my seniors. But that was a part of office life.

At that moment, stone-faced Asif walked in from the other side, trailed by his parents. I straightened my hair and adjusted the dupatta of my dress. Where is Mom? I couldn't handle these people. They made my blood boil.

"Beta, what happened?" Bushra's mother-in-law asked.

I looked at her and glanced quickly at Asif and his father. They stood a little away as if waiting for someone to include them in the conversation.

I stood and smiled. "It's a boy. Congratulations."

I did not wish Asif or his father separately; the 'congratulations' were for all of them.

"Delivered already? Oh!" Bushra's mother-in-law looked disappointed.

"Mom is inside with the baby. You can all go."

They went, and I sat in relief. Talking to them was like treading on eggshells. I wondered how Bushra *lived* with them. I checked the date on my phone. Twenty-fourth October, Monday. A new birthday to remember. I had a nephew now, and thinking about him made me smile.

Now that everyone was here, I decided to go home. I looked toward the labor room, contemplating whether to meet Bushra or not. My sister would be too exhausted to make conversation, but I would see her once before leaving. Even if I didn't, Bushra would be coming back to stay with us for the next two months. Plenty of time to talk with her.

"He's with his abbu," Mom said when she came out. "Thank Allah, everything went without a glitch. Yes, you were saying you wanted to go home?" She seemed to be thinking about what I asked her. "Yes, you should go. Meals will be given here to Bushra, but I'll need food. You go home, cook something, and come back here. Let me ask Asif if he'll be waiting too." She returned to Bushra's room.

I groaned. I wasn't going home to cook, I wanted to sleep. Oh, how much I needed that!

"No, they'll be leaving after meeting Bushra," Mom said as she came out of Bushra's room.

"Okay, so I'll come tomorrow," I said. Then I pressed my luck. "Mom, if you can handle it, I'll come in the evening tomorrow, I have to go to work."

She scoffed. "You are unbelievable."

"There's a cafeteria here. You can eat dinner and sehri, too." I tried to reason with her. But then I didn't want to be so mean. She was my mother, after all. "Okay, so I'll come early in the morning, get you tea, and then go to work from here. How is that? I'll also bring some clothes for both of you."

Mom sighed. "No need to come alone at 4:00 a.m. You come later with the clothes. Okay?"

I hugged her and left. I would meet my sister in the morning.

I rushed to reach the platform so that I could catch my usual train. But, like the last few days, I missed it. The crowd refused to part for me, no matter how much I elbowed my way. I was stuck on the stairs when the train came and left. Huffing, I sat on the just vacated bench, not noticing anyone around me. So, when someone tapped my shoulder, it startled me.

"Oh, hi," I said, wiping my forehead with a napkin. It was Sadiq. The heat was getting unbearable. "Why is it never cold in Mumbai?" I asked him.

"Looks like you ran your way here. Let your heart rate settle a bit. This feeling of heat will go away," he replied.

"Even you missed the train?"

"No, I wanted to wait for you."

I bit my lip and turned away. "I...I'm sorry, I kissed you out of the blue."

"No, it's not about that. I wanted to know if your sister is alright."

I slapped my forehead. Of course, he wouldn't think much of the kiss. Why was I making such a big deal out of it? He must have a girlfriend already, for all I knew. Did he really have a girlfriend? He seemed like he was open to dating before marriage, like me. I didn't think he was the strictly religious type. I looked at him and voiced my concern aloud, "Are you seeing someone?"

"What?" He gave an awkward laugh. "No, I don't have a girlfriend."

I hid a smile. "My sister is good. She delivered a baby boy. I went to the nursing home in the morning to visit her. That's why I got late."

The announcement of the train arriving started, and I moved to take my position. I squared my shoulders and inhaled deeply as if this was a war, and if I blinked, I would be killed. But Sadiq hesitated to leave my side.

"All good?" I asked him.

"Yes, I. Uh. I will not be coming by train next month. Have to go to live in a village. Rural postings," he said.

"Oh. Wow!" I replied. "That would be fun. Where are you going?" I wondered why he told me this.

Maybe he did remember the kiss then. He might even miss me when he was gone. Would he?

"I don't know right now. We will get our postings on first November."

The train crawled in. It was two minutes late, and people were hanging at the doors. I didn't want to travel in such a crowded train. My lack of sleep over the last few days had sucked the energy out of me. This hanging at the door didn't excite me anymore. Sighing, I stepped back and looked at Sadiq.

"Bye, and I'll meet you tomorrow?"

"Uh, I have a night shift."

"It's alright, I'll call you then?"

"No," he said while getting on the train, "I'll call you." With that, he disappeared into the crowd.

I messaged Roshni that I would be late and would meet her at the office. The next local arrived fast, and it was empty. I even got a place to sit.

I closed my eyes. Mom had been in a bad mood when I'd visited earlier. And why wouldn't she? The little fellow hadn't slept the whole night and did not let anybody else sleep either. *Thank goodness I went home.* I couldn't handle any more sleepless nights. But there would be plenty to come, I was sure of that.

Once Bushra came home with her baby, there would be loads of work. Cooking high-calorie food for her, washing the nappies, cradling the baby, handling the visitors...oh, the list seemed endless. It's not that I didn't like to do that work, I would do it happily if only my mother or Bushra would acknowledge my efforts. They seemed to think I didn't do any work, only sat in the office warming the seat and then whiled away my time at home. To them, I didn't do anything productive —like getting married and having babies.

I'd offered Mom that I would stay with Bushra tonight.

Mom scoffed. "Huh, as if you know how to feed the baby or change his diaper."

"I don't know, Mom, but neither does Bushra. We will learn, and there are nurses here to help. Go and rest tonight," I argued. But Mom wouldn't budge. "Fine," I huffed. "I'll bring another pair of clothes for both of you tomorrow morning."

"You better take leave for the rest of the week. We need to settle Bushra. I can't stand being here any longer."

"Okay, Mom," I'd replied, resigned. Mom would lose her mind if she went without sleeping anymore.

Now, on the train, I drafted the leave application in my head. Asking for any more leave meant my salary would be deducted as I had exhausted my paid excusals for the month, thanks to the false alarms raised by Bushra. It wouldn't be long before they fired me altogether.

Chapter 21
Of Eid and Banana Rides
Sadiq

I looked forward to beginning my rural stint. The last few days of my obstetrics postings were fruitful. My professors were impressed with my dedication and hard work, so they let me assist in a few hysterectomies. These opportunities helped me to build a rapport with my seniors. Most of them had contacts in various private hospitals and impressing them meant they'd help me find a job after I received my degree. So even though my obstetrics postings were a nightmare, they ended as a win-win situation for me. As everyone says, 'All's well that ends well.'

I was in an ecstatic mood for the last couple of days. Not even my abbu's subtle taunts about not attending Hamid's homecoming party had fazed me. I turned a deaf ear and kept my mind busy. Either studying or thinking about Afrah. Something or the other would remind me of her. I even chuckled in the middle of having dinner at home, thinking about her kiss. Ammi grinned at my behavior, but Abbu only showed perplexed silence.

As the first of November dawned, I started to pack my bag. I had packed three pairs of clothes and my books.

"Will this be enough?" Ammi asked. "Take one more shirt."

I shook my head.

"What will you eat? Will someone cook for you? It's a small village, there won't be a canteen also."

"Ammi, calm down. I'll figure it out." I wouldn't have to leave until tomorrow, as today we would only be allotted the village where we had to work for the next month. I'd decided to go to the library after the allotment and then come home. Plus, I would also need to work out how I would travel to the village. "Today, I'll come to know where I'll be staying for the next month."

"Oh, so you are happy leaving your ammi?"

"Hmm. I'll ask if they would let you stay as well. Will you come?" I teased, already knowing her answer.

"Sadiq, beta. You know I cannot leave your abbu here."

"You can, I don't know why you are so scared of him." Abbu wouldn't raise a hand on her, I'd made sure of that. But living with him was still a source of mental trauma that wasn't easy to bear either. "Anyway, Ammi." I forced a smile and kissed her on the cheek. "I'll see you at night."

Rubbing my neck, I walked out of the door and suddenly thought of Afrah. I hadn't seen her in the last few days. And I was unlikely to meet her today, as I was traveling early.

At the hospital, I was told of where I would live—a small village near Alibag, a coastal town south of the city. Many of my colleagues had theirs in the hamlets nearby. It was reassuring in a way that I did have company nearby if I were to need it.

"You will first have to report to the medical center in Alibag. From there, you can disperse to your respective areas," the officer who allotted us said.

We were six interns, and Saumil was one of them too. "We are planning to hire a car. You want to join us?" he asked me.

I reasoned with myself. I couldn't travel for free with them, I would have to pitch in since traveling by car would be expensive. Another option was the ferry to the jetty. And then a bus. I told Saumil about this.

"Yes, we know it. It would be more fun to enjoy the scenic boat ride as opposed to the potholed roads until Alibag. But how are we going to reach the village where we are posted?"

I nodded. He did have a point.

"Our locations are not too far from each other, around fifteen to twenty minutes each. Look here." Saumil showed me a map of that area hung on the wall near the officer's table.

"Okay. What time do you plan to leave tomorrow?"

After having our group discussion and booking a car, I walked to the railway station in relief. The trip wouldn't punch a hole in my pocket as I expected it would. I thought about going to the library.

"No, I'll go home today," I said aloud.

Ramadan was about to come to an end, and I hadn't had iftaar with my mother even once. It was either at the hospital if I had a shift or at the college canteen if I was at the library. Besides, I would be gone tomorrow and wouldn't be able to celebrate Eid with her. Spending my last free time with her would make her so happy. It was the least I could do.

We planned to leave at six in the morning. I didn't sleep after *sehri*.

"Call me every day? Okay?" Ammi sniffed, trying hard not to let a single tear fall from her eye.

"Yes, Ammi. I will. Don't worry."

I gave her a wobbly smile. It was the first time for

me, too, that I'd be away from home for so long. My colleagues planned to come back every weekend, but I refused. I did not want to waste time traveling to and fro, I would rather study.

"Let me first reach there and see how it is. I'll call you. Bye." I kissed her cheek and went out the door, not bothering to look for Abbu.

The journey was rickety, to say the least; the roads were that bad—still washed out from the rain. I heaved a sigh of relief and stretched myself as I got out of the car after nearly four hours of travel and bid goodbye to my colleagues.

The little village looked quaint. *If this place remains as quiet as it is, I'll finish so much studying.* The health center was in the middle of it. Each house was equidistant from one another as if it was a planned construction. A common toilet and a well were at opposite ends.

The Marathi language they spoke was a bit out of my league. I remembered Ammi looking at me in awe when I spoke fluent Marathi with the rickshaw driver once when we had to go to Bade-abba's house.

"Oh, Ammi, I learned it at the hospital. We have to. Most of our patients speak it," I'd said.

But here, I realized that the Marathi dialect the locals spoke would be difficult for me to understand. To my relief, I didn't have to work alone. The local medical officer in charge of the Primary Healthcare Center would supervise.

A ward boy showed me to my room. It was small, with a single bed against a wall and a tiny desk and chair next to the window that overlooked the entrance of the PHC. It had an attached washroom. But I couldn't see any plumbing fixtures in the washroom, and the toilet was outside—the common one that all villagers used.

The ward boy said in Marathi, "Saheb, you will have to fill the buckets from the well daily. But don't worry, I'll help you."

I nodded. One of the buckets was filled already. That would be enough for now to freshen up.

After depositing my books on the table, I sat on the bed. The mattress seemed stiff, but it would have to do. I'd slept on the cold floor at my house when my sisters came to visit. I lay down and wondered how my other batch mates had fared.

A knock on the door roused me from my contemplation. It was the ward boy again. I went with him and met the medical officer. He ran me through my duties for the time I would be living there. It wasn't much, and I was glad. It would leave me with enough time to read.

I used the phone from the health center and called Ammi to update her. She was about to start with her usual questions about my diet, sleep, and everything else under the sun when I told her I had to go and would call her later. I thought about calling Afrah but then decided against it. What would I tell her? And I didn't know how to deal with the light-headedness that often accompanied me whenever I saw her or heard her voice.

My days at the village passed slowly. The people of the village looked after themselves well. Their hygiene was good, and so I had second thoughts about the lecture I was supposed to give them on cleanliness. I had the notion that the villagers wouldn't even understand what I said, but the medical officer had put my worries to rest. He told me I wouldn't have to speak at all—only prepare a presentation. It would then be projected on the huge screen outside the health center, and the medical officer would talk. But I wondered how I would do it with the patchy electricity and the equally patchy computer.

To my relief, the electricity didn't play a spoilsport, and the program was a success. The whole ambiance of watching a screen under the open sky amazed me; I had never done or seen such a thing before. But it also made me melancholic. It was a feeling that came from the depths of my heart—wishing for a loved one to be with me like my ammi or Afrah. *Afrah?* So easily, she invaded my thoughts.

My colleagues paid me a visit over the weekend to cajole me into leaving with them. I wanted to, as I really wished to meet my ammi on Eid, but the medical officer had gone home, making me the highest-ranking health official. So, I remained stuck in the village.

"Eid Mubarak, Ammi," I greeted her over the phone.

"Eid Mubarak to you too, beta," she replied. "How are you? My poor boy will not be able to have *sheer kurma* this time...."

I chuckled. "It's okay, Ammi. You can make it when I come back."

She told me about the picnic the neighbors planned—a one-day trip to the National Park. I encouraged Ammi to go. While I had never been there, I had been to the zoo a few times, courtesy of my bade-abba.

Village life proved productive for me. I studied a lot and managed to clear the backlog of the last month. I fared even better on the practice test papers I had from Ashish. *Maybe I might clear it this year.* Then I shook my head. If I wanted to be a surgeon and stay in the city, I would have to be in the top 100 or 200.

On lonely and starry nights, I often found myself thinking about Abbu. Was he always like that? I'd read many topics in psychiatry, and on an occasional day when patients were few, I had even discussed it with my professor.

'He ticks most signs of narcissistic personality disorder. It's not uncommon,' the professor had said.

Later, I read about it and realized the professor could be right; all that my abbu did, the need to be regarded as important, that desperation to be admired, the way he manipulated Ammi and then adored her at times...I couldn't fathom that behavior. It didn't matter for Abbu how much trouble he stirred for us. Ammi seemed to hope he would get better, but I didn't have the heart to tell her otherwise. As for me, the lesser I spoke to him, the better for me. His staying away from my life made me happy and at peace.

Chapter 22
A Pleasant Surprise
Afrah

The days passed in a busy blur for me. After Bushra came home, we made arrangements for the aqiqah ceremony, where the child's head would be shaved. This was followed by the naming ceremony. Amongst all that, visitors came and went. I even helped my mother cook different foods to boost Bushra's breast milk production.

I was so exhausted by the seventh day. My leave was about to end, and I looked forward to going to work. Bushra's child refused to sleep at night, and although he now looked cute and cuddly, his crying irritated the hell out of me. I would suffer a breakdown if I didn't get a sound sleep soon.

Bushra stayed in the bedroom on the single bed that I had managed to purchase second-hand from a local shop. The mattress was new, and Mom had the foresight to cover it in plastic, as the little fellow always wet the bed the moment she opened his diaper. Sometimes I laughed aloud, looking at that stream covering my mother. At times, I was the victim, and then it was Mom who laughed.

Bushra couldn't even get out of bed until the eighth day. "Everything hurts," she always said.

With all the frantic activity, I was pleasantly surprised when my phone rang on the day after Eid.

"Afrah, how are you?" Sadiq asked.

"Oh, hi. I'm good. You?"

"Eid Mubarak belated."

I chuckled. "Eid Mubarak to you, too."

"So, all good at home?"

"Yes, we are getting by. He doesn't let us sleep, and I'm still on leave from work. I'm tired now, but what to do? Okay, enough about me, where are you? We never spoke after that day."

"Uh, yes. I'm in a small village near Alibag. It's so peaceful here."

"Wow, Alibag? Did you go to the beach? And did you see that fort? I so want to visit the place someday. I've heard there are speed boats and banana rides, too. What exactly is the banana ride? Did you—" I had to stop mid-question when Sadiq laughed. "Sorry, I know you are there for work, but in case you happen to go, sit twice in the speed boat, okay? One extra for me." I imagined Sadiq smiling as I said this, and my heart skipped a beat. What was wrong with me?

"Afrah? Are you listening?" His voice brought me back.

"Yes, sorry. Were you saying something?"

"No. I only wanted to say, take care. I'll call you again."

"Thank you, Sadiq. And thanks for calling me. I like talking to you."

"Um, I like talking to you, too."

I wondered whether he actually said this as his voice had become too faint for me to make out the actual words.

"Bye," he said, and the call disconnected.

I stared at my phone and smiled at it. He was such a shy fellow. But the one thing I liked about him was that he always listened and never interrupted me.

Once I resumed work, life became a bit better—I didn't have to hear crying every three hours. Most days, I had to stop on my way home from work to buy fresh fruits and vegetables for my sister. Bushra couldn't eat too much meat; it gave her loose motions, and the little boy would be affected, too. Of late, I wondered why Bushra had become so snappy. She got irritated by mundane things, like if the TV was left on or there were too many dishes in the sink. Sometimes she cried for no reason, and I often overheard Mom telling her,

'You should be happy. Crying will decrease your milk. And why are you crying? What for?' And then Bushra would cry more.

Maybe she misses Asif. I even asked her once, but Bushra shook her head.

"I don't know. I feel strange sometimes."

I knew she wanted to share more but was holding back for reasons I couldn't fathom.

The days after blurred into one another. I received calls from Sadiq once or sometimes twice a week. I enjoyed talking to him, though he still hadn't visited the beach or taken the speedboat ride. I had asked him about it every single time he called. He gave me some tips on how to calm a crying baby—rocking, putting them on their tummy, and so on. I was too scared to hold the baby, so I conveyed the tips to Mom. She didn't follow them at all because I refused to reveal my source.

"No harm in trying, Mom."

"I'm not doing experiments on my grandson," she chided.

I shrugged.

Bushra listened to everything I learned from Sadiq. But I didn't tell her about him, either, or how often I met him and spoke to him over the phone. I sometimes questioned my desire to keep Sadiq away from my family. *Bushra is married! She has experience in the boyfriend department, she might actually help me.* But I always put it off for later. Bushra's moods fluctuated like the force of the water flowing from the taps in our house. Sometimes too fast, sometimes in drips.

Amidst all this, there was an underlying excitement in the house. Papa would be returning home in mid-December. After living so many years meeting him only once or twice a year, I contained my elation, fearing it would be cursed. The memory of my first salary was still fresh.

One morning in the last week of November, I reached the station a few minutes early. The platform was crowded, as usual, with the train running late. I didn't have to board it anyway, so I stood near a bench, hoping to take a seat when anyone got up.

Someone cleared their throat right behind me. I turned around, and my heart fluttered. Oh, how much I missed seeing him this past month.

"What a surprise!" I said, tapping my feet. "I thought I'd see you in December."

Sadiq smiled. "I was of the same opinion. But I was relieved early. And I'm glad to be back home. I had started to feel a bit homesick the last few days."

"I'm happy, too, that you're back." *Should I tell him I missed him so much?* But my cruel mouth moved on its own, and I went on with, "So...?"

"Uh...uh...." Sadiq shook his head even before I

finished my question. "I did not get a chance to go to the beach or sit in a speed boat. I did sit on a ferry while returning home."

I laughed. "Hmm, never mind. So, what now?"

"You tell me. How are you doing? How's the little champ?"

"Oh, he's good. We are getting used to his sleeping patterns."

"Sadiq, bro!" Ashish appeared from nowhere. He stopped, realizing I was here. "Hi," he said, glancing between the both of us. "The trains are super late, so I had an idea that I'll come one stop down and get in from here. At least we'll be able to go *inside* the train...."

"Well, you can also skip this one and go in the next," I suggested.

"No, no. I have to reach before nine." Ashish sighed. "Have to relieve the poor guys who are on call for more than forty-eight hours. Unit 3 people."

"What is this Unit thing? I remember you spoke about it last time as well."

"I'll tell you. It's complicated." Sadiq answered.

"Wait, aren't you coming on this train?" Ashish asked.

"No, I'm going to the library to study. My next postings start on the first December," he replied.

"Oh yes, you were in some village until now? How was it, dude? I'm dreading it, to be honest."

Before Sadiq could reply, the train arrived.

"I'll tell you later," Sadiq yelled as Ashish prepared himself to get on the train.

"So?" I raised my brows.

"Yes, so let me tell you about the units."

I listened part in awe and part in horror as Sadiq told me about the unit system. Because he worked at a smaller hospital compared to other government ones, they had only three units. Each unit had night shifts twice a week and one Sunday a month, turn-wise. So, Unit 1 had Monday and Thursday, Unit 2 Tuesday and Friday, and so on. Now if Unit 1 had a Sunday shift, then the doctors in that unit had to be available the whole of Sunday, Monday, and until Tuesday mid-morning, sometimes a bit later, depending on the number of patients.

"Oh my God," I said. "No wonder your friend dreads the postings in those units so much."

"Yes, and if there are more patients on that day, they remain with the unit doctors 'till they are discharged."

"Much respect for you all." I sighed. The announcement for the next train started, and it was time to part ways with him. "I'll see you later." Sadiq nodded.

"Hey, you look awful," Roshni said as soon as I stood next to her.

"Gee, thanks. Little Zain keeps us entertained at night," I replied.

Roshni squealed in delight. "That's such a wonderful name."

I spotted Sadiq across from me. I forgot to tell him my nephew's name. *Next time.*

"You know your station man was here, he got in the previous train," I said and laughed.

It was a joke between us, Roshni called Sadiq bus man, and I called Ashish station man. Neither man knew they had such amazing nicknames.

"Are you joking?" Roshni narrowed her eyes. "Should I ask the bus man to confirm?"

"As you wish. It slipped my mind to tell the station man you would be on this train. Poor thing, he was squished and squashed from the moment he got in."

Giggling and talking throughout the journey, we reached our destination.

Chapter 23
Conflicts and Some Secrets
Sadiq

Somebody was singing a song on the train. It was too crowded to see who it was, but the tune was catchy and got stuck in my head. I had no idea which movie it belonged to, but that didn't stop me from humming it in my head. Afrah waved at me from the adjacent compartment as she got off her stop. My heart picked up its thudding as I waved back at her. How much I'd missed seeing her this past month! I didn't realize it until I saw her today. It was as if the clouds had unveiled to show the dazzling sun they were hiding, and my day turned so much brighter. But Afrah looked tired. Her eyes were puffy, and she had more pimples than usual—likely due to stress—on her beautiful face.

Before I reached the library, Rohan, another colleague, caught hold of me.

"Hey, can you spare a few minutes?"

"Sure," I said. I wondered why, though. *Maybe this is about the rural postings.* I prepared myself to tell him how it really was and not paint a rosy picture. Villages weren't for everyone. Yes, I had liked it there, but that feeling lasted only a few days. It got too boring later—I missed home-cooked food, even though the villagers were kind enough to cook for me, too, and missed talking to Ammi and watching Afrah giggling with her friend on the train.

"Ashish is throwing a party on his birthday, and he seems pretty stoked about it. We are planning to gift him something different, would you like to chip in?" Rohan asked.

"Oh," I muttered. It had skipped my mind even though Ashish would never stop talking about how he wanted to celebrate his birthday—the last one in medical college. Next year, who knew where everyone would be? Rohan and Ashish were good friends, too. "What do you plan to gift him?" I asked. If it were in my budget, I would contribute. I had to buy a gift for him anyway.

"See, that's the thing. We plan to do a spoof kind of thing. Give him all kinds of memorabilia so that he remembers us and this college. Do you know any particular incident with him that you both have experienced? Like while traveling together?"

I contemplated it. The idea was good. Funny even. And perfect for my friend. But what special incident could he think about? "One thing he hates is being posted in Unit 1 or Unit 3," I said.

Rohan laughed. "That's a good one. And true for most of us. Still, if you can think of anything else, do let me know." He turned to leave, then paused. "And by the way, the contribution wouldn't be more than two hundred bucks. So, you in, right?"

"Yes, count me in," I said. I could spend 200 rupees on my friend. Perhaps my only friend at the college.

Back home that night, Ammi waited for me. "You should have slept," I commented, looking at her yawn.

"No, it's that your abbu hasn't returned home yet, and I'm worried. He comes after prayers, has food, and sleeps. But today..."

"Relax, Ammi, he must be talking to someone and forgot the time. You know how he can be."

"I know, but please, can you go and check in the mosque?"

I sighed. "Okay, Ammi. I'll do that. You don't worry." As I was about to leave, Abbu walked in.

"Shukran Allah!" Ammi said, "Where were you, ji? I was so worried."

"Met an old friend and didn't realize the time. Sorry. I'm going to bed."

"What about dinner?"

"We had outside. I made my friend eat to his heart's content and packed some for his family, too. They are going through a tough time. And by the way, I have taken the 500 rupees you keep under the flour tin in the kitchen and gave it to him. At least he will buy groceries for his family and medicines for his sick wife."

Ammi leaned on the wall at the barrage of his words, her face contorted as if in pain, trying hard to not let the tears drop. I clenched my fists at Ammi's reaction. Here she was, worrying about her husband's whereabouts, and there—he was busy with his friend. Not that feeding anyone was a bad thing, but there was a limit to everything. He couldn't take the money for household expenses and spend it so leisurely. I didn't want to fight with him.

Unclenching my fists and making sure Abbu was out of earshot, I whispered, "Ammi, change the place where you keep the money, and don't tell him." Then hugging her, I said, "Come, let's eat food. I have missed you."

I would give her money for household expenses in the morning. I had savings for such unprecedented crises or medical emergencies. I sometimes felt guilty that I'd never told Ammi I'd received a scholarship— almost three-fourths of the fees—every year. Not that I didn't want to, but I also knew what would happen if I did. Ammi was naïve, she would tell Abbu unknowingly. And Abbu was an expert in extracting things from her. Especially money. I felt it was safer if she didn't know. Those funds were for emergencies, and they would ride us through until I finished my internship and started a real job.

It was by sheer chance that I came to know about the scholarship. I had spent the entire first year of medical college alone, not making many friends except Ashish. And after the fight I had with my father, who refused to contribute to the household expenses, I had a huge responsibility. Ammi had saved some money over the years, but that would tide us for a few months. And then what?

That's when I learned about this trust that helped students from Ashish; the degree of the help depended on the annual income and the marks scored. I was amongst the top five in my class, marks wouldn't be a problem, and neither would the income limit. We didn't even pay tax.

At first, I considered giving the money to Bade-abba for the loan, but then I changed my mind. I'd return the entire loan in one go later when I found a well-paying job. So, after opening a separate bank account, I kept all the scholarship money there. It helped me to buy most of my books and stationery, but not all. I still borrowed textbooks from the library and from my seniors. Besides, that money would be for emergencies only. And so, here I was.

"Shabana," Abbu called as we were finishing our meal. "That Amjad whom I had loaned money, will return it tomorrow, then I'll give you the 500 rupees I took from you."

I looked at Ammi, and she shrugged. This happened all the time. I had no expectations from my abbu anymore. The money taken was never returned to her but reused to loan to someone else. Any hope of him changing was left in the dark corner under the sink, where even Ammi's broom wouldn't reach. I didn't bother to argue with him over it.

My days in this house with him would be over soon. A few months more. That's it.

Chapter 24
Emergency or Not
Afrah

"I'm going to the airport, Mom!" My insides were bubbling with joy, like the water bursting in a *kadhai* of oil. The day I waited for so long was finally here. It was the fifteenth of December. Papa was coming! I tried my best not to let it show. Too much excitement wasn't good for my health. *Remember the first salary fiasco?*

"Wait, what's the hurry?" Mom began her interrogation. "His flight will land in an hour, and it will take him two hours to come out of the airport. What will you do there alone?"

"So, come with me. Bushra can manage alone for a few hours. She's better, and Zain has settled too."

I was only saying this to Mom as a formality, but the truth was that I wanted to ask Sadiq to come with me. We would get so much time to be with each other without the hullaballoo of the station and the trains that came and went. Papa would be amused to see Sadiq with me, but I also knew he wouldn't say a word. Or judge me. If only I could figure out a way to talk to Sadiq at home. I had always spoken to him over the phone when I was at my office. Mom watched me like a hawk. And it's not like I could tell Sadiq *I can't stop thinking about you. And I like you a lot. Would you accompany me to the airport to receive my father?* Mom would probably have a heart attack if she heard me saying that—either with shame or with happiness that I'd found a groom for myself. Biting my lip, I waited for her to go inside the bedroom. I wasn't sure if Sadiq felt the same way about me and I liked talking to Sadiq too much to risk anything.

"Ammi...look what he's done!" Bushra called. Her mood swings had reduced now, and she had started to appear a little like her previous self.

"Go, your favorite daughter and her son need you." I grinned.

"You are not leaving the house till I tell you," Mom warned me.

I quirked my brows and smiled.

The moment she went inside and said, "*Vomited again?*" I dialed Sadiq's number. I paused after each digit, second-guessing my grand plan. It was 9:30 p.m. *He should be home.* I really hoped he would agree. Otherwise, Mom would request the old man who lived next door to be my chaperone. He always complained about Zain's cries, and he grumbled at everything. How could I make polite conversation with him?

After a few rings, a woman answered the phone at Sadiq's home. *His mother?* I cleared my throat, speaking my rehearsed lines.

"I would like to talk to Dr. Sadiq. It's an emergency."

"And who are you?" the woman asked.

"I'm Dr. Farooqui from the hospital."

"Wait, madam, I'll call him..." The woman called out to Sadiq in the background, and I covered my mouth to stop giggling.

"Hello?" he sounded breathless.

"Sadiq!" I said, "How are you, my boy? Haven't seen you since the last few days, all good?"

For a moment, I thought Sadiq didn't recognize my voice, and a sudden sadness enveloped me as the other end of the phone was silent.

"Afrah?" he whispered. I almost missed that. "Farooqui madam," he then said in his normal voice. "Yes, what's the emergency?"

I took the plunge. "I wondered if you are free and if

you would go with me to the airport. My papa is coming, and I don't want to be stuck with my prickly neighbor. I'll have to leave with him, but at least I'll have your company out there."

Sadiq cleared his throat. "Dr. Farooqui, if it is an emergency..."

Then I snapped out of my fantasy world. What was I doing? Was I being selfish? Dragging a poor soul from his bed just for company. I shook my head even though he couldn't see me.

"No. No. It's not an emergency. Sorry for troubling you. I'll meet you tomorrow. Bye." I disconnected the call before he could reply.

I looked in the direction of the bedroom. Was this what Mom always told me about? That I did not care about others? Even Bushra had started to tell me that. Most of the time, I did what I wanted to, but did those actions hurt others? I didn't think so. Except yes, today I would have hurt Sadiq. What was the point of dragging him to the airport when I knew he had to study or sleep? He was already working so hard.

My phone rang before I could drown in more negative thoughts. It was Sadiq.

"Hi, are you alright?" he asked.

Mom came out at that moment. "Who are you talking to?" she asked.

"It's my friend, Roshni. She was telling me about a costume party at the office," I smiled at my mother. I cleared my throat. "So, Roshni, it's too late now. Let's talk tomorrow on the train. Our usual time?"

I didn't have anything to hide, Sadiq was only a friend. Then why did I feel so reluctant to share it with my family? I didn't have any answer to that, or maybe I feared that even now, I didn't know whether I was only 'friends' with Sadiq or if I could be something more.

Shrugging off my wayward thoughts, I knocked on our neighbor's door. Grumpy or not, I would have company on the way to the airport.

The next morning, I reached the station late.

"Don't go to work today, Appi...Abbu is here," Bushra said in the morning, holding a cup of tea.

"If I take any more leaves, they'll throw me out," I told her.

"It's okay," Papa chipped in. "I'm here to stay, and we have a lot of time to catch up. Go, my princess. Your palace of work awaits you." I giggled and hugged him. "You are the best, Mr. Ahmed Farooqui. I love you *so* much."

At the station and thriving on three hours of sleep,

I couldn't stop yawning. *Power naps at work might refresh me.* Deliberating on how to take the said naps without being caught by my seniors, I didn't hear Sadiq greeting me until he tapped me on my shoulder.

"Oh...hi," I replied. "Sorry about last night. I don't know why I called you. Silly me. You are busy with your studies, and I know how important sleep is for you, and still...."

"It's alright. I was ready to come, anyway." He rubbed his neck, and I had a sudden urge to do that for him. Then he spoke again, "Let me tell you this, I'm always available for my friends. I have very few of them anyway. Don't want to lose them."

Something overcame me. Such a strong feeling that I felt like I would burst into tears at any moment. Any small thing affected me in a way that it wasn't supposed to. And it was more whenever Sadiq was with me. *Maybe I'm going to get my period.* I had stopped tracking them, but I couldn't continue like this. I would have to write in the calendar to visit a doctor.

My eyes prickled, and I didn't want him to see my tears. "Thank you," I told him and averted my gaze.

Sadiq stood beside me. He didn't ask me anything more. I felt so relieved that he didn't. He just let me be. That was what I liked the most about him. When we met first, I found his silence a little awkward. But now,

I reveled in it—it was the most comfortable silence of my life.

The train arrived, and he bid me goodbye.

"I'll see you tomorrow," I said as we parted ways. I beamed when he nodded. That anticipation of meeting him again would make my day go faster.

Chapter 25
Hairy Legs and White Patches
Sadiq

The last week of December brought in a new exhilaration—my first practice exam. I had given in to Ashish's insistence and was glad I did. Even though I had no hope of cracking it, at least the experience of a 'live' exam hall gave me the opportunity to time myself finishing all the questions and experiencing the adrenaline of the situation.

Now, enthusiastic energy was palpable in our batch. In two months, we would graduate, and Ashish was thrilled to celebrate his birthday with such fanfare. He booked a banquet and invited the whole batch, promising everyone it would be the party of the year, complete with a DJ.

I was happy, too; I looked forward to the promise of being a real medical professional. A professor had arranged an interview for me at a reputable hospital in the suburbs. I would have to shuttle two trains if I got that job, but I didn't mind it one bit. It would pay well. And then there was Afrah. Meeting her in the mornings or even catching a glimpse of her made my days so much brighter. I couldn't pinpoint the thrum of something that I always felt when I saw her, but it strengthened the urge to hold her hand. I didn't know how she would react if I asked. She must be a bubble of joy for the people she spoke to. I was sure of that. So, I didn't know if she felt anything more for me other than being her friend. But she did kiss me. That had to mean she felt more for me... right? Another thing that made me a bundle of nerves was how would I handle *not* seeing her once I graduated? We wouldn't be traveling on the same train anymore.

It was the morning of the much-anticipated party of the year. I was about to leave home when there was a call for me on our landline.

"It's Dr. Farooqui again," Ammi told me while handing me the receiver.

"Hello," I asked tentatively. Afrah had never called me here after that day. I gasped when I heard her sobbing at the other end. What happened to her? I couldn't speak her name when Ammi was within earshot.

"I'm reaching the hospital, madam," I said instead. "What is the emergency?"

"Just meet me at the station," Afrah said and disconnected.

I ate breakfast in a hurry, not tasting the food but gulping it down.

"Eat slowly, they will manage with another doctor."

"No, Ammi, they won't. I need to go. Fast." I grabbed my bag and left, all the time thinking about what could have happened to Afrah. She did appear a bit low the last time I'd seen her. Her eyes were puffy, and she talked less, but I didn't ask her. *Maybe I should have!* But she always shared things with me whenever she wanted to.

After running to the station, I looked around wildly for her, breathless. *Where is she?* I saw the time on the indicator—I'd come early, way too early. She lived far from the station, and it would take time for her to get here, unlike me—where the station was a hop, skip, and jump away.

I sat on a nearby bench. With my legs tapping the floor of the platform and my gaze traveling from one direction to another, I waited. Finally, after what seemed an hour, even though it was only ten minutes, I saw her on the foot overbridge. I quickly stood and headed for the staircase. The moment our gazes met, she smiled. But it was not her usual bright one. This smile was dull, hesitant.

"Hi, I'm sorry. I must have scared you. It is nothing, actually. I was feeling sad. But my papa cheered me up," she said, smiling wide.

I found it hard to believe. She *was* sad, I knew it deep in my bones, like how I knew a patient was toxic and needed emergency care. And now she appeared cheerful, too cheerful. This wasn't her normal behavior. I couldn't help but snort.

"Spill, Madam Farooqui, spill. What *is* troubling you?" I looked at her, not taking my eyes away from hers.

She tapped her feet and crossed her arms. She wore a pink salwar kurta, the same one which we'd shared a joke about, a few days back. 'You look nice in pink,' I had told her in a rare attempt at giving compliments.

'It's not pink. It's a baby pink,' she'd scoffed, and I laughed.

"Baby pink looks good on you," I said now, attempting to genuinely see her smile. The real one.

It did the trick. But only briefly.

"Oh, my life is a mess. I want to do so much, but it looks like I don't have much time left!" she said exasperated. "You probably think I'm dramatic, but Sadiq, I really don't know what to do."

I tilted my head and urged her to say more.

Afrah looked around her and pulled me under the foot overbridge. It was less crowded here. She started, "I know it may seem ridiculous to you that I'm behaving in such a way, but I'm worried. Look at this." She folded the sleeves of her kurta and showed the white spots near her wrist. The one on her right wrist was bigger than the left. She then bent down and started to fold her salwar too.

"Afrah, what are you doing?" I said with wide eyes.

"Look, excuse my hairy legs, but can you see these white patches? They weren't this big at first. I assumed they were because of calcium deficiency, and so I took pills. Applied moisturizer, even showed the family doctor before he sent me a proposal for his son, then because I refused, Mom asked not to follow up with him, and now I don't know what is happening to me..." She had tears in her eyes by the time she stopped talking.

Her rambling left me speechless. I had seen patients make a mountain out of a molehill, and although Afrah didn't fall in that category, I didn't have the heart to tell her what those white patches were. *Vitiligo.* I was sure there must be more, smaller ones, on her back where she wouldn't be able to see.

"Do you know what this is?" she asked, dabbing her eyes with a napkin.

I didn't want to be the one to tell her. Besides, I wasn't a hundred percent sure of it. How could I stress her more with any of my assumptions?

"Look Afrah, the best person to tell you what this is and how to treat it is at the hospital where I work. Can you come?"

Afrah shook her head. "I can't come now. After work? Will the doctor be there in the evening?"

"I'll talk to her. Call me once you get free. I'll come to the station to pick you up." I wanted to hold her hand and assure her it would be alright. She would be alright.

"Okay, but how do I contact you?"

I adjusted the straps of my bag and craned my neck to see the indicator clock. Then I said, "Do one thing. I'll call you at four. See if you can leave a bit early from work. Okay?"

"Yes, I'll try to do that."

I didn't want to leave her like this, but what else could I do? As the train pulled into the platform, I let her board the women's compartment. I really wanted to tell her to come with me to the general one. It was crowded, but I wanted to comfort her. I smiled at her when our gazes met as the train moved, and she smiled back. That was a relief.

When Ashish got in at the next stop, I remembered again that it was the day of the party of the year. I grimaced; I couldn't *not* go. But I couldn't leave Afrah in the lurch, too. She needed me more.

I thought of telling Ashish I would be late but decided against it. Otherwise, he would ask me a hundred different questions, and I wouldn't be able to dodge all of them. Ashish was way too persuasive, and I wasn't ready to share things from my personal life. No one from my batch knew of my struggles; I had been good at hiding them and preferred it that way.

Ashish was busy talking on the phone. I wished him a Happy Birthday between calls and was secretly glad I wouldn't have to talk much to him. I looked at Afrah. She stood with her head low. Her friend was nowhere to be seen. Usually, they both couldn't stop talking or giggling. Sighing, I waited for the evening to come soon.

Chapter 26
Antiseptic and Embarrassment
Afrah

My day at work was restless. Numbers floated before my eyes on the Tally program. Images of those horrible white patches on my body occupied my mind. I hadn't paid attention to them in the last few months, so I didn't realize the ones on my legs had increased in size. The new ones on my wrists were scary. *What are all these? Would they go away?* I would have to cover them up with my long-sleeved kurtis until these patches disappeared. I hoped Sadiq and the doctor whose advice he was planning to take would help.

I hadn't spoken about this to Mom or Papa. Bushra and Zain took most of their time, and the lack of sleep made Mom cranky. Papa kept busy with varied business plans and went to meetings throughout the day.

He wanted to start a hardware shop and was on a hunt for a suitable place to rent.

Roshni, who normally would have cheered me up, wasn't well and didn't come to the office for the past two days. I sent her a text asking about her health. Roshni replied that she had a fever again and didn't know when she would get better to be able to come to work.

Now sitting alone for lunch, my favorite paneer tikka didn't bring me the joy it usually did. It seemed tasteless, and I couldn't even swallow a single piece. How could I, when I had no idea what my future held? Until yesterday I was so sure of my goals. A year or two more here, and then I'd have enough saved for the B.Ed. Course. I'd be the best aunt little Zain could wish for. But today, after seeing those patches, I wasn't sure anymore. *Would my health get worse?*

Sighing, I shuffled the paneer pieces on my plate. I didn't want to waste the food, so I finished it, gulping down as fast as I could, and went back to my desk. I had to keep myself busy or these thoughts would drive me crazy. Tally called out to me and with a deep breath in, I resumed work.

When the clock struck four, I stared at my phone, wishing it to ring. *Why hasn't he called yet? Did he forget?* I had no way of contacting him. It was so foolish of me. I should have taken the number of the hospital where he worked. My supervisor had agreed to let me off early when I told him about my appointment. I had packed up everything and was waiting for this call. And now, Sadiq was ditching me. Or was he? Maybe he had some emergency? *Arghh! Why can't I just stop thinking for a while?* After glancing at the clock, I put my head down on the desk. More like banged it.

At 4:20 p.m. my phone rang.

"Hi, I'm ready to leave," I said, without waiting for Sadiq to say hello.

"Ready to leave where?"

It was Mom.

Grimacing, I shook my head. Then I slapped my forehead. She couldn't see me. "Mom, nothing, I thought it was my friend Roshni. We go for a cup of coffee before coming home."

"Doesn't she work next to you?"

"She does, but she's not here now." I squeezed my forehead with my fingers; I didn't want to get into this with her now. "Why did you call?" I asked. "And this is not our home number. Where are you?"

"Bring some bread and bananas when you come. Your abbu had asked me, but I forgot."

"Okay, I'll get them," I replied, and wanted to add that I'd be late, but Mom had already disconnected the call. I thought about calling her back and informing her. But my phone rang again. "Hello?"

"Afrah, I'm free now. You can come," Sadiq said.

I heaved a sigh of relief. "Oh, thank Allah. I wondered if you forgot to call me."

"No, I cannot forget such an important thing. I guess it'll take you fifteen to twenty minutes to reach Nerul?"

"More than that. My office is a bit far from the station." I glanced at the clock. "I'll meet you near the ticket counter at Nerul station by five."

"Okay, see you."

I quickly grabbed my bag, rushed out of the office, hired an auto, and reached the station. My monthly pass only reached Vashi, and I had to go beyond. But the queue for tickets was snaking, so I skipped buying one and boarded the train. I got off two stations later.

Once I reached the ticket counter where Sadiq had asked me to wait, I heaved a deep breath of relief. There he was—hands in his pockets and a flicker of a smile on his face. I waved at him, and we walked the short distance to the hospital where he worked.

As soon as I entered the premises, the smell of the disinfectant assaulted me. The nursing home where Bushra had delivered didn't smell like *this*. Inhaling the hospital air made me nauseated. I took a few sips of water from the bottle in my bag and followed Sadiq. Patients in wheelchairs, ward boys shouting, and relatives muttering filled the lobby. The queue at the reception counter resembled the one at the railway station.

"Do I have to fill out a form and wait in this queue?" I asked. My palms had turned clammy.

"No, don't worry, I have it with me." He guided me to a wooden bench in a corner and handed me the form. "Fill in your details, and then I'll take you to the dermatologist." He also gave me a pen.

My hands shivered as I began to fill in my details: Name, age, sex, address, date of birth, contact number, and a hundred other things. Sadiq must have noticed it as he quietly asked whether I'd like him to fill it for me. But I shook my head. I could do it. What happened at this hospital would decide my future.

After I was done, Sadiq glanced through the form once and walked toward another door. I had to jog to keep pace with him, and more often than not, I ended up dashing or pushing someone. Sadiq looked behind him, and seeing me struggle, he held out his hand and walked with me. I was so nervous about meeting the doctor that I didn't feel the excitement I should have felt with him holding my hand in better circumstances. I did feel relieved, though. He was there beside me. I wouldn't get lost in this place. It was even more crowded than the railway station, and I wondered how he worked here day in and day out.

"Come, it's just here." He paused outside a cabin.

Eight to ten people waited outside. I went to sit on one of the chairs when he tugged at my hand. "We can go inside directly. I have already spoken to Swati Ma'am."

I followed him inside, and Dr. Swati asked me to go behind the curtain. She checked my front and back and looked at the white patches with a magnifying glass. When the doctor appeared to be sure of the diagnosis, she pushed the curtain aside and looked directly at me.

"So..." a quick glance at the form, "Afrah. You don't have to worry. These patches are called Vitiligo. It is not dangerous, and it will not spread to others."

I tried to repeat the word. "Vi...what? Vilitigo?"

"It's "Vi-ti-li-go," Sadiq gently corrected me.

I looked away, embarrassed. "Will this get better? Will the patches go away?" I asked Dr. Swati.

"That's the thing. It is not necessary to treat this as it doesn't harm your body as such. It is only cosmetic and is difficult to treat. But not impossible. You will have to adhere to the treatment plans. And keep in mind, this will spread throughout your body."

"Spread?" I asked, horrified. My heart thudded in my chest.

"Yes, it will spread. How fast or how slow, we cannot tell you." She paused. "But with medicines, we can control the spread. I understand it's too much to take in, but it is what it is. I don't want to give you false hopes." With that, she scribbled some medicines and handed the form to me. "You'll get some of the medicines from the chemist here, but the others, you will have to buy from elsewhere."

Sadiq held my hand again and guided me outside. The doctor began to see the next patient as if what she said to me didn't matter to her at all. *And why would it, you fool? That's her job.* My world tilted, and I leaned my head on Sadiq. He held me tight and released me once I sat on a chair. I was worried that my heart would jump out of my body the way it was beating. Sadiq's proximity, this news...

My mouth was dry, and I didn't realize that he offered me the water bottle from my bag. I took a sip. But I still couldn't digest what the doctor said. What was this illness? I rubbed my sweaty palms on my kurti. I wondered whether I should laugh or cry. Laugh because earlier, I thought I was going to die. Cry because these patches would spread...all over my body. My hands, my stomach, my legs.... Oh! My face, too. How would I look? I covered my face with my palms.

"Afrah... Afrah." Sadiq snapped his fingers in front of me. "Take a few deep breaths. Shhh...Do not think too much."

I looked at him, my eyes prickling. How did he know what I was thinking? "How will I become a teacher? Won't the little kids be scared looking at me?"

"Shh..." He held my hand and squeezed my fingers. "Deep breaths. No overthinking right now."

He was right. I was thinking too much and needed to take one thing at a time. Okay, so I have vitiligo. And it can be controlled. And it might not affect my face at all. It was unpredictable, the doctor had said. Who knows, except Allah? I took another deep breath, wiped my damp eyes with the sleeves of my kurti, and stood.

"Okay, so be it. I'll have to live with this vitiligo all my life. At least I'm not going to die." I tried to smile, looking at Sadiq, but it wobbled.

He stood next to me and gave me a lopsided smile. "You are an amazing woman, you know that? You can achieve whatever you want. And I'm always here to help you. Always. Okay?"

I nodded. He was correct. Whenever I put my mind to a particular thing, I achieved it no matter what. Like how I got a job. Like how I'm particular about wanting to work after marriage. So now, even if this vitiligo thing affects my body, I won't let it affect my spirit. I won't. I can't.

Now it was my turn to hold Sadiq's hand.

"Thank you for getting me here. Let's go and buy these creams and lotions."

"If you have any other problem for which you want a doctor's help, do it now," Sadiq suggested. "The chemist is outside this building in the opposite direction."

I gasped; it was as if he knew my situation. Yes, I did want to meet a gynecologist and ask about my irregular periods. I'd missed the chance at Bushra's delivery; with her in-laws and Mom hovering around, I didn't want to take a risk.

"You are such a sweetheart. Yes, I want to see another doctor. I'll meet you back here."

I quickly asked a nurse nearby where I would find a gynecologist. But Sadiq followed me. "I told you to wait there," I huffed, pointing in the general direction of where I walked from.

"Do you think anyone will entertain you here? You need to fill out another form for them."

"A separate form for each department?" I asked.

"No," Sadiq said, "Only obstetrics and gynecology have a separate one. Come, I'll talk to the resident doctor there, and she can help you with your problem."

So much for secrecy. Huffing, I once again followed Sadiq. It seemed a good thing, in a way, looking at the queue outside the gynec's. Sadiq spoke to someone and gestured for me to go inside. I was relieved when he didn't follow me in. Once I sat across from the doctor, I told her about my concerns— the irregular periods and severe pain with the bleeding.

"Okay. Come, let's do a quick sono for you. Lie down behind that curtain."

"Sono?"

"Ultrasonography." The doctor brought out a machine and a long wire with a probe. "This is going to feel cold," she said as she applied some gel over it.

Despite the warning, my breath hitched when it touched my skin. It *was* freezing. She moved it around, her eyes focused on the machine's screen.

"Alright, done," the doctor said after some time. "Afrah, you have cysts in your ovaries." Before I could ask anything further, she continued, "Cysts are tiny balloon-like fluid-filled things," she grabbed a pen and paper and showed me the normal and cystic ovaries. "Get it?"

I gulped and nodded. *Why are all strange diseases affecting me?*

"That's why you have a hormonal imbalance causing irregular periods, pimples on your face, and lots of hair on your body. It is called polycystic ovarian disease."

My eyes widened. "Even this body hair is because of hormonal imbalance?"

"Yes." The doctor began to scribble something on the paper. "These pills should help regularize your periods. Also, keep one thing in mind—control your weight, or you might get diabetes. You are good now.

Still, we will get your blood tests done. Give a sample at the lab before you go. I believe you also have to do thyroid tests as suggested by the dermatologist."

I had trouble following the doctor; she spoke so fast.

"Sadiq," the doctor called, "I have written everything here. Get her blood tests done and show me the reports, okay?"

"Okay," he said from the door.

I scoffed. I wanted to tell the doctor I wasn't dumb and understood what needed to be done, but I was also grateful that Sadiq was with me to walk me through it.

I snorted the moment I stepped outside. "I can't believe I've received two shocks in one day."

"I know. But you'll live, won't you?"

I grinned. "Yeah. I'm not gonna die." I started to walk but stopped when Sadiq didn't follow me. He stood where he was. "What?" I asked. "Let's get these medicines, then I need to go home with bread and bananas."

Sadiq opened his mouth as if he wanted to say something but changed his mind, shaking his head.

"Nothing. Yes, let's go."

Chapter 27
A Close Call
Sadiq

After we were done at the hospital, I accompanied Afrah to the station. The train was about to arrive, and the announcer said so.

"Come, Sadiq, let's run for it. I don't want to miss this train and wait another ten minutes."

Both of us ran from platform one, over the bridge, to Platform 3, where the train had started to crawl in. The station wasn't that crowded, so we reached the platform, but Afrah wouldn't reach the ladies' compartment in time, so she got in with me in the general compartment. She clutched her stomach once we got in. I did the same, too.

Breathless but still laughing, I asked, "Have you ever done this before?"

"Not from Kurla. From Vashi, sometimes. Roshni

and I run for the train on and off."

I stood beside her, just inside the door, both of us in silence. But a comfortable one.

"Do you want to sit?" I asked.

"No, I'm good," Afrah said, glancing at the few vacant seats.

When we arrived at the next station, we were greeted by a crowd waiting on the platform.

"Uh uh," Afrah muttered. But we were too late in deciding to go inside and sit. I didn't want her to be crushed by a bunch of strangers, so I moved to stand in front of her, with my back as a shield. The crowd stormed in, and the compartment was packed in no time.

"Thank you," she whispered, looking up at me.

"Are you going to be alright?" I asked. "We can get off the next station, and you can go to the women's or skip this train."

"No, I need to reach home as soon as possible. It's okay."

A shove from behind pushed me even closer to her, and I was almost hugging her now. "Sorry," I muttered and tried to push back. But the crowd wouldn't budge.

Afrah cleared her throat. Her hair had come loose, and before I could stop myself, I tucked a few strands behind her ear. She stared at me but didn't say a word.

I couldn't stop looking into her mesmerizing eyes. I

closed my own then and took a deep breath. Inhaling her flowery smell, I committed it to memory. When I opened them, she had a flicker of a smile on her face. My heart galloped, and I had an inkling, hers did, too. But we didn't say a word to each other.

The stations came and went, and the crowd increased and decreased, but we stood in the same posture—facing each other.

"It's our stop next," Afrah finally whispered.

It was then that I glanced outside; the cramped buildings interspersed with a few tall ones, and the minaret of the mosque—were an indication that it would be Kurla next. I nodded and asked her to come in front of me.

We climbed down the train and then went in the direction of the foot overbridge. I remembered I was supposed to get off at Vashi and go to Ashish's birthday party. But seeing Afrah so vulnerable, I didn't have the heart to leave her.

"Thank you for everything," she said once we were outside and had to go our separate ways.

"You are welcome. I'm happy I could help you."

"I'll see you tomorrow?" she tilted her head.

"Yes, you will." I smiled. "Bye."

After she left, I stood rooted in the same spot, wondering whether to board a train and go to the party or to go home. I decided on the latter.

When I climbed the stairs to the chawl with a smile on my face, Abbu's voice reached my ears.

"Shabana, cook the best food you can. I'm inviting all my mosque friends for dinner tomorrow. Bring *mithai* from the market, too. Or let it be, I'll bring it and some fruits."

I was too happy to let Abbu ruin my mood. I didn't say a word as I entered my house and headed straight up to the mezzanine. After lying down on the mattress, I closed my eyes. The image of Afrah, with her hair flying, standing in front of me on the train, flashed before my eyes. She always invaded my thoughts out of the blue, and after today, I wondered how would I even close my eyes without seeing her in front of me.

"Sadiq...Sadiq?" Ammi's voice floated from somewhere.

I opened my eyes—she was calling me. I stood and stretched, my joints clicking in protest as I had quite a hectic day at the hospital with not a moment to sit. I lay down again.

"Ammi...I'm very tired. Please let me sleep." I said, hoping she heard me.

"But you need to eat something, you didn't look well when you came."

Oh, I'm more than well. But I couldn't tell her that.

"Later, Ammi." I wouldn't be able to study much, so sleeping was the next best option.

Afrah

I reached home in a daze, all the while picturing Sadiq's face close to mine as he was pushed even closer to me by the crowd on the train. My heart had doubled its beats, and I had a tough time staying still. Unable to get him off my mind, I forgot to buy what Mom had asked me to.

"You can't even do one thing I asked of you," Mom muttered the moment I stepped inside.

I didn't want to spoil my mood, so I retraced my steps wordlessly, walked to the market nearby, and bought what she asked for.

"Why are you so late, anyway?" she asked as she took the bananas from me. "I'm not that busy to not notice where my older daughter is going."

"I went to the hospital, Mom. I didn't want to trouble you as you already have so many troubles."

"Stop exaggerating. What problem do you have that you had to go to the hospital?"

I showed her the patches on my hands and legs.

"For this? It will go away. Give it some time," she said when Bushra came out of the bedroom.

"Shh...Ammi, Appi. Zain is sleeping. What's the matter?"

"Your sister is being her usual self." Mom sneered at me. Then she turned to Bushra. "Go, you also sleep. Zain will keep you awake at night."

"No, Ammi, I'm good." Bushra sat on the sofa, and Mom sat next to her.

I freshened up in the bathroom, not wanting to entertain my mother's rude remarks.

"What did you do now that Ammi is so upset, Appi?" Bushra asked later when I was in the kitchen making a cup of tea for myself.

"I'm here and listening to both of you," Mom said from the sofa.

"Nothing, Bushra. I need to look after myself because everyone here is busy with their lives. What's wrong with that?" I couldn't help answering back.

"You should have gone to some doctor here only," Mom argued. "But it's like you have promised yourself you will not listen to your mother and do what you please."

Papa arrived at that moment. He was dressed in a three-piece suit. *Looks like he went to a business meeting.* Seeing us all, he asked, "What are my princesses doing?"

I rushed from the kitchen to hug him. "The cruel witch is harassing this princess..."

"Started, you two? Again?"

"Huh. This is not over." Mom said. "You need to

stop being so selfish."

"See, Papa? Did you hear that? I'm tired of telling her I'm not selfish."

"Appi...one of you has to shut up. If not her, then you," Bushra chimed in. "It's now becoming too grating to hear you both argue over stupid things."

I scoffed at her. "This has started from the day you married your boyfriend and left me alone to fend for myself."

Bushra laughed. "I know, Appi. I should have taken you as dowry."

On hearing the word dowry, I stopped laughing. "What else have they asked for now?"

"Uh...nothing. I was kidding."

I didn't buy that, but I would grill Bushra on it another time.

"Enough, you two. Who will give this old man a hot cup of chai?" Papa asked, loosening his tie and taking off his coat.

We laughed and got to work.

Later, Papa and I went to the terrace. We leaned over the parapet to watch the traffic below.

"Don't mind your mother," he said. "You know how she is. She says what's on her mind, but she has no ill feelings in her heart."

"I know, Papa, but it hurts. The doctor said I have vitiligo. It's going to be difficult to treat it. I'm scared.

What if it comes on my face, too? Mom is not even ready to hear me out." He patted my head. "She always tells me whatever I do is a waste of time. I don't understand it. What have I not done?"

Papa sighed. "She is worried about you, worried that she won't be able to find a match for you. Already there aren't many proposals coming your way because word has gone out that you want to study and work even after marriage."

"But that is what I want to do. I want to follow my dreams. I want to be a teacher. I'm not saying no to marriage. I want to get married too, start a family." Sadiq's face flashed before my eyes. I shook my head to drive his image away. "I know I'll need to adjust to my new family, but if they forbid me from being who I am, how can I live with such people?"

"See, this is what makes you different. You have clear goals in your life. I know that. But others around us don't understand it. Even your mother. Stay true to your ambition and principles. Focus on achieving your dream. It'll be difficult but hold onto it. Don't get affected by what others say or think about you."

"I know, Papa. I know that. But if my mother herself doesn't place her trust in me, how can I expect anyone else to do so?"

"Let's shift our focus away from your mother. Why don't you start applying to colleges for your B.Ed course next year? You know we can pay your fees. You don't have to work to save for the fees."

"I know." I turned to face the door of the terrace. "In a heated moment, Mom challenged me to earn my money and pay for the fees. And I accepted it."

"Ah, you and Nadira." Papa smiled. "A force to be reckoned with."

I chuckled. "Well, there has to be some 'live' entertainment within the family, too, nai? Only dramas on TV will not be enough."

We laughed.

Back downstairs, I played with Zain for a while. He was growing well and would turn two months soon. It would also be time for Bushra to leave.

"Appi...look," Bushra pointed, a great big smile on her tired face. "He's trying to turn."

I looked at my nephew, he did turn a bit. "He's one super active fellow," I said.

"Yes, Appi, but be careful. He can fall from the bed."

"I know, little sister, I'm here. I won't let him fall." I turned to look at Bushra, but she wouldn't meet my eyes. "What is it? I asked.

"Nothing," Bushra shrugged. Then she sat on the bed, and tears pooled in her eyes.

"Hey, little one, tell me, what's troubling you?"

Bushra shook her head and wiped her tears with

her sleeves. "I'm scared. After living here for the last few months, I feel like that newlywed bride again. Don't know what awaits me."

"Oh, come here." I hugged her. "You have spoken to Asif every day, so what's to worry about? You'll settle again in no time."

"Hmm...I hope so...." She wiped her face again and looked at me. "You know, sometimes I get jealous of you. No worries about in-laws. Not being on your guard always."

"Oh, the grass is always greener on the other side." I wiggled my brows. "And don't you worry, how long do you think Mom will let me enjoy being single? Huh?"

Bushra laughed.

I wanted to tell her she need not be on her guard at her husband's place. It was her house, too, after all. But I didn't want to spoil the camaraderie we just shared after months of being distant.

Bushra didn't ask me about the visit to the dermatologist, and I didn't say anything else on that matter. I lay beside Zain for a while and looked at him kicking his legs. I held his tiny hand, and he gripped it tight. Chuckling, I stroked his soft skin when my gaze fell on the patch on my wrist.

I sat up and examined them again. I hoped the medicines would work and all these patches would go away. I hadn't brought enough cash with me to buy the remaining medicines from the hospital chemist. "I'll get them tomorrow."

"What will you get tomorrow?" Bushra asked.

I had forgotten she also lay beside Zain. "Oh, it's nothing." I didn't want to bother Bushra with my problems when she was already so stressed. "I'm going to finish cleaning up the kitchen."

While scrubbing the dishes, I wondered what really troubled my sister. A new demand? Or was it her envious sister-in-law? Today was the first time in a while that Bushra had shared things with me. Did motherhood change her, or was it something else? I kept the vessels in the plastic basket and left them to dry. I would figure out Bushra sooner or later.

I looked forward to meeting Roshni tomorrow. It would be so exciting to tell her about the intense moment I shared with Sadiq on the train. That instant when he brushed my hair off my face and the way he looked at me. If I'd stood on my tippy toes, and with another push or nudge from the crowd, I could have kissed his lips. I hitched my breath now, as I had then. I didn't know if he had noticed. Goosebumps rose on my body as I lay on the mattress, thinking about him. Did he like me more than a friend? Maybe I should ask him...knowing him, he might not even share how exactly he felt if I didn't.

Chapter 28
Invitation
Sadiq

Ashish glared at me because I had missed his party. A month had passed, but he wouldn't let it go.

"I'm sorry...I couldn't help it," I said for the tenth time since then. I'd told him Afrah needed my help, and I couldn't refuse her. "If Roshni asked for it, wouldn't you help her out?" I argued.

Ashish narrowed his eyes at me. He sometimes believed me and sometimes didn't. That wasn't my problem now. I wouldn't keep justifying myself. If he didn't believe me, then so be it.

"Where is Afrah, by the way?" he asked.

I glanced across the compartment where Roshni stood by the door at her spot, minus Afrah. "She is not well. I had spoken to her last night."

"Oh wow, man! I didn't know you do talk on the

phone." Ashish teased.

I rubbed my nape. "She called me. But we couldn't talk long, Ammi was trying to listen."

"Maybe it is high time you got yourself a mobile phone."

"Hmm...I will. But not now."

"Okay, so we are planning an overnight party after graduation. You coming?"

"I don't think so."

"Don't be such a bore, man. Come, it'll be fun. We'll have a DJ night, too. You missed the one at my party," he said, pointedly.

I groaned. "Not this again."

Ashish laughed.

I had to attend a dinner organized by Bade-abba after my graduation ceremony. And this was something I couldn't back out from.

I met Afrah at Vashi station a few days later.

"Did the sun rise from the west today? Dr. Sadiq asked me to meet him," she said, walking toward me when I spotted her. "Do you want to eat this dabeli?" She pointed to the stall selling it. She didn't wait for my answer and bought two. "It's so yummy," she moaned after taking a bite, waiting for me to eat mine.

The taste of the vegetables, peanuts, and spices melded in my mouth.

"I have never tasted this before. Actually, I never thought I would eat it, considering the way it is made. How can anyone put vegetables in a bread bun and eat that? The last one which you gave me during Ramadan got spoiled, and I had to discard it."

"So, what's the verdict now?" she asked.

"It is good, really good."

She grinned at me and finished her dabeli.

I rushed to eat mine and said, "I want to invite you to my graduation."

"Wow...your graduation?"

"Yes, we will also have to take the Hippocratic Oath and all."

"Hippo...what?" Afrah said after finishing the last bite of her dabeli.

I chuckled, the thud-thud of my heart increasing just a bit. "Hippocratic Oath. It's a promise that we doctors make on our graduation day. You'll get to hear the entire thing once you come."

"You want *me* to come?" It appeared like Afrah couldn't believe it. "What about your family?"

"My bade-abba has organized a dinner for it."

"Oh..."

I really wanted her to come. Being alone on such an important day—when all my batch mates would be surrounded by family—did not sound appealing to me. And Afrah was my very good friend. *Only a good friend?* I suppressed the doubt. *Not now.* It would make my day so much better if I had someone to share it with. Besides, if Afrah said yes, I would insist that Ammi come. It would be a good opportunity to introduce them. *So, tell her, you fool.*

I cleared my throat. "So, will you come? It would make me really happy." She tilted her head, and I continued, "It's on twenty-eighth February. You don't have to tell me right now. Think about it, though."

"Okay, I will think about it. But you could have asked me over the phone, too."

"Yes. But it's been a while since I saw you."

Her eyes twinkled, and she beamed at me. "I missed you, too. When I come early, you aren't there, and when you are there, I am late. Never mind, I like this. We can meet on and off."

"Uh, yes." I started to walk toward the platform, Afrah beside me.

"Are you going home?" she asked.

"Yes." I didn't want to tell her why I was going home when I was supposed to go to the library to read. I hoped she would travel with me in the same compartment—her proximity made me feel good, even though my heart fluttered as though I might get an arrhythmia every time she was close to me.

As the train arrived, I saw her eyes flicker toward the women's compartment. But then she looked at me and climbed into the general compartment. This time, we found seats and took them, instead of standing.

"I find some improvement in those patches," she said. "Oh, but the medicines are so expensive. Half my salary goes into buying them."

"It's good if you are responding."

"But there are a few more on my stomach now. How can I treat those? I can't sit in the sun, you know."

Yes, the treatment involved applying the cream and sitting in sunlight for at least half an hour.

"Silly me, it is what it is. I have to deal with it without complaining. Sometimes I do think, why did I get it? But then I remember my papa's words. He always says Allah gives difficult problems to only those he thinks can handle them and come out stronger. It's so true, don't you think?"

I gazed at her, she wore huge rings in her ears today, and the way she spoke, I could listen to her all day, keep drowning in her voice. Her abbu was right. Each day *was* a struggle for me too, but I still made it out stronger than I was before.

"I look forward to starting my life after graduation," I said. "I want to move my family to a better place, even if it's on rent. Start returning the loans." I'd told her I lived in a chawl, and it was better if she considered that as the reason for shifting homes than telling her about my troubled relationship with my father.

"You know I dread the weekends these days. With my sister gone, my mother's entire attention is on me. She arranges for some or the other proposal, and I have backed out until now, though I don't know how long I can do that." She sighed. "Sadiq," she gasped. "We officially broke our pact of not talking about our families."

I shrugged. "I know. But can we exist without them? At some point or the other, they will be a part of our lives, won't they?"

"Hmm. True." We stayed silent for a while, Afrah gazing out of the window. Her hand was on her lap, and I had this urge to hold her and tell her things would be fine. Her vitiligo would be under control, and she would be a teacher someday. And I wanted her to hold me back and tell me that I would make it, too. If not anything, we would be there for each other. Always. That made me smile.

"What?" Afrah raised her brow.

I hadn't noticed she was watching me. "Uh..."

"Tell me?" she pleaded.

"I...I like being with you," I said. *Finally*.

Afrah chuckled lightly. "I like being with you, too," she said, taking my hand in hers.

I smiled. *That went well*. I squeezed her fingers, and we sat like that until it was time to get down.

Chapter 29
Of Carrot Halwa and
Graduation
Afrah

I skipped my way home, literally. Passersby gawked at me, but the smile plastered on my face remained where it was. *Sadiq likes me!* I chanted this like a prayer until I reached home. But since I wasn't a hundred percent sure whether it would go any further, I didn't want to share it with my parents yet. Besides, my mom's reaction worried me. Although she *should* be happy, her moods were worse than Bushra's.

So, I willed myself to calm down. Taking a few deep breaths, I climbed up the stairs without the bounce in my feet. When I opened the door, I inhaled deeply. Mom was cooking something in the kitchen.

"Wow, smells nice. What are you making?"

"Your abba is getting two of his friends for dinner tonight. Care to help me?"

"Of course. Let me freshen and change."

Together, we cooked chicken pulao, corn soup, and a carrot halwa. The kitchen filled with the smells of the sautéed spices, and the pure ghee of the sweet dish. It made me drool. My mind drifted to Sadiq on and off during our cooking spree. *Maybe if this halwa is left over, I'll take it for him.*

"If this halwa remains, keep it in the fridge." Mom burst my bubble. "Bushra and Zain are coming tomorrow."

"Oh, tomorrow?" I didn't know what to say. It had been over a month since Bushra had gone back. Not that it was a problem, I just hoped Zain would sleep through the night. The last month was so peaceful. *And it meant Sadiq wouldn't be able to taste the halwa.* I wondered if I could tell Bushra about him now.

Bushra had adjusted well at her home after going back from here. Her in-laws, although demanding, were good with kids. I didn't get a chance to talk to her like I was hoping. Zain took most of her time—the remaining was spent with Papa and Mom. Bushra wouldn't leave Zain even for a few minutes to go to the terrace where we could talk freely.

"What if he cries when we are gone? No. no. It's a nightmare making him quiet."

One morning, as I hurried to leave for work, I heard Bushra in the kitchen.

"Now it is Appi's turn. My mother-in-law has a distant relative. She says he will be a good match for her. He is a bit older, though."

"Doesn't matter. Tell her to arrange a meeting."

"Ammi, I can tell her, but if Appi behaves the way she does with all the rishtas, it will not be good for me. Even my reputation is at stake here."

"Oh, my bachcha, don't worry. I'll talk to her."

I cleared my throat, announcing my presence. I wasn't interested in listening any further. "Talking about me?" I asked, plastering a smile on my face and relishing the sight of both Mom and Bushra squirming because they were caught.

"N-no, Appi. Not about you," Bushra said, averting her gaze.

I shrugged. "Mom, let me be very clear. I will only marry the one who will fit my criteria." With that, I turned around and walked out the door.

Shoving the conversation into the farthest corner of my mind, I made my way to work. I wanted to concentrate on my goals. But it did hurt me to think that Bushra didn't care about me anymore. She had become like the others, looking at a particular situation like a horse with blinders.

"Hi," Sadiq said. I blinked away my thoughts.

"Hi, how are you? Okay, tell me, what's wrong if I want to work after I get married?" I didn't mean to ask him like this, but I wanted to know what he thought.

"Nothing's wrong. If that's what makes you happy, you should do it. Why are you asking?"

I sighed. "I'm tired of dodging proposals when my mom knows this 'future husband' will not let me work." Then I pulled him into a less-crowded area. "Forget we had this conversation. It has been on my mind for a long time, and I feel as if I am getting ahead of myself in having such dreams. Only my papa supports me. But you are right. My happiness matters, too. And I will not sacrifice it, no matter what."

Sadiq smiled, and I had this sudden urge to stand on my tippy toes and give him a kiss. "I feel like kissing you now," I voiced the thought aloud to see how he reacted.

Sadiq widened his eyes.

I giggled. It was fun teasing him. "Relax, I won't do it here." I had a vivid memory of me kissing him on the cheek at the station a few months back. That was a kiss that happened out of happy emotion. Now it would be different. Special. Because I felt different about him.

And I was sure he did the same, judging by the way he couldn't stop looking at me.

"You know whenever I get a call at home, Ammi says, 'Go, Sadiq. Dr. Farooqui is calling you.' I think she suspects something else."

I chuckled. "Ha. That's so sweet. At least she suspects. At my place, everyone is too busy to notice what I'm doing as long as I stay out of their way, and then they expect me to listen to them." I slapped my forehead. "We are doing it again, talking about home and things."

Sadiq shrugged. "As I told you, they are a part of our lives."

"Hmm...come on, the train is here." I grabbed his hand.

"Uh, no. I'm not going on this one, I have to go to Borivali. I came only to see you."

"Borivali? Why?" It was a distant suburb of the city.

"I have an interview at a hospital there. So, I can join the day after I get my degree."

"Wow, that's amazing."

"Yes, my professor has arranged for it."

The train stopped. "Okay, bye. And I hope everything goes well with the interview." I said before getting on the train.

"Bye and thanks," he waved.

I told Roshni about my feelings for Sadiq. She was the only person with whom I was comfortable sharing things.

"I feel bad things didn't work out between Ashish and you," I added.

"Oh, it was fun while it lasted. But we have different goals in life. He wants to go abroad to do his post-graduation. I cannot leave my family."

Roshni had told me how she was the only bread-winner in her family. They had their savings and the insurance money rolling in after her father's untimely death, but someone needed to work to keep things going.

I'd taken leave from work but was still on the office premises, in the women's restroom. My feet wouldn't stop tapping, and I continued to crack my knuckles. "Ow." I grimaced as Roshni untangled my hair.

"You need a haircut, woman. Look at these split-ends."

"Let it be now. Just do something with them so that I look nice."

"Are you going to wear one of the full-sleeve things?"

"Oh yes, I don't have a choice. Don't want people staring any place else other than my face."

I was excited to attend Sadiq's graduation. It was like wading into the unknown. My college graduation was simple. I hadn't even rented a graduation coat and hat. We went to our classrooms and were handed the certificates by our professor. Today would be something different.

"Okay, done." Roshni put one last clip in my hair. She had styled them in an elaborate bun and left some flicks to frame my face. "I need to go now. You'll have to handle the make-up by yourself."

"Thanks, I'm not putting on much make-up. Just a bit of kohl and lipstick." Make-up flared my pimples, and I tried to avoid it as much as possible. I made a mental note to ask for treatment of pimples when I visited the doctor at the hospital for a follow-up.

Satisfied with my appearance, I snuck out of the office and rushed to the station. Mom thought I was at work, and Papa was too busy setting up his shop to notice what I did or where I went. I didn't like hiding things from my family, but I wouldn't share any news of Sadiq with them until I was sure of our feelings for each other.

Sadiq looked dapper in a blue-striped shirt and a pair of trousers. I had never seen him like this; he wore the same three pairs of shirts for the past six months that we'd been talking. It gave me an idea of his financial condition, but I didn't want to pry.

"You look...different," he said when he spotted me at the station.

"Good different, or bad?" I smirked, enjoying the sight of him flustered.

"Uh, good. Of course."

"Thanks. Am I late?"

"No, perfectly on time. Come, let's go."

We walked a short distance to the college—it was right behind the hospital. The ground-floor auditorium was packed with the graduating batch and their families. Sadiq took his graduation coat and hat. He looked funny in the oversized gown, and I couldn't stop chuckling.

"It's rented," he told me.

"Okay, come stand here. You need to have a pic of this." I lifted my phone and clicked. "Can you smile? Why are you so *khadoos*?"

"I'm not," he said.

"Okay, as you say." My jaws hurt from giggling so much. Sadiq grabbed my hand and entered the auditorium. "Ooh, I like angry Sadiq," I whispered in his ear.

Sadiq narrowed his eyes. "You don't want to meet angry Sadiq, believe me."

"Oh, okay. I believe you. I don't want to meet angry

Sadiq." I fake-shuddered, wondering how often he lost his temper. *So much more to learn about him.*

He found a seat for us in the middle of the auditorium. A few of his batch mates greeted him and nodded to me. No one asked who I was, and I was glad for it. The anonymity made me happy. We still hadn't labeled our relationship—friends suited me for now.

The ceremony began with speeches by the dean, the chief guest, and a few others. I was excited about their oath-taking, and when that moment arrived, I clicked more pictures. But it was over as soon as it began.

"That's it?" I asked, disappointed.

"Yes, what else did you expect?"

"When will you throw your caps and all?"

"After we receive our degrees. They'll call us individually on the stage."

"Great. Then, I'll click your picture."

Once the degrees were distributed, they clicked a group photo. Sadiq participated in a few, but I noticed he remained aloof for most of them. I caught sight of Ashish.

"Hi. Can you click a picture of us?" I handed him my phone.

"Nice phone," he commented. "Now convince your boyfriend to buy one for himself. How do you guys even talk?"

My mind was stuck on the word boyfriend. "He is not my boyfriend," I grumbled.

"Really? That's what you are telling yourself now?" He snorted. "Look at him."

At that moment, Sadiq began to leave his batch mates and walked toward me.

"I have never seen him so happy since I've known him. Something or the other has always troubled him, but when he is with you or talks about you, he seems a different person. Also, know one thing, he will not make the first move. It's up to you." As Sadiq approached within earshot, Ashish told him, "Hey man, we were waiting for you for so long. Don't leave your girl alone, dude. Come now, stand next to her, and let me click a picture."

I turned toward the camera, Ashish's words reverberating in my mind. "Sadiq, stand closer. Or else you will not be seen in the pic."

Sadiq moved closer to me, but Ashish didn't look satisfied and put my phone down. He walked over to us and put Sadiq's hand on my shoulder. I glanced at Sadiq. He swallowed hard. Smiling, I put my arm around his waist.

"Ah, that's perfect!" Ashish grinned and clicked a few pictures. I made funny faces in some.

Later, on the train, when I showed the pictures to

him, Sadiq couldn't stop laughing. I couldn't stop grinning, hearing his laugh.

"You want to get down at Vashi?" he asked, tapping his leg.

"Vashi? Why?"

"It's a...a surprise."

"For me?" I couldn't believe it.

"Yes. We can go to the new mall and eat something?"

"Sure. That would be fun."

We got down at the station and walked to the mall. I wondered what he was up to. We went to the food court, and Sadiq asked, "What do you want to eat?"

"What are *you* going to eat?" I asked. I wasn't really hungry, but maybe he was.

Sadiq paused for a moment. "Pizza?"

"I don't mind. But take only one. I'm not very hungry, will share a piece from yours."

He went to get the pizza, and I looked around the mall. I had come here a couple of times with Roshni, window shopping and then eating here at the food court. However, we had never tried the pizza.

Sadiq brought our order, and we found a table to sit in the food court. After we finished eating, we sat there, looking at the other shoppers.

"Thanks for this," he said. "You made my day so much better."

"Oh, I enjoyed it, too. Besides, now I can say I have actually listened to the Hippocratic Oath being recited."

"You know, Afrah, you are so true to your name."

It took a moment for me to realize the exact meaning of what he said. His gaze was on me, and his voice was in a different tone. Tender. I could feel my cheeks heating up. My name meant 'to bring joy.'

"Uh...I have something for you," he added, bringing out a small packet wrapped in a newspaper.

"Oh, ideally, I should be giving you a graduation present." I took the packet and unwrapped it. There was a pink and blue colored silk scarf, neatly folded. I gasped and touched it, caressed its softness. "It's beautiful."

"There's more. Open it." He smiled.

I unfolded the scarf, and a small bracelet lay at the center of it. There were five beads on a string, each having a letter of my name. I hitched my breath as my eyes pricked with unshed tears.

"Wow."

I didn't want to cry; not here, not now. This was one of the most thoughtful presents anyone had ever given me.

"And Happy Birthday in advance," he said, reaching over to hold my hand.

My birthday was tomorrow. "How did you know?"

I remembered I hadn't shared that piece of information yet.

"I read it on the hospital form you had filled back in December."

"And you remembered." I squeezed his hand. "Thank you. I love this." I caressed the scarf on my face, inhaling its smell, and asked him to help me tie the bracelet on my wrist. "You could have given me tomorrow," I said.

"I'll be traveling in different trains from tomorrow. I'm starting a new job at a hospital in Borivali." He replied.

"How silly of me. Yes, I remember now. I'm so glad you got the job. So when will I see you again?" I couldn't bear not seeing his face as often as I did. He had a calming presence in my life.

"As often as I can. I'll call you."

"You better get a new phone when you receive your salary. It's so difficult to contact you at times since I don't know if you're home."

"I'll try. Have some other things to sort out first. Buying a phone is not a priority. And now, if I'm not at the hospital, you'll find me at home. At least until I find a library nearby."

My phone rang. Mom—asking me to bring fruits while returning home.

"Let's go," he said, but I was as hesitant as him to move.

We didn't have a choice. I had an inkling that this would be one of the last times we met in a long time. *Be proactive and ask him how he feels.*

"Sadiq," I remained sitting as he stood, gesturing for him to sit back again. He did. *I should tell him now. No better time than this.* Taking a deep breath, I said, "I like you. Really *really* like you."

He rubbed his neck. "I know. I like you, too."

I wanted to bang my head—it didn't go as I imagined. I tried again. "I like you more than a friend. I mean...I want us to be together."

Sadiq grinned. "I know. Me, too."

"Really?"

"Uh...yes, what else do you want me to say?"

I didn't know that either. This wasn't a movie or one of Mom's melodramatic shows where there'd be background music or Sadiq would break into a dance.

"So, I can now call you my boyfriend?"

Sadiq shrugged. "If that's what you want."

I banged my head on the table, for real this time. "Why you are talking in circles, you tell me. What do you want?"

Sadiq suddenly stood from where he sat across from me and took the chair next to me. I caught him looking around and wondered what he was up to when he placed a quick kiss on my cheek.

"Haww! Look who's become bold!" I laughed, holding my fingers over the place where his lips had brushed.

Sadiq chuckled. "Someone's company is rubbing off on me."

I held his hand again and placed my head on his shoulder. I closed my eyes and sighed. I felt as if a burden had been lifted from my mind. Oh Allah, I wanted so many more moments like this.

Chapter 30
The After Party
Sadiq

I made my way toward the chawl. My ears buzzed, and my heart fluttered—I wondered whether it was the atria or the ventricles that got wings—thinking about the last few hours. Graduation turned out to be the best day of my life. I did feel that Afrah liked me, and I was right! She was so fearless. And I was glad she took the initiative because it would have taken me years to gather up the courage and express what I felt for her.

Standing near the stairs of the chawl, I greeted my neighbors, smiling at them but not really looking at their faces. Then someone pulled my ears.

"Ouch," I grumbled and looked for who did that. "Ammi...!"

"Now that you are a doctor officially doesn't mean you can forget your ammi. What are you doing down here, smiling like a fool? That Mumtaz Aapa told me you are here. I'm waiting for you for so long...come up now."

I followed her, rubbing my ear but still smiling. The moment we entered our little house, I hugged and kissed her on the head.

"I'm so happy, Ammi. I have graduated. I'm so looking forward to starting a new job tomorrow." *And I have found a wife, too, whom I like so much, you won't believe it. You'll like her, too.* I wanted to share it with her but stopped myself from doing so. First, we had to move away from this place. Improve our living conditions before I brought Afrah into our lives. "I'll start looking for a new house soon. And then we are off from here."

The shocked expression on Ammi's face threw me off for a second, but I had to convince her. I would try my best. When I looked at her again, she'd masked her face with a neutral expression.

"I'm so happy for you. And yes, you'll find a good place for yourself soon. I know it, here." She placed her palm on her heart.

"Only for me? You'll be coming too, Ammi." I stopped. I didn't want to argue with her now when we were both in such a good mood. "We'll talk about going from here later." She nodded but didn't meet my gaze.

She wasn't sharing something with me, but I shrugged it off. She would tell me sooner or later.

"Come now, let's get ready. Then we need to go to your bade-abba's house," she said.

A visit to Bade-abba's house didn't faze me today. It was a party for me, and this time I'd enjoy it.

At Bade-abba's house, the atmosphere was jovial. He had decorated the entire house with balloons, ribbons, and the like. For a moment, I was shocked—so much fanfare for me? Delicious smells wafted from the kitchen. I wanted to eat first and talk later. The pizza I'd eaten with Afrah had all but evaporated in my stomach. I turned to find a place to sit when my sisters Anam and Madiha pulled me aside and asked about my convocation. They hugged me and pulled my nonexistent cheeks.

"Don't do that, Aapa."

"You look great, doctor saab...."

"What do you mean? I have always looked like this. Not changed overnight."

"No, but there is something different about you," Anam said.

"Yes, you are glowing. And why not, we have seen

you slog for five and a half years," Madiha agreed. "You deserve every bit of happiness now."

I didn't want to share the real reason for my 'glow,' as they put it. Not yet.

"Yes, I know. But I still have a few more years to study."

My sisters clucked their tongues, but I was happy to see them. It didn't surprise me much that I met them only at Bade-abba's house. They didn't come by much to our place at the chawl because it was too cramped, and Abbu was always around. My sisters were lucky, they didn't really have to deal with him. Thinking about him, I looked for him but found Bade-abba close to me instead. It appeared he had overheard our conversation in the way he shook his head.

"Your studies will go on," he said in his roaring voice. "But today, you will only enjoy yourself, my young man!"

We sat making small talk and eating as the dishes were served. Farheen sat next to me, dressed in a full-length, red dress that my sisters gushed about. I was struck with annoyance as she kept giggling for no apparent reason.

Not able to take it any longer, I asked, "What is so funny?"

"Nothing," she giggled again. "Did you like the butter chicken? I made it."

"Yes, it is good." I nodded, trying hard to remember whether my cousin had graduated yet. So, I asked her.

"No...I left my studies after the twelfth grade, don't you remember? Everything went over my head. I like to cook and design dresses. I'm happy with my life."

"Of course. You should do what makes you happy." I smiled.

After dinner, Bade-abba stood. "My family and friends, it's time to share some good news." Everyone stopped talking and looked at him. "I have bought a new house for my daughter, Farheen, in the adjacent building, where she will stay with her husband after marriage."

Abbu and Ammi were amongst the first to congratulate them.

"Arshad Bhaijaan, you are the best!" Abbu said and hugged him.

"Oh, ho. Wait." Bade-abba laughed. "There is more. My nephew here," he gestured at me. "Come here, bachcha." I stood next to him. He patted my shoulder. "My nephew here is now a proper doctor. Dr. Sadiq." He clapped, and the rest followed. He whispered to me among the ruckus, "I'm happy I could help you to fulfill your dream."

"I know Bade-abba, and I'm going to be eternally grateful to you for that," I said, with my hand on my heart.

"Don't make me cry now." Turning to his family, Bade-abba continued, "I also want to announce another happy news. I have fixed the nikah of my daughter, Farheen." Again murmurs of congratulations and mashallah floated. "The most important thing is that my son-in-law is also here."

Complete silence descended on the room. Farheen had many suitors, it was heard, but Bade-abba never entertained anyone. Even I was curious to know who that person would be. The unlucky one, I imagined Afrah saying. No, I didn't have anything against Farheen, I didn't *know* her as such.

"Dr. Sadiq here, and my darling Farheen are going to get married soon! Let's pray for the well-being and happiness of the new couple."

My jaw dropped when Bade-abba announced my name. Suddenly, I found myself next to Farheen again, and people around us were congratulating and back-slapping me. Whereas all that I could hear was a buzz in my ears. My mouth had gone dry, and my breath became labored. The room around me spun and I gripped the chair nearest to me when someone pressed a glass of water in my hand. It was Ammi. The way she appeared calm and collected, I realized Ammi knew of this before. It was *this* thing that she wasn't sharing with me.

I reached home in a daze and went straight up to

the mezzanine. My jaw pained with the effort I had to put in forcing a smile. I couldn't do anything else. There had to be some way out of this. Not that Farheen was bad or anything, but I couldn't imagine myself with her for the rest of my life.

"Sadiq...Sadiq, listen to me," Ammi called from somewhere behind me.

"Not now, Ammi. I'm tired," I replied. Yes, I was angry with her for not telling me. But I also didn't want to talk about it, hoping it would all disappear in the morning like a bad dream.

Only, the next morning, Abbu was waiting for me. I didn't utter a word. We breakfasted in silence. I had to report for my first day at the new hospital by ten. There was an introduction session, and I would be shown around the hospital, and I looked forward to it. I wouldn't have to do *actual* work at the hospital today.

"So, did you like our surprise?" Abbu asked. "Wasn't it the best gift you've ever received?"

I didn't reply. Afrah crossed my mind. *I won't be able to meet her today.*

"What? Nothing to say?" Abbu continued.

This was bait, and I didn't want to fall for it. I convinced myself to keep my mouth shut. Talking to him was going to add to my problems.

But Abbu couldn't keep quiet. "Good for you, you get a wife and a home together," he spoke with derision. "Don't forget your poor abba and ammi then, doctor saab—"

"Sadiq, here. I have brought some haleem for you," Ammi interjected, trying to diffuse the tension. She offered a plate of the meat and lentil dish.

"No, I don't want any. I'm done. I'm getting late for work." I went up again.

When I came down, Abbu had left. I heaved a sigh of relief. I didn't want to talk to him. Not now, not ever.

"Sadiq...about last night," Ammi started.

How long could I run away from it? It had to be dealt with—the sooner, the better. So, I looked at her and said, "Yes, Ammi. Why didn't you tell me before?"

"This was decided the day your bade-abba offered to help you with your education. Your abbu asked him what he could do to repay the loan, and your bade-abba said he didn't want any money back. Instead, he asked for your hand in marriage for Farheen."

I couldn't digest this. "Oh, so I was bought? I can't believe you hid such a huge thing from me!" I wondered if this would have happened if I'd told them about the scholarship and given Bade-abba the money as soon as I'd gotten it. Maybe, maybe not. The transaction of my life was already done by then.

"They would have told you. But it was at my insistence they didn't. I didn't want your focus to be disturbed. So, we decided we'll tell you the day you graduated."

I picked up my bag from the floor and snorted. "Yes, and I looked like a complete fool. Why were Anam and Madiha so happy? Did they also know?"

"Of course, they were happy. They adore Farheen. And no, they didn't know. Farheen didn't either, except a few months back when she started getting rishtas. Her abba had to tell her."

Marriage among cousins was not uncommon, but I had to find a way out of this. I wasn't going to let others decide my future. Without saying another word, I stormed out of the house.

I found a public phone at the station and dialed a number.

"Hello..."

"Hi, Afrah. Happy birthday."

"Thank you," she replied. "I loved your gifts, and I'm wearing the scarf and the bracelet today. I wish I could have met you..." I could hear the announcement on the platform. "My train is here. I'll call you later."

"I'll call you," I replied. "Bye."

What will I tell her? I wondered. *Or should I tell her? No.* Not until I found other options. She was my one source of happiness, and I didn't want to risk losing that. I was only thinking about myself, but I couldn't help it.

Later at home, Bade-abba waited for me. "Here comes my son."

I wanted to groan but caught myself. I had thought hard about how to approach my uncle in between lectures at work. After greeting him, I sat on the floor, drinking the tea Ammi offered.

"When do you want the nikah?" he asked.

This was my chance. I could tell him I didn't want this. It was only my ammi and bade-abba here. Sure, they would understand.

"Yes, when do you want it, Sadiq?" Ammi looked at me, pointedly. "Your abbu and I have promised this. It has to happen some day or the other. The sooner the better." Her voice carried a steely resolve.

I blinked. "No," I said. Ammi gasped. I cleared my throat and looked at them. "I mean not now. I still have to study for three more years. I have entrance exams at the end of this year."

"That's alright." Bade-abba laughed. "You will have a separate room for yourself now, to study."

"I'll be staying at the hospital for the first year of residency. There is no changing that. Besides, I need to concentrate a hundred percent if I want to clear this entrance, or else a whole year will be wasted." I could do this. Ask for more time. And they would have to agree.

"Hmm…we'll discuss this again. I need to go now." Bade-abba stood and left.

A moment of silence passed between Ammi and me.

"Why did you say all of that?" she chided. "He sensed your hesitation."

"So, what, Ammi? I am still stumped that you guys sold me off because you couldn't afford to pay my fees. I am so angry at you, Ammi. The least you can do is buy me some time. Is that too much to ask?" I clenched my fists and banged them on the wall. "I don't like her, Ammi…how will I spend my whole life with her?"

"You'll learn to love her. I hadn't even seen your abbu before marriage."

"Yes, so you see where that got you?"

Ammi flinched and squeezed her eyes shut. When she opened them, they were glazed with unshed tears. I grimaced. I didn't want to hurt my mother.

Ammi stepped forward and held my hand. "This is not about me. It was a promise, and you cannot get out of it. I'll ask for more time, but that's all I can do. You will have to marry Farheen eventually. Meanwhile, you also need to figure out what you'll tell the girl who is on your mind right now."

It didn't surprise me that she knew.

"I'm returning his loan, Ammi, so now he cannot hold me against it. Also, if I had known there was a

"Yes, I know. But..."

"I know there is something going on with you."

Should I tell her now? I swallowed, and my heart picked up its rhythm. *No, I can't tell her this over the phone.*

"Uh, no, Afrah...it's just my studies and new work."

"Okay, fine."

"I'll meet you soon. Bye," I said and banged my head over the phone.

Chapter 31
One Last Suitor
Afrah

These were the best months of my life. Time flew so fast, and it was July already. The rains played havoc with our lives, as usual. But I didn't mind it one bit. I didn't know being in love could transform my days so much! When Bushra was dating, she appeared guarded. To think of it, I might appear the same, too. My cheerfulness was limited to only when I stepped out of the house. I hadn't shared with Mom or Papa that I'd found a husband for myself. It was something I intended to be a surprise all planned out. Sadiq would come home one Sunday with his parents and ask for my hand. I imagined the gob smacked expression of Mom and giggled.

"What?" Mom said while watching her favorite drama on TV. I was seated next to her, pretending to watch.

"Nothing. This is just so stupid," I said, pointing to the TV.

The phone rang, and as Mom answered it, I pondered over the last few times I'd met up with Sadiq. He seemed disturbed as if something on his mind was not letting him be free with me. I did try to prod him, but he shrugged it off as workload or studies. But I doubted that was the reason.

Mom flopped next to me, shaking me out of my thoughts. "Bushra is coming tomorrow."

I groaned. "Please tell me she's coming alone. Ask her to leave Zain with Asif."

"Rubbish! A mother can never leave her child alone."

"Not alone, Mom. He will be with his father. He eats everything now anyway, so what's the problem?"

"You have become too thick-skinned to understand all this."

"Okay, thanks, Mom." I chuckled. Crossing my arms over my chest, I blew my cheeks. It had been long since I'd exasperated my mother. Sadiq would have called me 'naughty girl.' I smiled, thinking of him.

Papa walked in the door bearing food parcels. I squealed like a little girl waiting for presents.

"What did you bring for me?"

"Your ammi called me to bring fruits and fresh vegetables for Bushra and Zain. But how could I leave my favorite daughter without anything?" he rummaged through the bags and handed a parcel to me.

The aroma of mint and minced meat hit my nostrils as I grabbed the bag. "Seekh paratha! Oh, yummy!" I kissed him on the cheek. "I'm having this now. Mom, do you want? And Papa?"

"Watch what you are eating. You are putting on weight," Mom said, just as Papa asked me to plate for him, too.

"Relax, Mom, I know. Do you want me to leave a bit for you, or should I eat everything?"

The drama on the TV ended, and Mom put on her dupatta. "I'm going down to Rukhsana. Have something to discuss." She stopped on her way to pass me by. "Look, that white patch is coming on your neck, too. Maybe you should start wearing a burqa. No one will notice then."

"Yes, mom. I'll wear one when the next family comes to visit me for a marriage proposal." I gave her an innocent smile.

She left in a huff muttering, "Useless girl."

I giggled. Papa laughed, too.

"Leave your poor mother alone."

"Oh, I don't like to annoy her anyway. When she leaves me alone, I'll return the favor."

We sat on the floor with the meal.

"You'll finish a year at your job next month. Why don't you start applying to the teacher's colleges?"

"I don't have enough saved yet, Papa. Half of the salary goes into treating this." I showed him the patches that were becoming slightly pigmented with the treatment. "But I'm tired. I'm spending so much time and effort, and still, there isn't much improvement." I sighed. "Besides, the time period of applying is over. I have to wait for next year now."

"Next year, Inshallah," he concurred. "And you don't have to work. I can afford to pay your fees."

"I know, but I like to work. Did you wonder what would happen if Mom and I were left alone for the whole day?"

Both of us burst out laughing. Feeling comfortable, I decided it was time to tell Papa that I was in love. Only Roshni knew about it.

"Papa, I have to tell you something." Sadiq was a doctor, and I was sure my family wouldn't have a problem with that.

"Hmm. Go ahead."

He looked at me, but I found myself tongue-tied. Why couldn't I share the most important thing in my life with him? He deserved to know this. Regaining my courage, I opened my mouth.

"Yes, tell us," Mom's voice startled me. "What were you saying?"

I bit my lip. *When did she sneak in?* No, I wouldn't be able to say it now. I smiled wide as my brain worked overtime to think of something appropriate to say.

Clearing my throat, I finally said, "I might get a raise at my job the next month."

"That's good," Papa said and patted my head.

"What? Aren't you planning to leave the job?" Mom interjected. "Enough now. It's time to settle."

I shrugged and raised my brows at Papa. "Not again." We laughed as Mom went to the bedroom.

"I know this wasn't what you wanted to share, but I'm here to listen. You can tell me anytime. Okay?" Papa whispered.

I nodded.

The following day, a Saturday, with the arrival of Bushra and Zain, the house was a flurry of activity. I helped to make soft chapattis for the little brat and mashed veggies.

"Not that way, Appi," Bushra slapped my hands. "See, you roast it lightly, or else he will not eat."

"But it has to be cooked."

"Yes, but if you cook on a full flame, it will burn. Keep the flame slow."

"She doesn't spend much time in the kitchen,

Bushra. Leave it." Mom took the rolling pin from my hands and pushed me aside. "I'll do it."

I shrugged, but it felt as if they'd whacked me on my head with that dratted rolling pin. My mother and sister treated me as if I were an outsider. They had formed a team—a team against me. I blinked fast and went to the living room.

Papa was sitting on the sofa. "Afrah, come here," he called out to me. "Don't listen to them. See what little Zain has to say to his *maasi*."

I sat next to him and observed Zain. He had started to sit and mutter unintelligible words. He left everyone in a bauble of laughter whenever he did that.

Later in the day, when Zain slept, Bushra asked me to go to the terrace with her. After what she did earlier today, I didn't want to, but I was curious to know what she wanted to talk about.

"You look good," I said. I didn't know what else to tell her.

"Yes, I have started some exercising, and I also watch what I eat. You look radiant, too," Bushra added as an afterthought.

"So...tell me, why are you here?" I asked. Another demand from her in-laws?

Bushra shrugged. "I don't need a reason to visit you all."

"I know, but these days I think you and Mom have

made it a mission to humiliate me. Make me feel dumb."

"You are thinking too much about it. Back in the kitchen, what you were doing was wrong. So, I had to correct you. Somebody has to, Appi."

"Why do I think this 'correcting' part is not about what happened in the kitchen?"

Bushra sighed. "Appi, we all want you to be happy."

"Oh, thanks, little sister. But I am happy. Can't you see that?" Then when realization dawned, I chuckled. "Do you think getting married is the only thing that will make me happy? Look at yourself. The other day you said you envied me. And now?" I raised my brows.

"Marriage has to be worked upon. That was a low moment in my life." Her phone rang. "Let's go, Zain has woken up and is crying."

The evening passed amidst chatting and watching Zain. He had to be under constant supervision or else Allah knew what lint or fabric he would put into his stomach.

After dinner, Mom started, "You have another suitor who is coming to visit tomorrow."

"Yes, Appi, they are relatives of my mother-in-law. Please do your best."

I laughed. "So that's why you came here. Oh, your 'reputation' is at stake."

Bushra averted her gaze. But then she cleared her throat. "Appi, he is a bit older than you, but their family is nice. Well-to-do. And I have spoken to him. He is even ready to let you study and work after marriage." She stroked Zain's hair. "Please, Appi...do not ruin this. Please."

I took a deep breath. "Alright, I'll do my best." *To ruin it.* I imagined a burst of evil laughter following that. I had Sadiq now. I didn't need to please anyone, even if the said person would meet all my requirements.

"Please, Appi..."

I felt sorry for Bushra. She didn't have any idea what was coming for her.

"Yes, don't worry. I'll be on my best behavior."

I got myself busy organizing the clothes in the cupboard I shared with Mom, all the while planning my attack on the poor unsuspecting man who dreamt of marrying me. I'd done it before, but now I had more ammunition. Finding my 'uniform,' I put it aside.

The next morning, I sat on the sofa, ready. When the suitor's family arrived, a gasp escaped my lips. The suitor was the same creepy fellow from Bushra's baby shower. I'd forgotten his name. *What is it?* He looked at me and gave me a knowing smile. I didn't smile back.

"Appi...please," Bushra whispered in my ear.

I went to the kitchen. Papa was filling a jug with water. "I don't like him."

"It is okay, princess. You can refuse. I won't let you marry anyone whom you don't like. But for now, be kind until they leave."

I sighed and went back to the others. Bushra and Mom waved me to go to the bedroom with him to talk alone for a few minutes.

"Look," I started.

"Mirza," he said, smirking.

"Is that your name or surname?"

"What does it matter? I want you as my wife. You can call me whatever you want to."

I grinned. "How about creep?"

"I like you. You're fiery."

"I want to study to become a teacher, and I plan to teach all my life."

He smiled. "I know, I don't mind it. You can do as you please."

Most men went out the door when I told them this. But Mirza seemed unperturbed. So, I took the next step.

"Hmm...did you know about this?" I showed him the patches on my wrists. "I have this on my entire body."

He scoffed. "Doesn't matter. I can't wait to touch them all."

My body gave an involuntary shudder, and goose-bumps rose on my neck. How could he speak to me like that? Sadiq and I never talked in such a way, and we actually *liked* each other. What if he said things like this to other potential brides? I took a deep breath. *No problem, I have one more weapon in my arsenal.*

"Okay. But one more thing." This was something I'd found on the internet when I searched for the symptoms and effects of polycystic ovaries that the gynecologist had diagnosed. I had even discussed it with Sadiq—he had said pregnancy was difficult but not impossible. I had taken his word, but the scumbag in front of me didn't need to know that. "I cannot give you children. I'm infertile."

I watched his expression with interest and relished it. He opened his mouth to say something but then closed it, not meeting my gaze. The cuff link of his shirt was now more intriguing than me. I really wanted to laugh. *Gotcha.*

"I can show you my reports and the medicines I'm taking if you think I'm fibbing."

He cleared his throat. "There's no need for that. I believe you." He stood and went out without saying anything more.

No parting thoughts? Huh! I pumped my fist in the air. *Mission accomplished.*

I went out smiling. Mirza didn't meet my eye a

single time post our conversation. His family left soon after.

The moment the door closed, Bushra held me by the shoulders. "Seriously, Appi? How can you be so selfish?"

"Now, what did I do?" I gaped at my sister. "*He* rejected me."

"I heard what you told him, Appi. I heard everything."

Heat simmered in my heart. "You did, huh? Then you must have also heard how he spoke to me?"

"He didn't say anything offensive," Bushra crossed her arms.

"Really? 'He didn't say anything offensive.' So now I'm stupid if I say he was eyeing me as if I were a piece of meat."

"He has a casual way of talking, Appi. He didn't mean anything bad."

Mom interfered, "I don't understand what pleasure you get by driving good people away?"

"Good?" I seethed. If my anger burnt everything around me, so be it. "Papa," I looked at him, "He told me, 'I can't wait to touch all the white patches on your body!' Does that make him a 'good' person or what he said to be a 'casual' conversation?"

"Nadira and Bushra, if he said what Afrah said he did, then I'm on her side. We cannot let her get married to someone who treats her like this even before anything is official." His tone suggested a finality.

"Abbu, she also told him she cannot get pregnant! There has to be a limit to the lies," Bushra added.

Papa tilted his head at me. I looked away. To Mom and Bushra, I said, "You both think I'm up to nothing good. Always wasting my time. But Bushra, I've told you how irregular and bad my periods are, so I got myself investigated. I'm better now, thank you very much, but I'm not in the mood to justify myself or my actions any further."

"You are a selfish bitch!" Bushra cried. "This was important to me. What will my in-laws think of me now?"

"The same they thought of you until now." I shrugged. Bushra stepped closer, and for a moment, I wondered if my sister would hit me. I braced myself. I'd hit her back.

"Ammi, look at her attitude!" Bushra whirled around to complain to Mom. "Why is she like this?"

"Since when have you become a stuck-up bitch who cares only about her reputation?" I countered. "Where was this strong attitude when your in-laws asked us for money or jewelry like uppity beggars?"

"Afrah!" Mom yelled.

"That's enough," Papa said. He stepped between

us. "Go inside, Bushra. Now. Wash your face. You stay here, Afrah."

Zain howled his lungs out at the commotion.

"I hate you, Appi."

I scoffed. "Likewise, little sister."

Later, in the living room, when my heart rate had settled to normal, I rehashed the argument. I couldn't believe why my sister, who looked up to me until a few months ago, now treated me the way she did. What had changed? Why didn't Bushra tell me what she was planning? Maybe I might have told her about Sadiq instead of looking for a rishta from her in-law's side of the family.

My eyes prickled with tears when I thought about how Bushra took that creep's side. *How could she?* A muffled cry left my lips. I didn't want to announce to my family how much their words affected me. At least Papa tried to understand me, or Allah knows what I'd have done. Wiping my eyes with my dupatta, I dialed the one person who would make me feel better.

"Hello," I said, sniffing. It was a Sunday, and as far as I knew, Sadiq had an off day. And he always answered the phone when he was home.

"Who's this?" the woman at the other end asked.

I cleared my throat. I didn't recognize her voice—it didn't sound like Sadiq's mother. "Is Dr. Sadiq there?" I said.

"Yes…one minute."

I could hear many voices in the background and wondered what he was up to.

"Hello," he said, breathing hard.

"It's me." My voice came out in a whisper.

"Are you alright? You don't sound good," he said so softly, that I had to strain to hear him against the noise in his house.

"I'm not," I replied. "Can you meet me today?"

"Today? I can't. Not now. Can we meet at the station tomorrow? Before you catch your train?"

"Oh. Okay," I said, my heart sinking. "I'll see you tomorrow then."

Sadiq muttered a yes and disconnected the call.

I went to the kitchen to distract myself. Washed the utensils and mopped the kitchen. Wiped the crockery and put them back on their designated shelf. The house was quiet, and I peeked into the bedroom. Bushra was lying on the single bed with Zain beside her. The little boy appeared to be sleeping. Mom was folding the laundry. She looked at me and shook her head.

I went back to the living room.

Mom walked behind me and said, "You better don't talk to your sister for a while."

"She better don't talk to me. Why is she being so rude these days? And if she has a problem, she can go back." Mom tut-tutted. "Mom, one more thing. No more proposals for me. Until now, I cooperated with you. I stayed home and spoke to them with respect. But not anymore. I'll find a husband for myself on my own."

Mom raised her brows. "Do you have anyone in mind? Then why don't you introduce us to him?"

"I will soon," I said. And with those little bits of words, a weight lifted from my chest.

"Great then. Both my girls have a love marriage. I cannot be happier."

Mom's comment struck me as odd. I narrowed my eyes. "Why do I feel you are taunting me?"

"He better be from a good family."

Mom went back to the bedroom, and I lay down on the sofa. I still couldn't digest Bushra's behavior with me today. This seemed something else. The bitterness in her voice and actions had to have some other cause. What had I done to upset her so much?

The next morning, I was excited to meet Sadiq. I had even rehearsed what I wanted to tell him.

"Hi," I grinned when I spotted him.

"Hi, so all good? You sounded sad yesterday."

"I was, had a bitter fight with my sister. Okay, so I'm getting straight to the point as I have to catch my train. When are we telling our parents?"

Sadiq appeared momentarily shocked. "Parents?"

"Yes," I shrugged. "We've been going on since what...." I raised my fingers, "Six months now? It's high time to tell them."

"I think we can still wait."

"No, Sadiq. I can't wait anymore. I don't want to sit through any more rishtas in my house. I'm tired of playing the same cassette. My mother doesn't get it. She continues to ask people to look for suitable men for me. I told her yesterday that I'll introduce you to the man I want to marry." I tilted my head. "What do you think?"

"You told her already?"

"I didn't tell her your name or anything. I was non-specific. But she got the hint. So, when are you telling your parents and coming to my place? Next Sunday?"

I saw his hesitance. The way he rubbed his neck and shuffled his feet. I chuckled to hide the hurt I was feeling. "Have you changed your mind? Don't you want to spend the rest of your life with me? Does my vitiligo bother you? Maybe my hormonal imbalance? You can tell me, you know. I can take it. I have been taking it for long—other people taking out their frustrations on me. So, you can do that, too."

Sadiq remained quiet. He then said, "Afrah...it...it's not that."

But I wasn't going to stand there, taking a kind-worded rejection from the one person I had come to love. I shook my head to stop him from explaining and ran to catch my train, all the while blinking hard to not let a single tear drop.

Chapter 32
The Choice
Sadiq

I stood dumbstruck, looking at Afrah's retreating back. *Great, now I have driven her away.* I wanted to tell her the truth, but not now when she was already so vulnerable. With shoulders sagging, I dragged myself out of the station. I had night shifts at the hospital for the next three days. But Afrah had sounded so dejected last evening, I couldn't *not* meet her. And now, I made her even more dejected.

Shaking my head, I sighed and briefly closed my eyes. Slowly, I made my way back home and up to the mezzanine. My books stared at me as if begging for my attention. *Yes, I'll give an equal amount of time to you all.* At least I had this goal to achieve. My new workplace was perfect for me. The patient load wasn't heavy, and I got enough time to read. Besides, it paid well, and I learned a lot of procedures, a hands-on type of job. I couldn't have asked for more.

Except I wanted more. I wanted Afrah in my life. And now, it was time for some hard decisions.

The surprise visit from Farheen the previous day forced me to face reality. There was no way I could get out of it unless I cut all ties with my family. But could I really do that? What about Ammi? I loved her so much. She was the most important person in my life. *And Afrah?* My inner voice chided. Wasn't she important too? I rested my head on the book in front of me.

"What is it, Sadiq?" Ammi asked me. I hadn't heard her climbing the steps. "You've been disturbed since the call yesterday evening."

I sighed. "I don't know what to do, Ammi."

"Is this related to Dr. Farooqui?"

I snorted. "You bet. She drives me crazy. Why do I have to marry Farheen? Why?" Even though I knew the answer, I couldn't stop myself from asking this question a hundred times over.

"Because if your bade-abba had not funded your education, you wouldn't have been a doctor," Ammi replied.

"But I'm going to return the loan, right?"

"Yes, you will. But this is like that question, did the chicken come before the egg?"

"Huh. I wish I had known what I was putting

myself into. I wouldn't have fallen in love. I would have distanced myself from her if I had known my marriage was fixed."

"Yes, but you *didn't* know you would fall in love. It's not in our hands," Ammi said. "But what you do now will be totally your decision."

She held my head and placed a kiss on my forehead. "I trust you. You will do what is best for all of us." She tidied the little mezzanine and went back down.

I pondered over what Ammi said, then my mind drifted to Afrah. Sooner or later, I would have to tell her my dilemma. And I knew she wouldn't force me to be with her if she were aware of my predicament. I didn't want to string her along anymore if, at the end of it, I was going to break her heart and mine, too.

Was there no middle way out of this? Maybe I should tell Farheen. She wouldn't agree if she knew I would only be living with her while my heart belonged to Afrah. If she refused to marry me, surely bade-abba wouldn't force her. *Oh, what a wonderful idea. Why didn't it strike me before?*

I rushed down the stairs and searched for Farheen's number in my diary. As I was about to dial, Ammi stopped me.

"Are you going to tell Farheen to back off?"

"H—how did you know?"

"She knows because we had a long chat about it. I told her that you don't want to marry her, and you don't like her, probably may never like her, no matter what she does. She doesn't know you are in love with someone else, though. But she told me that her father will force her to marry you, no matter what. He will not accept any reason she gives. And now that he has announced your nikah, his reputation is also at stake."

"But still, Ammi, why me? He can get any other man for Farheen."

"Maybe because you are a doctor?" she suggested.

And it finally made sense then. This insistence of me marrying Farheen and not bothering to know what *I* want...Bade-abba was more interested in the 'doctor' tag than me as a person. I scoffed, "But this is utter nonsense, Ammi."

"I know. But we can't do anything. You know your Bade-abba. He always gets his way."

I went out to clear my head. All arguments laid out by Ammi were correct. I had two options. If I chose Afrah, I would have to leave behind my entire family. If I chose to stay, I would have to let go of Afrah. I *had* to decide. I had to call Afrah.

Having decided, I found a public phone and dialed her number. I knew it by heart. But she didn't answer her phone. I tried a couple of times more, to no avail.

Crestfallen, I went back home and with a heavy heart, went to work.

The next morning, when Ammi went to the market, I dialed Afrah's number. This time, she answered.

"Hello," she said.

"It's me."

"I don't want to talk to you, Sadiq."

"Wait...meet me today evening. I have to tell you something important."

I was willing to beg her to meet me if she refused, but after a moment, she said, "Oh, is it? Okay then, I'll meet you. But I'll be late today. Can I call you when I'm done with my work here?"

I sighed, my lips curving into a smile. "Yes, okay."

"Listen, when will you buy a new phone?"

What should I tell her? That I wouldn't need one because we wouldn't be together after today to talk with one another?

Her chuckle saved me from giving a reply. "Okay, I need to go, and I'll call you when I'm about to leave from work. Bye."

Later, while having lunch, I braced myself.

"Ammi. I have made my decision. I'm going to tell her today evening."

She nodded.

I wondered how I would tell Afrah everything. What if she didn't even listen and went off like she did yesterday morning? No, I couldn't let her do that until I was done speaking. *Maybe I can write all of it down and hand her the letter.* The more I contemplated it, the more I found this idea practical, considering Afrah and her unpredictable behavior.

I planned it all out—I'd meet her at Kurla station, then take her to Dadar. From Dadar, we would take a train to Bandra. There was a cozy café outside the station. I had visited it with my colleagues from the hospital where I worked a few days before. I wanted to give her something she would remember, something special. Then while departing from the café, I'd give her the letter and ask her to open it only after she reached home. It broke my heart, knowing I was going to break hers. But I didn't have any other choice. Ammi was important, too. And it was her promise I didn't want to renege on. If it were only my abbu's, I wouldn't have thought twice. But with Ammi, it was different.

Afrah didn't deserve this. Had I known my marriage was already fixed, I wouldn't have spoken to her, ever. I had made this point to Ammi, but she was equally in a fix. What little power she had, she had used already. She had resigned that she would follow me in what I considered to be right. Neither of the options was right, though.

So, I began to write.

> *Dear Afrah,*
>
> *It pains me to be writing this to you when I am supposed to tell you this face-to-face. But knowing you, I wouldn't be able to explain myself. Hence these words on this paper.*
>
> *I came to know on the day of my graduation that my marriage was fixed to my cousin. It will be a third-degree consanguineous marriage—*

I cut the last part. Consanguinity didn't matter to her when I was writing to break her heart.

> *I was aghast at this news, and I still am because I am tied to it by a promise made by my mother. Please don't think that it has anything to do with any of your health concerns. No, it isn't. Farheen, my cousin, knows I don't love her and will never be able to. Despite this,*

she still says she likes me and wants the marriage to happen. I'm sorry for not telling you this earlier. But I doubt our suffering would be any less. Had I known it before, I would have never spoken to you when we met at the station.

I was searching for a way out all this time, but then I realized there wasn't any. So now I have to let you go. It breaks my heart to write all this, and I wish you all the happiness in the world. My best wishes are always with you. Don't ever think of yourself any less due to your skin condition. You are and will always be beautiful, inside and out. And I will always love you. Always.

Remember that.

Sadiq.

I read the letter a number of times. My eyes prickled. I hadn't cried since I was little. I wanted to bang my head on the floor. Or run away from everything. Instead, I folded the letter and kept it aside. The blue shirt that I had laid out to wear brought back the happiest day of my life—my graduation.

When Afrah called, I was ready. After reading the letter one more time, I put it in my shirt pocket. I'd decided I would go to the hospital after dropping her back at Kurla station. That way I would know she won't open the letter before reaching home. I wore the new shoes I'd bought a few days back. I wanted her to remember me in my best form.

Reaching the station early, I bought our tickets. It was 5:45 p.m. on the indicator clock when I spotted her. She had wrapped the silk scarf I'd gifted around her neck and sported a huge grin.

"Hi," she said. "So, what did you want to tell me?"

I quirked my brow. "What's the hurry? Come with me, I want to take you somewhere." But my heart broke into a hundred pieces under my ribs as I held her hand and crossed the bridge to board the train, knowing it would be the last time.

Chapter 33
Black
Afrah

I wanted to jump for joy. *He is going to propose to me. He is going to propose to me.* I kept repeating it in my head and couldn't stand still. We boarded the general compartment together. It wasn't that crowded today.

"New shoes?" I gasped, looking at his blue canvas shoes with neon orange laces.

"I wondered when you would notice that."

"All dressed up and all, huh?" I teased. "What's the occasion?"

Sadiq rubbed the back of his neck. He didn't meet my eyes when he said, "You'll know soon."

"Oh, come on, don't keep me waiting. Tell me now, please?" I looked at him and batted my eyes. He melted like an ice cream on a hot day whenever I did that.

But this time, it didn't work.

Pouting, I showed him my phone. "See, I made a separate album for our pictures." I browsed through the gallery. "Look at this," I smiled. It was Sadiq and me outside the college on graduation day. Sadiq laughed at my expressions in a few of them. When I looked at him, he wiped his eye. "Hey, what happened?"

"Something went into my eye," he said, blowing his kerchief and putting it to his eye.

"Do you want me to do that?" I asked, pointing to the kerchief.

"No, it's better now."

He kept patting his shirt pocket. I couldn't make out whether anything was in there.

"Come, we have to get down now."

I looked at the platform sign. "Dadar? It's so crowded here, and where are we going?"

"Don't worry, I'll hold your hand. I won't leave you alone till we reach Bandra."

"Bandra? Wow, are you taking me to Bandstand?" The sea-facing promenade was one of my favorite places to visit.

"No, it's far from the station, and I have to reach the hospital. I have a night shift today. How about coffee and pastries? There's this beautiful café close to the station."

"Hmm...okay. Let's go have coffee then." I imagined him dropping on one knee in the café and proposing. I giggled at that image.

"You'll have to board the ladies' compartment. The train will be crowded soon; it's peak hour."

I waved my hand at his suggestion. "We'll go together. You are here with me. I have nothing to worry about."

As we walked over the bridge, I saw waves of people moving in one direction and then the other.

"After traveling from Kurla daily, this place doesn't seem that bad," I commented. "I don't know why I dreaded this so much."

Sadiq looked at me. "You were young when you came here and got lost, so it's natural you are scared."

My feet stopped moving when he said that. I couldn't believe he remembered this little thing I'd told him so long ago.

"What?" He pulled my hand.

I shook my head, then narrowed my eyes. "Look, is that our train?"

"No," Sadiq said.

"Yes," I laughed. "Come on. It will be fun."

"We cannot run in this crowd until the platform *and* catch the train..."

"Don't be a spoilsport. Let's try!"

Without waiting for his reply, I started to run, "Wait!" Sadiq cried. He caught up to me, held my hand, and we ran together, dashing against people, muttering apologies, and hearing cusses thrown at us.

We missed the train.

"Oh, never mind," I laughed, breathless.

Sadiq held his middle. "6:20 p.m."

Looking at the crowd of people, I considered going to the women's compartment. But by the time I could decide, the train pulled in.

"Come," Sadiq stood next to the first-class compartment.

"Can't we go in there?" I gestured to first class.

"I can, but you don't have a pass."

"Who's going to check in this crowd?" I asked.

"No, Afrah, not first class, please," he insisted. He was a stickler for rules.

I didn't want to argue with him, and I was delirious with happiness. So, when I was pushed into the compartment with Sadiq behind me, I didn't complain.

We stood near the door, the breeze making his hair fly. Mine was greasy—I hadn't washed them since Saturday and had oiled them on Sunday so that I could look as ugly as possible to the family who had come to see me. But now, no more. I would soon proudly show off my doctor-husband. I gazed up at him and found him looking at me, tenderness in his eyes. For a moment, I thought he'd cry, but then he only smiled.

I locked my elbow with his and rested my head on

his shoulder. He threaded his fingers with mine. I didn't care about how we would look to others, a newly married couple, a couple on honeymoon, or a starry-eyed girlfriend and boyfriend. The first two would be true soon, anyway. I couldn't wipe the smile off my face.

I raised my head to look at him when a huge fire-cracker went off. Or that's what I thought. The train shuddered, the occupants yelled, and everything went black.

Sadiq

A shooting pain radiated in my right leg. It took me a few moments to understand what happened. Some-thing went wrong with the train. Had it derailed? Yes, but the smoke and debris around me suggested some-thing more sinister. I turned my head to look for Afrah. First to the right and then to the left. My ears buzzed, and I thought someone was calling out my name. But the commotion was too much to make out from where the sound came. I felt like vomiting, but nothing came out.

Trying to sit up but failing, I touched the part of my right leg where it hurt the most. I couldn't sit to see what happened to my leg, but my hands felt sticky. And I knew in an instant what it was. Blood.

Forgetting my pain for a moment, I knew I had to look for Afrah. But the smoke limited my vision. Urging myself, I managed to sit up. Tears fell down my cheeks from the effort, and I coughed. Pausing to take in the scene again, I dragged myself toward a man who lay there, half-burnt, muttering something. My medical training kicked in, but I couldn't do much. Checked the man's pulse and tried to shout for help. But ended up coughing more.

As the bout of cough subsided, I pushed myself to stand. I couldn't. My legs gave way, and I fell again. I turned to my right and called for Afrah. But my voice came out as a whisper. *Where is she?* Scores of people lay around me—some screaming for help, a few moaning, a few others motionless. I cleared my throat and tried again.

I pushed myself one more time, attempting to stand, but failing once again, I began to crawl. I winced in pain, dragging my right leg. The smoke and debris were too much to make out anything. And the chaos. A few paramedics rushed to help the others. Soon they would come for me, too, and then I wouldn't be able to find Afrah. *Ya Allah, please keep her safe.* I changed direction to go opposite where the paramedics went. I could feel the blood trickling down my right leg, but I didn't pause to check it. *I have to find Afrah.*

I didn't know how much time had passed when I caught sight of something familiar. The silk scarf I'd gifted Afrah. It had torn in parts and was covered in soot, but I could still make out the red flowers on it. *She must be close.* I tried to increase my speed and kept shaking any unconscious or injured person who I thought was female, muttering Afrah's name. Oh Allah! What if she was already taken by the rescue team? Or what if.... No! I couldn't assume the worst.

But she was nowhere to be found. The paramedics moved closer; they were triaging the victims. Soon they would take me, too. Then my gaze fell on another woman. I tried to call her name but coughed instead. Her dress, even though blackened by the smoke, was similar to what Afrah had worn today.

"Afrah!" I tried again. This time my voice was more than a whisper, but still not loud enough. The woman showed no signs of motion. I crawled toward her, my heart beating fast. A few beads of the bracelet I'd given her lay scattered. Now, I was sure the woman in front of me was Afrah.

I shook her, then turned her around and gasped. Her face and upper body were burnt. I frantically checked for a pulse. The paramedics were upon me.

"You need to come with us."

They checked the woman in front of me. "Leave her, she's dead. We can save you." The paramedic called for a stretcher. I remained at Afrah's side.

"Please check properly, she must be alive...please," I kept repeating. I clutched the scarf in my left hand.

"Come on, hurry. He's going into shock! We could lose him!" the paramedic yelled as my eyes fluttered shut, and then everything went dark.

Chapter 34
Finding Light in Darkness
Afrah

oughing, I opened my eyes. My ears were filled with a tinkering sound. *Where am I?* We were on the train... There was smoke all around me. Or was it dust? I shook my head. The buzzing in my ear increased. I couldn't make out anything. My hands felt wet, and when I raised them to see, they were soaked in blood. I tried to yell but ended up with a lungful of smoke and coughed. Pain shot down my left hand, and tears dropped from my eyes as I tried to support myself to stand. It didn't work, and I fell. I tried again until I could walk in small steps, keeping my left hand still. *Where's Sadiq?*

The smoke made it difficult to see, but I saw a hand moving on the ground. I bent to hold it, but it was only that...a hand. My legs gave away at the realization, and I fell. The contents of my stomach forced their way out. Breathing hard, I changed course. *What the hell happened?* My breath came in short puffs, but I had to find Sadiq.

"Sadiq…" I opened my mouth to call, but my throat hurt, and I coughed again. Praying to find him soon, I crawled further through the smoky haze. The tinkering in my ears had reduced. Screams and cries echoed around me. My hands brushed something else—it was hair. And the woman it belonged to looked dead. I let go and retched again, but there was nothing left in my stomach to come out.

I had lost all sense of direction trying to move away from the smoke. My eyes caught something familiar. A shoe. It looked like Sadiq's. *He must be close!* I tried to stand so I could reach it faster, but my legs wobbled, and I was back on my knees again. Crawling toward the shoe, I grabbed it. A part of it was dusty, but I was sure it was Sadiq's. The neon orange laces were intact. I held it close to my heart and kept calling out for him. A few people helped me to get up and tried to take me away.

"No. No, my Sadiq is here…help me to find him. Please… help!"

"Madam, you need medical care," someone said. "If he has survived this, you will find him at the hospital."

"Survive?" I asked, but the man had gone away to

look for others. "Of course, he is alive. He has to be. We are going to get married!"

"Shh...ma'am, we are taking you to the hospital." A wheelchair appeared out of the smoke, and I was made to sit on it.

I didn't remember giving them the landline number of my house, I didn't remember when my parents came to see me, and I didn't feel the pain in my left hand when it was put in a cast. I didn't feel anything...except the irrepressible feeling that I had to find Sadiq.

"Where is...?" I asked the nurse who came to check me.

She looked at my file. "Afrah, where is who?"

"S...Sadiq. Where is Sadiq?"

I didn't know how long I slept. Or which day it was. The machine attached to my finger beeped.

"Shh," the nurse said. "He must be at some other hospital. Many people were injured that day. If you know the phone number of anyone in his family, you'll be able to find out where he is. Okay?" She patted my arm.

I nodded. It did seem like a good idea. I asked for a phone.

"Wait, I'll send your father in. He has a phone."

"Papa!" I cried, even though my voice was hoarse as soon as he appeared in my line of vision.

"Oh, my princess, relax. You'll be fine, and we'll take you home soon."

"What happened?" Even now, I didn't have any idea of how I'd landed here.

"Bomb blasts at multiple stations in the trains," he said, and I hitched my breath.

I remembered those screams for help and those bloodied bodies. Tears flowed from my eyes as I saw myself clutching Sadiq's shoe. Where was it now?

Holding my good hand, he continued, "Calm down. It's all over now. It happened yesterday, the eleventh of July. Today is Wednesday."

Sniffing, I tried to wipe the snot from my nose. Papa helped me.

"The nurse said you needed a phone. Whom do you want to talk to?"

I gestured for the phone in his hands. My fingers trembled as I dialed Sadiq's number. The line rang, but no one answered. But that didn't deter me. I redialed, the phone almost slipping from my sweaty hands. The line kept ringing, and as I was about to hang up, someone answered.

"Hello?" a soft voice asked me.

Before I could open my mouth to reply, sobs and wails from Sadiq's house pierced my ears. What would I ask this woman? How would I ask? Those heart-wrenching wails were proof of what had happened. Disconnecting the call, I cried.

I dozed in and out of consciousness. When alert, I knew I had a fracture in my left arm that was fixed with screws. I also couldn't stop howling, and the doctors preferred to keep me sedated. Sadiq's shoe was fixed in my memory, and I kept asking for it.

"What exactly are you looking for?" a nurse asked.

The last I remembered of it was that I had it clutched to my chest. "Shoe—blue and orange," I whispered. Orange laces. It was precious for me—Sadiq's last physical memory, proof that he existed, and he was going to ask me to marry him.

And no one could find it.

My phone had so many pictures of him, and I wished with all the hope in my heart that it would be intact. I asked Papa about it.

"It must have shattered into pieces, dear."

Shattered into pieces...like my heart. Tears streamed from my eyes. Crying and then going off to sleep were the only things I could do. I didn't have the strength to get up, and no morsel of food passed through my throat.

I lost track of time. Mom and Papa brought me

home, but I behaved like a statue. *How many days has it been since I lost Sadiq?*

"Afrah...you need to talk to your colleagues at the office. Your friend Roshni had called," Mom said one morning.

Yes, Roshni. I remembered how excited she was on that day when I'd shared that I was meeting Sadiq, and I had this feeling that my life would change after that. *It did change, didn't it?* I had a vague memory that Roshni had come to visit me at the hospital. And it was Roshni who had informed my family about what was supposed to happen that fateful day.

"I don't want to."

"Afrah, you need to. You should talk to her. It will take your mind away from things." Papa insisted.

Bushra approached my bed, and I grimaced. The last thing I told my little sister—*I hate you*. What if those had been the last words I ever said to her? I couldn't help myself and started to sob again.

"Appi...Appi, I'm here. Zain is here, too. Please, he wants his *khaala* to play with him."

But I turned away and refused to talk to Bushra as well.

My hand in the cast felt heavy, and there was still some pain. My body had largely recovered, but what about my heart? My soul? Would they ever recover? I couldn't stop wondering.

I tried to sit. Flashes of the time spent with Sadiq appeared before me like a reel of a movie. How I wished I had printed at least one picture of ours and framed it. Now, I had nothing except his memory to hold on to. Maybe I could visit his house? Could I do that? I didn't know where he lived exactly, but I could ask. But then what? What would I get looking at the sad and broken faces of his family? How could I meet their eyes? How could I tell them I was the last person to see him alive? No. It would break me further if I visited the place where he lived.

The cast on my left hand was cumbersome to manage. I didn't like my mother or Bushra helping me and snapped often. "I can do this on my own."

"Let us help you," Mom said in a tone I'd not heard recently from her. So gentle as if she was talking to a child. Her child. "You can go back to normal once the cast is off."

"Really? Can I go back to normal?" I yelled at her instead. "Didn't you wish I died in that blast? After all, I have given you nothing but shame and tension..."

Mom blinked back tears, and I turned away from her.

"Appi, see I have made your favorite food—biryani," Bushra cajoled me.

"Yes, so now you can claim you are a better cook than me."

I wanted to hurt them deliberately because I was hurt, too.

One evening, Papa sat beside me. "It's going to be a month tomorrow. We are sorry that your chance at happiness was snatched away from you, but you have to move on. You need to."

"I feel itchy inside." I gestured at my cast.

Papa went to the living room and came back with a marker. He drew a big smiley face on my cast. "There... see...I want to see you like this."

I frowned. "But it's itching inside. Give me something to relieve it."

He gave me the marker, but it didn't reach the place where I wanted to scratch.

"The cast will be out in a few days," Papa tried again. "Have you thought about what you are going to do?"

I'd spoken to Roshni a few days back. She was as stubborn as me. Even more. "We are waiting for you to return. You are our most valuable employee. So don't you dare tell me anything otherwise!" she had scolded me.

I'd pondered over it, and Roshni was right. I had to start with something. Sadiq wouldn't have wanted me to be sad all the time. I would return to work and, next year, apply for the B.Ed course. I'd be the teacher I'd told him I would be.

"You can do the accounts at our shop," Papa suggested, "in case you don't want to go back to your job."

For the first time in a month, I gave a flicker of a smile. Asking me to help him was a validation that I mattered to him. I always knew I mattered, but still. Hearing it made a difference.

"Can I come tomorrow? I need some light and air."

He smiled. "Of course, you can."

"I'll resume my job too," but my voice drifted. Would I be able to travel on a train again?

Mom walked toward me hesitantly. And, of course, she would. I had been like a tigress waiting to bite the head off anyone who came near me. I bit my lip in guilt. I was rude to her and Bushra. Life was unpredictable, as I had experienced, and I didn't want to hold grudges against anyone anymore.

"I'm sorry, Mom," I said, hoping that would suffice.

She hugged me. "You don't have to say sorry. I should be sorry. I am, for being too harsh on you. Now, come out. Bushra has come to visit you."

I smiled through the tears that were about to fall from my eyes. My rudeness had driven Bushra away. She'd come to visit only for a day, never staying the night. I walked out slowly. Bushra glanced at me but then looked away. The sofa on which she sat was new.

I sat beside her and pressed the cushioned seat with my right hand. "When did this happen?"

"The old one tore completely, and Zain tried to pull out the stuffing and put it in his mouth. It wasn't safe." Mom said. She sat in between us.

"Appi," Bushra looked at me. I raised my good hand to silence her. "Appi...listen to me..." she said again.

"No, you listen to me first," I muttered. "I'm sorry for snapping at you so often. You didn't deserve it."

"I'm sorry, too, Appi. I had become envious of you and your carefree life. Your happiness and freedom as a career woman with dreams. It got the better of me, and I tried everything to sabotage it. It was all me, I kept filling Ammi's ears to get you married. And I'm sorry about Mirza, he...he was a debacle. I don't know what got into me."

Bushra glanced at me with dewy eyes, and I knew she was being sincere. How much longer could I be angry with her? I took a deep breath. "It's alright, little one. What's done is done. Let's start over."

"Yes, Appi. Let's start over." She hugged me, and Mom joined in too.

I felt a twinge in my heart. I'd lost the love of my life but also found some more.

Chapter 35
Another Pleasant Surprise
Afrah

Two months later

I trudged to the station with Roshni after a busy day at work. A few people stared at me, but I snorted. It didn't affect me that much now. The patches of vitiligo had begun to appear around my mouth and eyes. It bothered me initially—I didn't like to be stared at. Mom suggested I wear a burqa, but I refused. It felt like it would be the wrong reason to do it if and when the day came for me to wear one. Yes, people stared. Some even turned in the opposite direction when they saw me as if vitiligo was contagious. But I couldn't blame them. They didn't know any better. Even a few colleagues at the office behaved as if I was a walking-talking contagion. I shrugged them off. They didn't matter to me.

"Want to have a dabeli?" Roshni asked, breaking my stream of thoughts.

I looked at the man at the stall who made the dabeli. It brought back memories with Sadiq. The day when he admitted he was trying it for the first time. I wanted to commit each and every moment we had spent together to my memory.

"Afrah?" Roshni asked again, "Here, I bought one for you too."

I shook my head. "I'm not hungry."

"Please eat half? I'll eat the remaining."

"No, I don't want to."

"Okay."

I was glad she didn't push me further. Roshni was a gem of a person, and I was so lucky to have her by my side. I remembered the first day I returned to work after the blasts. Train after train entered and crawled out of the station, but I stood like a heavy rock on the platform. I couldn't bring myself to enter the train. My heart raced, and I gasped for breath each time the horn of an incoming train sounded. I was about to turn my way back home when Roshni came to me. She'd returned from Vashi when she didn't find me on any of the subsequent trains. She'd even called my home only to find I hadn't gone back. She held my hand and gently coaxed me inside the next train. I didn't know how long I would have stood on the platform. 'I'll come early and wait for you here,' Roshni had said as she hugged me. 'Till you are comfortable doing it on your own.'

I was thankful for such a wonderful friend.

Over a few weeks, I regained my confidence and stopped freezing when I saw an approaching train. I'd overheard the news channels talking on a loop about those blasts—acts of terrorism. Nobody knew by whom. The number of injured and dead kept increasing, and I requested Papa not to watch the news in my presence.

Now, as the train pulled in, we got in and found seats. I rested my head on Roshni's shoulder.

"Sleep, my child. Sleep," Roshni patted me.

I smiled, but it was quick. My new phone rang. A gift from Papa a few days back. I clicked on the call button.

"Appi! Zain...some...something has happened to him!" Bushra sobbed.

I sat up, alert. "What happened?"

"I don't know, Ammi is wailing non-stop."

"Just take him to the hospital near the station. I'm reaching in some time. Go, hurry. Take him from Mom and rush. There's no time for her melodrama."

"What's wrong?" Roshni asked when I ended the call.

"Something has happened to Zain," I bit my lip, my

heart racing. What happened to that little bundle of joy?

"Bushra is smart. She will take him to the hospital, don't worry. Do you want me to go with you?"

"No, I'll manage."

"Call me if you need anything, okay? Anything," Roshni insisted.

"Yes, I will." What I needed right now was for the train to increase its speed or, better yet, fly me to the hospital.

Bushra visited us often because I loved to play with Zain. He was the only one who could make me laugh with his antics. And if something happened to him....

Kurla station arrived, and I jumped from the train even before it halted, all my fears forgotten, as I dashed toward the stairs. Roshni yelled for me to be careful, and I waved my hand, hoping she had seen it.

At the hospital, I asked for the children's ward and also dialed Bushra's number. She answered at the first ring.

"Appi, he's in the ICU."

"I'm here. Where are you?" I asked.

I then saw Bushra walking out from the opposite door. I rushed over to her. "Is that the ICU?"

"Yes, Ammi is with him. But she will have to leave. Only the child's parents are allowed. He will be here for a few days."

I hugged her. "Zain will be alright."

"Doctor said he had a *fit*."

"I did tell you he seemed a bit warm in the morning," I said.

"Yes, but we thought it was because he was teething."

"He is in the hospital now and will be taken care of. Don't worry."

"Yes, they said he'll be kept for a day for observation, and then they will do some tests because it's not common for babies younger than one to have a fit."

"Okay, dear. Calm down. Let's sit here."

"Should we call Abbu?"

Papa had gone to another city to place an order for materials for his shop. He had delayed getting them because of the blasts, and I didn't want him to suffer any more losses.

"Let's not call him for now. Or else he will abandon his work and rush here. We all will manage."

I'd been handling the accounts since the last month. It kept me busy. My job was followed by a visit to the shop. I returned home so tired that I barely had any time to think. Not that I wanted to forget Sadiq, but thinking about him made me so glum that my parents became worried. I didn't want them to be concerned about me so much and tried my best to put on a brave face.

Three days later, Zain was discharged. The doctor counseled us on what to do if another such episode occurred. We had to follow up regularly to make sure there wasn't any other problem.

Thank Allah, Zain was back to his usual self. The same non-stop babbling, trying to stand and falling on his bums and then laughing...he was a tiny entertainment package for all of us.

For our first follow-up visit, I accompanied Bushra with Zain. When it was our turn to go in, I chose to wait outside. The cabin reminded me of another hospital visit, that time with Sadiq. I didn't want to relive that. But Bushra insisted I go in with her.

"Please, I won't know what the doctor will say. Zain doesn't let me sit in peace," she said, bouncing Zain on one shoulder.

A mother standing with her child exited and, taking a deep breath, I followed Bushra inside. My gaze fell on the doctor, and I paled. My bag dropped to the floor as I gasped. I leaned against the door, breathless.

A nurse who was in the cabin made me sit on a stool near the door. "Are you alright? Do you need some water?" she asked.

"Appi?" Bushra called.

I couldn't stop staring at the person in the doctor's seat. At the nameplate on his desk. It was Sadiq!

He hadn't noticed me yet, as he was busy scribbling on some papers on his desk. But then he looked up at the commotion I'd caused, and our gazes met. He widened his eyes and opened and closed his mouth like a fish.

I picked up my bag and went closer to him. I wanted to pull him up and hug him. But before that, I pinched myself to make sure it wasn't a dream. Sadiq was here, right in front of my eyes. He was here! Alive!

For a few seconds, time stood still. And then an ear-piercing cry filled the cabin. It was Zain. Bushra gaped at Sadiq and me, probably wondering why we were engaged in a staring match. Sadiq pulled himself together and began doing what he was supposed to do. He went through Zain's file and then gave some instructions to Bushra. I heard him talk, but none of his words registered with me. I wanted to talk to him. Alone. Right now.

My mind wouldn't stop churning with questions. He finished talking to Bushra and looked at me. I took a few steps closer and saw the crutches at his side.

Before I could ask him anything, he cleared his throat and said, "My shift ends at five in the evening. Meet me outside."

In a daze, I nodded. Sitting on a just vacated chair

outside the cabin, I covered my lips with my palm. Bushra shook me to make me listen to her.

"Appi?" She sat next to me, bouncing Zain on her lap. "What's wrong? Who is that doctor? Do you know him?"

"Bushra," I said, managing to smile even with the tears in my eyes. "He's alive. He's alive!"

Bushra stared at me for a few seconds before she put two and two together. She gave me a sideways hug. "Oh, Appi..."

Wiping my tears, I asked, "What did he say about Zain? I wasn't paying attention."

"He said Zain is doing well and to continue the medicines and follow up after a month."

I pulled Zain's cheeks. "Thank Allah, my sweetie pie. You are going to be fine!"

Bushra smiled. I glanced at my watch. I'd taken the day off to be with my sister. It was still noon. How could I wait till five to meet Sadiq?

"Appi, I'll go home. You stay here. I know you wouldn't want to leave now," Bushra said as if hearing my thoughts.

I nodded.

I waited outside, and after a while, when there were no more patients waiting, Sadiq came out. He balanced himself on crutches and limped forward. When his gaze fell on me, he stopped midway, not expecting me to be there. Then, he hobbled toward me. His right leg was gone. I stood as he neared.

"Let's go to the canteen," he said.

I walked beside him, itching to hold his hand. But I didn't because he needed both his hands to hold the crutches.

We took a seat in the canteen, and I looked around as Sadiq adjusted himself and his crutches beside him. Doctors, nurses, and hospital staff occupied the tables and chairs. A few glanced at Sadiq and nodded at him. He acknowledged them with a wave. When we finally looked at each other, I grasped his hands. He held mine, too.

"Oh, Sadiq! I can't believe this. I thought you... you...were dead..." I swallowed a lump.

"And I thought that about you, too..."

"How?" We both asked together.

I squeezed his fingers. "You first."

Chapter 36
Of Recaps and the Future
Sadiq

I took a few deep breaths. I didn't want to relive that horrible day. But Afrah wanted to know. She had the right to.

"You know how we stood near the door," I started. Afrah nodded. "One moment, we were holding each other, and the next...I was in immense pain and outside the train. It took me a while to get my bearings, and then I began to look for you. I don't know how much time passed, but then I saw the scarf you wore that day. Forgetting all my pain, I scrambled to reach it. I took the scarf in my hands; it was torn and blood-stained. I also saw a few beads of the bracelet I gifted you scattered around. And there was this girl a few feet away, face down, burnt. Her dress was covered in soot and dust and blood...but it looked yellow to me, the one you wore. I dragged myself near her and checked her pulse on instinct. I couldn't find one. Panicking, I yelled your name and kept doing it. A few paramedics found me, but I was not ready to leave you. They told me you were dead and nothing could be done. And then I fainted." I paused. "I don't want to think about it anymore, Afrah."

I didn't want to tell her about the nightmares I still had, the guilt-ridden days and nights I spent. And the way my life changed after that day.

I could still visualize Ammi's puffy face when she first met me at the hospital. They had found me after two days of the blasts. Ammi told me how she was worried when I didn't call her from work as I usually did. But she consoled herself, thinking I must be busy. Then when I failed to return home the next morning, all hell broke loose. She imagined the worst and couldn't stop crying or beating her chest. Abbu and Bade-abba visited various hospitals to find out about me. I didn't remember being awake until forty-eight hours later when I gave the nurse my landline number.

"I had called at your place," Afrah interrupted, "to ask about you. I heard the cries and wails, and I assumed..."

"Shh. It's alright. It doesn't matter now."

I had a faint memory of how my sisters, Farheen, Abbu and Bade-abba—all of them visited me. And all, except Abbu, behaved as if I was dead already. They couldn't stop crying even for a moment. It was much later that I realized the reason. In my anesthesia-induced haze, I didn't notice I'd lost one leg.

'It was crushed, and we wouldn't have been able to save you had we not amputated it,' the doctor had informed me. 'Saving your life was a priority.'

I'd nodded, as I did now, in front of Afrah.

She squeezed my fingers tighter. "It's okay if you don't want to talk about it anymore, Sadiq. Believe me, even I don't want to think about it. I am just so happy we found each other again."

I smiled. Yes, what a miracle! I had found her again. But this time, would I be able to keep her? I didn't want to tell her the real reason why I had invited her that fateful day. I didn't want to tell her how guilty I felt, how I couldn't stop blaming myself for her death. If I had given her the letter at Kurla itself, if I had not raised her hopes and then driven her into the mouth of death....

These thoughts plagued me non-stop since that day. I didn't want to tell her the little relief I'd felt that she'd died knowing I loved her. I accepted it as my fate.

And now here she was. That very 'fate' had brought her back into my life.

"Sadiq...I still can't believe I'm seeing you again. Forget about everything that happened, maybe it was a test to see how we fared. I haven't stopped thinking about you. I have cried myself to sleep most nights and still do. But now..." she smiled, holding my hands tight, "...now, let's start over."

"Afrah." I started. Should I tell her why I was meeting her that day? Yes, I had to. No, I couldn't bear not to see her again. How could I have ever made such a decision? How could my family have made me choose? Whose fault was it?

A thrumming started in my head. I winced. I had developed these headaches due to a lack of sleep. I had to avoid thinking too much as it was a never-ending cycle. *Afrah is right, we should start over.* If only I could erase everything. If only I'd known my marriage was fixed with my cousin, perhaps we wouldn't have found ourselves here.

My eyes filled with tears, and I didn't even realize it until Afrah said, "Sadiq, it's okay. It's okay. I'm here now. You're here. We are alright."

"I know that. But...." I took a deep breath. I had to tell her the truth. I owed her that. Withholding information had created havoc in my life, and if we wanted to start over, she deserved to know the truth. "You need to know something."

Afrah sat with her chin on her hands. The vitiligo had claimed her face.

Clearing my throat, I started, "I..." This was the moment to get the truth out. "I...um...let's meet again tomorrow?" One day more. I needed a day more to process this. Then I'd tell her. For sure.

"Yes, of course. I am going to meet you every day. Did you buy a phone or not?"

Her question made me grin as if the sun was back in my life after an eclipse. I pulled out the phone from my pocket. Afrah snatched it from me, and I chuckled. She typed with her deft fingers.

"I have a different number now. Papa gifted me." She went on and on. She then gave a missed call to her number from my phone.

Oh, how much I missed this!

I stood, balancing myself on the crutches. "My break time is over. More patients are waiting for me."

"Yes, I'll see you tomorrow. Once I return from work."

I went to the OPD and laughed as Afrah skipped her way to the exit.

Sick kids with their parents came and went. I saw each and every one of them with a smile on my face. My heart felt light as if a constriction around it had been freed. Today was a beautiful day. One of the best days of my life. And I wanted it to stay that way. So, I pushed the thoughts of telling Afrah the truth into a corner of my mind. And also ignored the pain at the amputation site until I couldn't take it anymore. Wincing, I told the nurse not to let anyone inside for a few minutes. The patient load had reduced, so it shouldn't be a problem. I rolled the pant sleeve of my right leg. The stump appeared swollen.

"Oh, no. Not again."

I immediately dialed the number of the orthopedic surgeon who had operated on me. If this swelling did not reduce soon, it would be difficult for the fitting of the temporary prosthetic leg. I had recovered well after the surgery, at least physically; I didn't have any infections at the amputation site. I did experience pain and the feeling as if my leg was still there. The medical term for it was phantom pains. I'd read about it so many times, not knowing that one day *I* would be the one experiencing it. Shaking my head, I listened to the instructions the orthopedic surgeon gave me. After tying a compression bandage with the nurse's help, I was ready to finish seeing the remaining patients for the day.

Later, at home, I couldn't stop grinning. My study corner was right next to the kitchen. It wasn't that peaceful compared to the mezzanine above, but I didn't have any other option. I couldn't climb the stairs often. I had the mock test papers in front of me, and although I had not given up on my dream of becoming a surgeon, my speed of learning had reduced.

"What's so funny?" Ammi asked.

I looked at her and knew I had to share it. "Ammi, she's alive!"

Ammi's face appeared confused, but then she must have realized, judging by the way she gasped. "Your Dr. Farooqui?"

I laughed. I hadn't told her Afrah's name.

"It's Afrah. And she is not a doctor. She wants to be a teacher."

"Afrah, hmm...Beautiful. So, when am I meeting her?"

I looked down at my papers. I didn't know when. Or if ever. I'd bought some time to sort out my feelings, but the truth was I didn't know whether I deserved her after what I'd done.

Ammi watched me for a few seconds and then said, "Sadiq, it's not your fault. You tell her everything and then accept whatever she decides with a smile on your face. Alright? Promise me you will not delay this any longer." She held my face in her hands. "Promise me."

"I can keep *this* promise of yours." I gave her a knowing smile and then burst out laughing.

"I know you will never let me live down *that* other promise." She was smiling too.

Abbu came stomping inside the house. "Shabana, are you going to help with Farheen's wedding or not? Or just sit here chatting your days away with this cripple?"

Ammi flinched and looked at me. But I'd turned a deaf ear to Abbu's antics. I was glad Abbu hadn't softened toward me, as I wouldn't know how to handle a caring father. Ignoring him was much easier.

"I'm sorry, but I need to go," Ammi whispered.

I shrugged. I would finish off solving the paper in front of me. Farheen had rejected me because of my absent limb. Not Farheen per se, as she was equally bound to follow her father's orders as my parents, but Bade-abba didn't want me to be his son-in-law anymore —the same person who had bragged to the whole world about me. I scoffed. So much for my bade-abba's proclamation of love for me.

Not even three months had passed, and Farheen was about to wed another man of Bade-abba's choice. I planned on attending the wedding, walking on both my legs. My temporary prosthetic leg would be ready by then. And a little part of me couldn't wait to see their reactions. I hadn't shared this development with anyone else, not even Ammi. Farheen and Bade-abba had opened my eyes to how they really were—not worthy of me sacrificing my happiness for. They didn't stand by me when I was damaged, and now, I didn't need any of them.

I still couldn't believe I had agreed to marry Farheen. How could I have made *this* choice? Not just for me but for her, too. She would be trapped in a loveless marriage and maybe grow to resent me. Like Ammi, even though she can't say it to Abbu's face. Promise or not, I should have stayed firm to stop this family's mistakes from repeating.

But what was done was done.

Finger-combing my hair, I looked forward to meeting Afrah again. Tomorrow I would be spending the day in Orthopedics. And I needed to come up with a plan to tell her the truth about that day and my feelings for her.

Afrah

I reached home carrying a cake, humming a tune, and smiling all the way. If it were up to me, I would have called Sadiq a hundred times on my way home just to be sure I hadn't dreamt all of it. But Bushra had seen him. So, it wasn't my imagination. After the last few months spent in grief, I finally sat in front of him and held his hands. It was surreal. Shaking my head, I kept my phone in the bag. He was busy and wasn't going anywhere. The hospital was on the way, and I'd visit him daily while returning home from work.

"Oh, someone is in the seventh heaven!" Mom exclaimed, looking at the chocolate cake.

I hugged her. "Yes! Your dream of getting me married is going to come true soon."

"I know, Bushra told me. So, when are we meeting him?"

I plonked myself on the couch. "Soon, Mom, soon." Closing my eyes, I leaned my head back, and Sadiq's awestruck expression made its way into my mind. I was sure that expression mirrored mine. I grasped my fingers, trying to feel his touch....

"Ammi had started to ask around if anyone is still interested in marrying you," Bushra said, waking me from my daydream.

I raised my brows. "Really, Mom?"

She looked away. I sat on my knees in front of her and grinned.

"Had I not met Sadiq today, I would have probably agreed to it as well."

Mom laughed. Probably in relief. "That's like my wonderful daughter."

The next evening, I reached the hospital before five. I'd spoken to Sadiq last night.

"I still can't believe I met you again," he'd said, his voice tender.

"And I still can't believe you got a mobile phone!" I laughed.

Sadiq chuckled, and we didn't talk much after that, still reveling in the fact that the other was hale and hearty.

He sent me a message this morning, and I replied that I would see him soon.

Roshni was surprised to see me in such a cheerful mood, and when I told her the reason, she couldn't believe it, so she accompanied me to meet Sadiq. I pouted all the way and made faces at her. Of course, I didn't want her to come with me. *Kebab mein haddi.* Who likes a bone in their boneless meat?

"Relax, I'm not going to snatch him away from you. I'm not interested in him. But I want to make sure you are not fooling me," Roshni said.

"I'll click a picture of him today."

We went to the pediatric OPD where I'd met him the day before. To my horror, he wasn't there.

"See, I knew you had made it up. What an imagination you have!" Roshni exclaimed.

"Shut up, I swear he was here yesterday. You can ask Bushra." I looked around, biting my lip. When a nurse passed by, I asked her, "Do you know where Dr. Sadiq is?"

"He is in OPD number seven," the nurse replied, much to my relief.

I then glanced at Roshni, and we made our way to the said OPD and found Sadiq checking a patient. He looked up and gestured for us to wait outside.

Roshni gasped as Sadiq limped out of the OPD. "You did not tell me this," she looked at me with an accusing glance.

"It doesn't matter. He is breathing and talking, and becomes nervous the same way as before."

Sadiq cleared his throat. "I'm right here, ladies."

He sat beside me, and Roshni excused herself.

"Well, I'm really glad to see you, Sadiq. I just wanted to make sure Afrah wasn't joking. I'll see you tomorrow, Afrah." She nodded at Sadiq and left.

"You didn't tell me," I started, "why are you working here when you want to be a surgeon?"

Sadiq gave me a crooked smile. "I had to leave that job after those blasts. No matter how much I tried, I couldn't climb into a train."

"I know," I said. "I couldn't either. Then Roshni helped me out."

"Hmm...Ashish tried to help me too, but I froze every single time a train halted on the platform. The compartment for the handicapped is always empty, and it was inviting to be able to travel even at peak hours without the crowds. But I simply couldn't. Then, even Ashish stopped coming. And I don't blame him, he had his exams to prepare for."

"It's alright," I said. "It was a painful experience for both of us. I still get goosebumps when I think about that day. I'm just thankful we made it out alive."

Sadiq shook his head. "I motivated myself to buckle up, and I did feel better for a while, but not confident enough to board a train. My colleagues would call me at home, and a few even suggested I go to therapy, but I wasn't ready for that either. Then, my professor, with whom I was close, found me this vacancy. I handle this hospital's outpatient department, wherever the load is heavy. I don't need to take the train to get here, I get paid, and it keeps my mind occupied. I'm so tired by the time I reach home that I take a quick nap and then begin studying, though my progress is not that great. But that goal is what keeps me going."

I couldn't see him this sad and wanted to change the topic. So, I held his hand, and when he looked at me, I asked, "When are you coming home to ask for my hand in marriage? My mom was asking," I added innocently.

Sadiq rubbed the back of his neck. "I...uh."

"What? Have you changed your mind?" I asked in mock panic.

"No, oh dear, no. Relax," he said. I laughed but could sense he wanted to tell me something more. "It's just that..."

A nurse called for him.

"Afrah, I have to see many more patients, and it'll be a while. How about we meet tomorrow?"

I was reluctant to leave him, but then I stood. "Okay, tomorrow then."

Chapter 37
A Little Bit of Love
Sadiq

Tomorrow. I had to tell her tomorrow. I couldn't drag it any more than I already had. If she wanted me to meet her parents, then she deserved to know the truth. Various thoughts looped in my head. What if I didn't tell her at all? That way, I wouldn't risk losing her again. She would never know what my intentions were before the blasts. Only Ammi knew, and she wouldn't tell Afrah anything. But could I start my life with her on lies? It wasn't lies per se. It was an omission. I'd done it many a time before.

But what if Farheen told her about our marriage that would have happened if not for those blasts? Afrah was talkative and inquisitive, and in some way or other, she would come to know about it. And then what would happen? She would hate me and never give me a chance to redeem myself. *No. She has to hear it from me. No one else. Then she can make her decision.* Now, I needed to think about the best way to break the news to her. Writing a letter like last time seemed like the best course of action.

> *Dear Afrah,*
>
> *Before I come to your place to ask for your hand in marriage, you need to know something. That day, I wasn't meeting you to propose to you. I was going to break your heart and mine as well. But I didn't have much of a choice.*

I wrote my heart out. Poured everything on the paper. About the impossible situation I was in, how my marriage was fixed to my cousin in return for the fees for my education. How my ammi was bound by a promise and how I struggled to find a way out, but there was none.

> *If, after reading this, you can forgive me and give me another chance, I promise to make it up to you. You can't imagine how much I have blamed myself all these months when I thought my cowardice was*

*the reason you might've been killed. Please,
Afrah, I love you a lot. Please forgive me.*

*Yours,
Sadiq.*

This was the first time I had said the words 'I love you.' I didn't like the circumstance in which I would be saying this to her, but what other choice did I have? It might be my only chance. Besides, I had no idea how she would react to this *bomb* I was about to drop on her.

The next evening when Afrah came to visit me, I was ready. I patted my shirt pocket in which I'd kept the letter. Afrah noticed me doing that, but she didn't say anything.

As I sat next to her, she asked, "So do you have any good news for me?"

I cleared my throat. *This is it.*

"I do have some news for you. Good or not, that's for you to decide. But before we take our relationship further, it is your right to know this." I handed her the letter.

I gazed at her as she unfolded the paper and read

the contents of the letter. A gamut of emotions crossed her face—shock, confusion, and hurt. She sighed and then looked at me. She didn't say anything for a few seconds. Then she burst out laughing.

"From when did *you* learn to joke?"

I hadn't contemplated this kind of reaction from her. I felt my face flush.

"No, Afrah. I am not joking. Everything in the letter is true. I *was* going to break your heart. I couldn't marry you. I'd written everything and was going to give that letter to you after I spent more time with you at that café. But..." I paused, "I am sorry. It was all because of me that you were on that train. I was being selfish—if only I had handed that letter to you at Kurla itself rather than...." My shoulders slumped, and silence descended between us.

The cacophony of patients and their relatives rang in the background. Afrah stared at me, and for a moment, I wondered if I *should* laugh and call it all a joke. But I didn't avert my gaze. She had to know it was the truth.

Afrah finally spoke. "So, you knew about the arranged marriage from the day you graduated, and for four months, you gave me false hope?" Her lips quivered as she struggled to control herself.

I nodded and looked into my lap. What else could I say?

"So now what?" Her voice came out as a whisper. "Should I leave and pretend to have never met you?"

"Do you want to do that? It's whatever *you* wish to do," I replied with a flicker of a smile on my face. I'd imagined her storming away, and if that happened, I had decided not to follow her because I deserved it.

"What do you mean by that? If you are getting married to her, what's the point of my being in your life?" she crossed her arms. "I cannot be friends with you."

"We are not getting married. It is off," I mumbled.

"Be loud and clear," Afrah said.

I repeated.

"But why?"

I kept a hand over my heart. "Aren't you happy I'm available?"

"This is *not* a time to joke," Afrah replied, her voice stern.

Sighing, I ran my fingers through my hair.

"Bade-abba has found another suitable match for her, and they are getting married soon. I wasn't myself after the blasts, and when I did become more aware, I sensed their hesitancy in taking forward the arrangement because of this." I gestured to my amputated right leg. "So, I told them it's alright if they call our wedding off. I wouldn't feel bad. And guess what, they agreed."

I scoffed. "Even the 'doctor' tag didn't seem that important."

Suddenly, Afrah stood. "I need to go."

I made no move to stand. Instead, I asked, "Will I ever see you again?"

"I don't know. I need some time to process this," she said and walked out.

Out of my life, or just the hospital—all I knew was that it forced a silent cry out of me.

Afrah

How naïve of me! My heart broke into pieces—again. Sadiq didn't choose me. He claimed to love me, yet he was ready to let go of me so easily. Tears threatened to drop, but I blinked rapidly. Yes, I was happy to see him alive, but I couldn't get over the fact that he was going to break my heart. *He has broken it already.*

I sat in an auto-rickshaw. Not wanting to go home, as Mom and Bushra would ask me a barrage of questions about Sadiq that I wasn't ready for, I changed direction and went to Papa's shop.

Papa was surprised to see me. I had not visited the shop in the last two days since I met Sadiq.

"Ah, my princess, all well with you?" he asked.

But I didn't reply. I sat at my usual spot, at the far end of the shop, and switched on the computer. Perhaps entering numbers in Tally would calm my racing mind.

"What's wrong?" Papa asked again as I didn't utter a word. He was used to me blabbering non-stop. "Afrah, what is it?" He held my hand, stopping me from opening the application on the monitor. "Won't you tell your old abba?"

I undid my hair and tied it in a bun. Then I cracked my knuckles and looked everywhere except him. What would I tell him?

"Come on, princess," he insisted. "I'm here to listen."

I slumped on the chair. Tears that hadn't dropped before ran in a stream. Papa hugged me. I wiped my face.

"It's about Sadiq. He told me a few things today..." And then I told Papa everything I learned from Sadiq, hiccuping in between.

"Oh, my dear. It's alright." He patted my head. "You know how short our life is? And you have seen death from such close quarters. If you still love him, give him another chance. Isn't this your kismet that you met him again without the troubles that separated you?

Maybe this is what Allah wants, for you both to be together."

I shook my head. "I don't know what to do or think anymore. He planned to discard me, and now because his marriage is off, he wants me back. What if he hadn't lost his leg and I had met him today? Imagine knowing he was married to someone else, and here I am, still unable to stop thinking about him." I was ranting more for myself than for my father. "What a cruel joke."

Papa appeared to be deep in thought, the creases on his forehead deepening. He then sighed.

"Afrah, I'll tell you only this. You can choose to spend your life in the 'what ifs' and 'had-beens,' or you can grab this second chance handed to you on a platter. Make a decision that you won't second guess yourself on. Be firm in it. I'm with you, whatever you choose."

I nodded and sat in my corner, entering numbers in Tally while Papa got busy attending to customers. In between, he offered me a sandwich. It lay untouched.

The last few months of my life played before me. Yes, I loved Sadiq. He understood me as Papa did. But then he had also betrayed me. Or had he really? Maybe it was our destiny to be in that train blast so that he wouldn't be able to break my heart. Or he would have—if the blast didn't happen. And today, I would probably have been married to someone else. I gave a humorless laugh. Papa was right. No point in digging into the 'what ifs' when I had life right in front of me.

Having decided, I glanced at the clock. It was 7:00 p.m. I wouldn't find Sadiq if I went to the hospital now. *Tomorrow*.

At home, I retired to bed early, feigning a headache and dodging all of Mom's and Bushra's prodding about when they'd get to see the love of my life.

The following evening, I again visited the hospital where Sadiq worked and, this time found him in the pediatric department. He didn't notice me; he was busy writing prescriptions. A queue of patients still waited. It would be a while before he was free again, so I sat on one of the vacant chairs outside.

When Sadiq shuffled out, he drew in a breath as his gaze fell on me. I gave him a tentative smile. He asked me to follow him, and we went to the canteen. It was deserted, save for a few people who had dropped in for tea. Sadiq asked for two cups of tea, and we sat.

"I'm so happy to see you again," he started.

I cleared my throat and wiped my hands on my kurti, not knowing why I was nervous. I'd rehearsed my speech on the way here and wanted to tell him I was ready to give him a second chance.

Instead, I blurted, "Are you sure your cousin won't come back to lay her claim on you?" I had to cover my mouth with my palm.

Sadiq burst out laughing. The few people in the canteen glanced our way. I grimaced. Sadiq looked at me, his eyes shining. He leaned toward me and tucked a few strands of hair behind my ears. That gesture reminded me of that day on the crowded train when we traveled together. My heart beat faster in my chest.

"Don't you trust me?" he asked.

"Of course I do, but I want to be sure. It shouldn't be that I say yes to you, and then she snatches you away again."

"No, she won't." Then he looked me in the eye. "Do you have a problem with this?" he asked, gesturing to his lost leg.

I snorted. "No. Do *you* have a problem with this?" I gestured to the vitiligo on my face.

Sadiq shook his head.

"Then we are even." I shrugged. We hadn't realized we were holding hands until the waiter had placed two cups of tea. "Can we get something to eat? I'm starving."

Sadiq laughed. "I feel so at ease now."

"You are lucky I have realized over the last three months that life is too unpredictable," I said and sipped the tea. Its sweetness made me hum. "And I don't want to waste any more time not being with the people I love."

"Hmm...someone has become too serious in life."

"Huh, yes, a certain someone's company is rubbing off on me."

We laughed, not caring who stared at us.

As I finished the tea, I could feel Sadiq's gaze on me. I tilted my head and furrowed my brows.

"What's going on in that head of yours?" I asked as the sandwiches he ordered arrived. I took a bite.

"I still can't believe it. You are finally going to be a part of my life. And now I can get back to studying even harder and achieving my dreams with you by my side."

"Yes, achieving dreams and all is fine. But we'll get married first."

"You'll have to live in a chawl. I haven't shifted to a better place yet."

"It's okay."

"You don't know my family."

"I'll know them." I stopped eating. "Are you trying to scare me away? Because I'm not leaving you no matter what." Then I laughed. "You know what, you don't know my mother, too."

"Ah, what a lovely family we have."

"Indeed."

"I forgot to tell you the most important thing. I'll get a prosthetic leg in a few days, then I won't need this." He raised his crutches at his side. "I'll be fairly independent."

"That's good for you. But then I hope your cousin won't come back running for you because you can walk with both your legs."

Sadiq laughed. "I never wanted to marry her in the first place. And now, that chapter is closed forever. Besides, we'll be married by then. And we'll attend my cousin's wedding as a couple."

"Yup."

I finished eating, and we walked to the OPD. I held his elbow. "I can't wait to see you at my place soon."

"Yes, I'll be there, don't you worry."

"That's good, Dr. Saab because now, I'm not going to let you get away so easily."

"I look forward to it," he said as he lowered himself into the chair. "Now, Ms. Farooqui, I need to see a few more patients."

I had a good look at him and clicked his picture—with his coat and the stethoscope around his neck. That picture would do to show my family.

Sadiq squeezed my hand, and I squeezed his back, too, making a silent promise to be together no matter what happened.

I skipped the way back home, my heart lighter than it had ever been. A little bit of love was all I had ever wanted, and finally, I had it. From everyone in my life.

THE END

Acknowledgments

Thank you, dear reader, for showering your love on my book. It means a lot to me. I do have a few people to thank for making my book a reality.

My editor Samiha Hoque, and the entire team at Shaherazad Shelves for believing in me and my book. Samiha was so prompt to reply to all my queries, and editing was a really enjoyable experience.

My earliest readers, Shalini Mullick and Divisha. They helped me see what I needed to do to make the beginning more interesting. My Word Warriors: Rashmi, Sonia, Manisha, Bhavana, Sudha, and Pavittra who always had my back and supported me in the revision process. Writing is such a lonely process, and I'm glad I have these gorgeous women in my corner. They are never behind to give a shout-out across all social media platforms. I can't wait for them to release their beautiful stories in the universe.

A huge gratitude to my family, who has been an enormous support. Without them, I wouldn't have been able to fulfill this dream of mine.

And how can I forget my friends and colleagues from medical college? Each one of you have given me so many memories, and maybe you might find yourself in this book and in my future ones as well ;-).

About the Author

Arva Bhavnagarwala is a pediatrician and writer based in Mumbai, India.

Between seeing patients and being patient with her two boys, she finds time to scribble words here and there. These words then become stories, and these stories are a way for her to connect with readers. Her short stories have appeared in various anthologies and literary magazines like Woman's Era, Active Muse, and The Hooghly Review.

Arva loves to travel despite her unpredictable motion sickness when not busy with pediatrics or writing. She is also a voracious reader and can devour books, sometimes entire novels, in one day, with food and water forgotten. An avid chai lover, she loves potatoes in her biryani. You can find her on Twitter (X) at arva_writes and on Instagram at arva.writes.

A LITTLE BIT OF LOVE is her debut novel.

www.ingramcontent.com/pod-product-compliance
Lightning Source LLC
Chambersburg PA
CBHW011206190726
48288CB00013B/3339

* 9 7 8 1 9 6 0 3 2 3 0 9 5 *